FLAMES OF FURY

CARRIE VIXENHART

CONTENT NOTE

Please be advised that this book contains explicit content that may not be suitable for all readers. Dark themes include violence, death, grief, mature subjects, supernatural elements, and explicit sexual activities that are shown on the page. Readers sensitive to these topics are encouraged to proceed with caution. For more details, visit Vixenhart's website at vixenhart.com/books or scan the QR code.

DEDICATION

To my favorite sister, whoever reads this first.
There's nothing in the world like a sister: equal parts soulmate,
sparring partner, and unsolicited life coach.
Thank you for showing my daughters how fierce, ridiculous, and
ride-or-die sisterhood can be. May they be as lucky—and as loud—
as we are.

FLAMES OF FURY

CHAPTER

ONE

Luka was watching her. She couldn't see him, not through the thick stone walls or the towering windows veiled in shadows. But she felt it. A presence crawling over her skin like an unseen tether, a weight she couldn't shake. Was it a comfort or a curse? The blood bond pulsed, unseen but ever-present. Gritting her teeth, she forced herself to push through the sensation.

Because she had work to do.

She wasn't sure when it started, this sense of being watched even when alone. But lately, it felt like every moment was under glass. Luka didn't press the bond, didn't speak into her mind, or try to summon her. But his silence was a tether in itself. Sometimes she wondered if he haunted the halls just to keep her close. Not in a possessive way, not exactly. More like a question that never got asked aloud. It left her suspended, part fury and part ache.

She dreamed about him again last night. Not the dark visions of battle or blood, but the kind where their magic tangled in ways she couldn't explain. Where he touched her wrist, and the thread between them lit up like gold spun from shadow. Waking up felt like loss. And she hated herself for that.

As she tightened the laces of her running boots, she glanced toward the window once more, almost daring him to show himself. But there was nothing. No flicker of movement. No shadow amongst the glass. Just that hollow press against her magic, like an echo waiting for a sound that would never come.

Rolling her shoulders as she stretched, the crisp morning air stung Ophelia's skin. Her midnight-black hair was pulled into a tight braid, a few stray strands sticking to her tan skin. She had an athletic build and long legs that carried her through the world with the same restless energy that hummed inside her. Yellow-green eyes flickered toward the estate's towering windows, knowing Luka was somewhere beyond them. Always watching.

Across from her, Brisa cracked her knuckles, the intricate black tattoos that covered her golden skin shifting with the motion. Barely taller than five-two, Ophelia's cousin radiated an energy far larger than her frame, her sharp brown eyes full of mischief and challenge. Wearing her leather and a lip ring that glinted when she smirked, Brisa was all sharp edges and unfiltered words. Though they'd only met a year ago, Brisa had become one of the most formidable forces in Ophelia's life.

"You know, we could just skip to the part where we actually hit something," Brisa grumbled, shaking out her arms. "Running's overrated. And I can't do it in my boots."

Laughing and adjusting her stance, Ophelia addressed her cousin. "You know you can't really fight in thigh-high leather boots either," she said.

"Speak for yourself," Brisa said, her signature look of boredom firmly in place.

"I know you use your air magic to cheat when we run," Ophelia said, pinning her cousin with a stare as she held back another laugh.

Brisa shrugged lazily toward the sky, admiring her neon-green nails like they held the secrets of the universe.

Alex stood beside them, her hair now fully silver, a transformation that had taken over after the trauma of the last year. She was taller than Brisa but still more compact than Ophelia, her cerulean blue eyes watching Ophelia closely. Alex had been her best friend since childhood, unwavering, steady. Even now, when everything else felt uncertain, Alex remained a grounding presence.

Ophelia still carried the guilt of Alex abandoning medical school after the supernatural world barreled into their lives, upending everything. But Alex didn't seem to mourn the loss. Instead, she was embracing her fae bloodline, learning how to wield the power that had always been buried deep within her. She studied the fae magic of healing and decay with the same relentless focus she once gave organic chemistry and med school applications.

Alex shook her head with a soft laugh. "Ophelia's the strongest she's ever been. Pretty soon, I don't think your magic will keep up," Alex said, grinning at Brisa.

Brisa's face softened for her girlfriend, the only time her mask of disinterest disappeared. But it vanished beneath a devilish grin as she pinched Alex's ass and took off at breakneck speed, wind power shoving her forward like a rocket. Alex squealed and laughed before running after Brisa.

Ophelia grinned to herself as she pushed off into a relentless pace, but her mind wasn't entirely with them today. Gabriel. Luka. The blood bond. The uncertainty of what came next. It all refused to settle in her mind even as she felt her powers stir in response to the rhythmic pounding of her feet against the ground.

Gravel crunched steadily beneath their feet. As they moved down the long drive, trees framed their path in a tunnel of green. The scent of saltwater grew heavier the closer they got to the Ionian Sea, and the tang of salt burned her nose. Gulls screeched above, the wind tugging strands of hair loose from her braid.

By the time they reached the cliff's edge, her breath was even and her muscles loose, but her thoughts were anything but. Below, the sea crashed against jagged rocks, the sound like distant thunder. Spires of stone jutted from the mountain where they stood. She shot a long, deliberate side-eye at her cousin and her best friend, knowing what she needed to do. Knew what she craved. With barely a break to catch her breath, she backed up from the platform in a running start stance.

"Don't you dare," Brisa said, with an exaggerated eye roll.

"Ophy," Alex said in a one-word warning.

She was one of the few people Ophelia allowed to call her by that nickname. The other—the man who had helped raise her and then betrayed her—was dead.

Ignoring them both, she launched herself over the cliff and sailed through the air, allowing her full power to surface.

Halting her plunge, she used her air power to turn mid-air to face them, suspended by the combination of earth and air magic. The air obeyed her. But she still didn't trust that it always would. Bringing her hand up, fire flamed from the tip of her middle finger as she lifted it to her closest friends.

As Brisa yelled, "Show off!" and Alex grinned, Ophelia dropped toward the ocean below. The water welcomed her like an old friend, cool and bracing. She summoned its power, letting it thrust her upward.

Just a year ago, she'd still believed there was something

wrong with her—some damage left behind by her mother's disappearance and presumed death. Her mom's best friend, Elijah, had raised her as his daughter, along with his husband, Sebastian.

Elijah hadn't understood what was happening to Ophelia as a child. Her magic had manifested immediately after her mom disappeared. She'd tried to explain the warnings to him. At first, he didn't believe her. But then he witnessed it, time and again—her ability to sense danger or impending change. And he'd tried to cure her.

But everything had changed since then. Sebastian died, but not before Ophelia discovered he'd been a plant in her home, a low-level witch sent to watch her, though she still didn't know by whom. And her magic was growing more powerful than ever.

She was a hybrid, both witch and vampire. She was a fusion of power that shouldn't exist but did. It was rare for a witch to wield more than one elemental ability. Most controlled only a single element, and two was considered an anomaly. Ophelia, however, controlled all four: earth, air, fire, and water. And that was only the beginning.

Elijah had disappeared six months ago, distraught over the loss of Sebastian.

And her mom wasn't dead. At least not yet.

Breaking the surface of the water, Ophelia wasted no time finding a hold on the sheer rock wall before her. She climbed, one muscular leg and arm at a time, the moss-slicked surface offering little grip. Her fingers screamed and her back barked, but still, she pressed upward, refusing to use magic.

Halfway up, her breath hitched. Her muscles were on fire. Her shoulder throbbed where an old wound had never quite healed right. Magic thrummed beneath her skin, demanding to be unleashed, to make this easier. But she didn't. Wouldn't.

Her body had become something other: hardened, honed, sacred, and strange. She both loved it and resented it. She hadn't asked for this kind of strength. But now that she had it, she would use every bit of it to survive.

At last, she hauled herself over the final ledge and collapsed onto solid ground, chest heaving.

For just a moment, she allowed herself to lie on the ground, catching her breath. Alex still wore the same grin. Brisa stood over her with an unimpressed look, both hands on her hips.

"You're insane," Brisa said, muttering under her breath.

"Genetic blessing," Ophelia said, winking at her cousin.

Ophelia sprang to her feet, using a flicker of fire magic to warm her body and dry her soaked clothes. Then she took off toward the estate at a sprint. Technically, it was hers now, left to her when everyone believed Luka had died at the Eye of the Earth. Complicated didn't even begin to cover it.

Brisa cursed behind her and ran to catch up. Alex kept pace at her side, her breath even and steady. She'd trained almost as hard as Ophelia these last months. Her fae bloodline had only come to light after she was kidnapped by supernaturals. But the magic had been there all along, quiet and waiting. And stronger than anyone expected. She'd never match a full-blooded supernatural in raw power, so she made up for it with relentless training and obsessive study.

"You good?" Alex asked, eyes scanning Ophelia's face as they neared the courtyard.

Ophelia forced a nod. "Yeah."

Alex didn't look convinced, eyes drawn down in skepticism, but she didn't press.

They slowed as they passed through a tall wrought-iron gate, and the rest of the estate came into view. Straight from the 1500s, the stone-clad fortress loomed before them, its weathered façade unyielding. But the castle still bore the scars of its past. Arrow slits had been bricked over long ago, and scorch marks still marred the edges of the ramparts. Four cylindrical towers, one at each corner, cast shadows on every corner.

The windows above were dark, but Luka's presence clung to her like a phantom breath. A pull she couldn't escape—no matter how much she wanted to. She exhaled hard and shook it off. She wasn't running anymore. Not from him. Not from anything. Not again.

The morning sun stretched long fingers of light across the courtyard. Once, it had been a peaceful space—meals, meditation, quiet. Not anymore. Now, training mats covered the stone, scuffed from daily sparring. Suspended above them, bean bags floated lazily in the air, held up by ever-present magic, ready to be used for agility drills. This place had become their battleground, a place to push limits, to prepare for what was coming.

"Now comes the fun part," Ophelia said, cracking her knuckles. "Hope you're warmed up."

Brisa groaned. "I hate when you say that."

Ophelia smirked. "Then brace yourself," she said. "It only gets worse."

They stepped onto the mats. This was no longer practice. This was survival, sharpened daily.

TWO

Ophelia's fists moved in a blur, her strikes landing with brutal precision against the suspended bean bags. The magic keeping them aloft adjusted their weight and position, forcing her to react, to anticipate, to move as though she were fighting a living opponent. She thrived in this—the raw exertion, the sheer force of will behind every blow.

Brisa circled her, watching with sharp eyes. "Good. But you're still thinking too much."

"I'm not—" Ophelia started to argue, but Brisa cut her off.

"You are. I can hear it," Brisa said with a smirk. "Literally."

Brisa's power was rare, even among witches—the ability to hear thoughts as they flickered through nearby minds. Ophelia knew better than to leave hers unguarded. She'd learned that lesson the hard way. But right now, Brisa didn't need to push very far to know Ophelia's thoughts were tangled in something deeper than training.

A few feet away, Alex leaned against the stone wall, watching. "She's stronger than she was," Alex said, tilting her head toward Brisa. "Give her a little credit."

Brisa scoffed but didn't argue.

Nearby, Mo—Ophelia's uncle and her mother's older half-brother—sat at the long table, poring over an ancient book written in a language long forgotten. He was a warlock with the command of earth, manifesting in the ability to manipulate the ground beneath him, summon roots to entangle enemies, and draw strength from the land itself. But today, it wasn't the dirt beneath his boots that mattered. Mo possessed the ability to read and speak any language, even those lost to history. It was a rare and invaluable skill, making him a keeper of knowledge in ways few others could match.

Ophelia struck the next target with a force that rattled the magic suspending it. Her strength wasn't just in her body. Sure, her ability to wield all elements was practically unheard of. But that wasn't the only thing that made her different. Hybrids of any kind were forbidden, as supernaturals weren't meant to cross bloodlines. Yet she existed, something that should never have been possible.

And beyond that, she had something rarer still—a sense of when danger was coming. When the world shifted beneath its surface. A warning system she'd relied on since childhood.

Right now, it was silent. But her instincts were screaming anyway.

Because Eris was still out there. She'd vanished in the aftermath of the battle at the Bell of Time, wounded and furious. And she'd been quiet for too long. The silence made Ophelia uneasy.

Ophelia had only recently learned about her troubled sister. Their mother, Celeste, had hidden the other powerful hybrid in a misguided effort to protect them all. But Eris was too powerful; her magic was tied to the darkest part of their bloodline.

She was dangerous. And sooner or later, she'd return.

Brisa stepped forward, rolling her shoulders. "All right, let's see if you can handle something that fights back," she said, transitioning the training from kickboxing to hand-to-hand combat.

Ophelia smirked, stepping onto the sparring mat. "I was hoping you'd say that," she said.

Brisa lunged first, swift and relentless. Ophelia countered, slipping easily into the rhythm. It was familiar, second nature. They had repeated it in training countless times before.

Except today, Ophelia wasn't fully there.

Luka. Gabriel. The blood bond. A tug in her chest that wouldn't let her breathe fully.

She barely dodged a strike, her movements slower than usual.

Brisa didn't hesitate. She landed a hit against Ophelia's ribs, hard enough to force her to stagger back. "You're not here," Brisa snapped. "I can see it all over your face."

Ophelia clenched her jaw, righting herself. "I'm here," she said.

Brisa lunged again.

Ophelia moved to counter, but then pain lanced through her. Sharp, sudden, a crackling surge that pulsed through the bond she barely understood. Gasping, she bent at the waist as the sensation crashed over her like a wave.

Brisa took the opening.

A solid blow struck Ophelia's shoulder, sending her stumbling back. Brisa pulled up short, her brow furrowing. "What the hell was that?" she asked.

Ophelia steadied herself, breathing through the pain. "Nothing," she said, gritting her teeth.

Brisa didn't buy it. "'Nothing' doesn't make you double over mid-fight," she said.

Alex stepped forward, her voice softer. "She's right, Ophelia. Something's wrong," she said.

From the edge of the courtyard, Mo slowly rose, his chair scraping the stone with deliberate finality. The ancient book closed beneath one weathered hand, dust curling up like a breath held too long. He moved with quiet command, towering over the table, his slacks soil-stained at the hem. His expression was unreadable, carved in shadow, but his deep brown eyes gleamed with something sharper than concern.

"Enough sparring. We need to talk," he said, voice like gravel shifting beneath ancient roots. "I think I know what's happening."

Ophelia exhaled slowly, already dreading whatever he was about to say.

They joined him near the table. Ophelia sat, chest still rising from the sparring match. Brisa stood a few feet away, arms crossed. Alex perched on the edge of the training mat, watching them.

"The blood bond," Mo said at last, his voice careful. "It's coming back fully. And much stronger than before."

Ophelia tensed. "I thought it was broken. When Luka died," she said.

Mo shook his head. "That's usually how blood bonds work," he said, his gaze flickering toward her. "But we don't have enough information about when a person comes back."

A chill ran down her spine. Luka had bound her to him with a blood bond, without her understanding what it meant. She had discovered it only after he was gone, believing him dead. It had been devastating. But that betrayal had helped her move on. She'd fallen in love with Gabriel. He was her twin flame, her life mate. And now...now Luka was back. And she was more confused than ever, unsure what her true feelings were.

She swallowed hard, glancing toward the estate. Luka was still recovering from the torture he had endured at her sister's hands. But he wouldn't be weak forever.

Brisa let out a frustrated sigh. "So what? Why is it so much stronger this time?" she asked.

Mo's voice stayed level. "Blood bonds are complicated. They aren't just physical. They tie two people together in ways we don't fully understand." He hesitated before he spoke again. "I think it wasn't as strong before because you were always together. But now…" he said, voice trailing off.

Ophelia clenched her fists. "And if I don't want to be bound to him?" she asked.

Mo's expression was unreadable. "Then you need to break it. But that's not easily done. I've been searching, but the answer isn't clear yet," he said, gesturing to the piles of books.

Alex spoke softly. "If Luka is feeling the bond, too…"

Silence settled over them. Ophelia's stomach twisted. She had no idea what this meant. Not really. But she knew she needed answers.

Mo exhaled and leaned forward. "There's only one person who might be able to tell you the truth. Someone who has been around longer than she should have been and has seen enough of the supernatural worlds to piece this together."

Ophelia already knew the answer before he said it.

"Sofija," she whispered. Sofija, High Priestess of the witches, had ruled for over two hundred years. She was powerful, sustained by earth magic. And she'd always creeped Ophelia out.

Mo nodded. "I know very little about blood bonds. I can continue searching for answers. But we also have to search for answers about Eris. I think you should go to Mt. Slivnica and ask for an audience. Of course, she'll want something in return. You'll have to be on guard," he said.

Ophelia sighed. She understood, of course. The blood bond was the least of their concerns. They were balancing so many threads. The blood bond. A missing, enraged Eris. Her mind needed stillness.

She stood abruptly, heading for one of the cylindrical towers at the corner of the courtyard. They all knew where she was going. Brisa and Alex followed while Mo watched. This was their rhythm.

Reaching the small stone door veiled by vines, she braced herself and pushed it open. The hinges groaned. A narrow staircase twisted upward, coiling like a serpent through the tower's core. At the top, she stepped into a round room bathed in light from ocean-facing windows. Sunlight spilled across woven mats and timeworn stone. Shelves bowed under the weight of books. The air shimmered, alive with magic.

It was one of her favorite places at the estate.

But Luka had created this room for her.

And he had lied to her in it.

It wasn't empty.

The scent of night-blooming jasmine and cedarwood curled around her, sinking its claws into her memory, thick and familiar, curling through her lungs like smoke.

To her left, green eyes met hers—shame and something like longing flickering in their depths. Those same eyes had once looked at her just before he fed from her blood. Somehow, he was at once formal and indecent. Even weakened, his presence pulled at her. Luka.

And to her right, the vampire who pushed every button, glaring at Luka in a silent warning. Although he was lounging on the mat, his frame spilled over, all muscle and restless energy. Tattoos crawled up his arms, disappearing beneath the too-tight T-shirt that did little to hide his bulk. His broad arms were crossed, every line of his body radiating challenge. Then he looked at her and smirked, his intense brown eyes catching hers like they always did. Gabriel.

They flanked her like rival truths. Past and present. Guilt and desire.

She exhaled slowly and lowered onto her mat, forcing her body to relax as she settled. Mira had insisted on this daily. With everyone.

Mira knelt beside her, a presence as steady and unshakable as the earth itself. She had been in Ophelia's life since she was a teenager, one of the few stabilizing forces in the chaos that had followed her for as long as she could remember. Sebastian had been the one to take her to Mira's yoga studio, back when she was unruly, angry, and lost. Mira had been more than an instructor. She had been a guide, someone who had helped Ophelia channel her power into something manageable. Someone who had never asked for anything in return.

But Mira was more than human. Like all of them.

Strands of white streaked her long black hair, subtle proof of how time and power weighed on her. Her golden-brown skin held an ethereal glow, and her deep, knowing eyes could cut through any illusion. As a moira—a supernatural capable of seeing fragments of a person's fate—Mira had spent her life avoiding those who wanted to use her for her gifts. But she had still helped Ophelia, even when she hadn't asked for it.

And now, she had joined them at the estate for protection. Because if someone wanted to use her to get to Ophelia, they wouldn't hesitate.

Alex and Brisa sat on their own mats nearby, mirroring Ophelia's movements. Alex, ever composed, eased into a stretch, her silver hair catching the candlelight like moonlit silk. Brisa, in contrast, shifted with restless energy, her gaze fixed on the two vampires like a predator waiting for prey to twitch. She didn't bother hiding it—she was waiting for the inevitable clash, for one sharp comment or smug glance to ignite the brawl they all knew was coming.

"Close your eyes," Mira said gently.

Ophelia obeyed, but her mind didn't quiet. Luka. Gabriel. The bond. Eris.

"Let your body be still, even if your mind isn't," Mira said. "Breathe with intention. Inhale through your nose. Slightly constrict your throat as you exhale—let it sound like the ocean. That's Ujjayi. Victory breath. It calms the nervous system. Anchors your focus. Reminds your body it's safe, even when your mind isn't sure," she said.

Ophelia tried to follow, pulling air through her nose, then exhaling slowly. The sound rasped low in her throat, soft but uneven. Her fingers curled against the fabric of her leggings.

She should have answers by now. She should feel something shift.

"Keep breathing," Mira's voice came again, calm and unshakable. "Even when your thoughts pull you elsewhere, bring yourself back," she said.

But all Ophelia saw behind her closed eyes was chaos. Flickers of memory. Flames. Water. Screaming. Magic. Grief. Her mind bucked against stillness like a wild thing cornered.

She tried again—inhale, exhale, ocean breath. Steady.

She had fought for so long. For her mother. For the truth. But who was she fighting for now?

Feeling a presence, Ophelia opened her eyes to find Mira directly in front of her. Mira reached out, fingers pressing lightly to her wrist. A slow, steady warmth spread beneath Ophelia's skin—like roots anchoring her to something deeper.

"You are more than what brought you here," Mira said

softly. "Fate may think it knows your path. But only you decide how to walk it," she said.

A muscle in Ophelia's jaw tightened. Mira wasn't demanding a choice—she was offering clarity. For once, someone wasn't pushing her to pick a side, to define herself in absolutes.

She still didn't know the right path.

Maybe she never had.

She'd grown up lost—her mother gone, her magic misunderstood, everyone around her treating her like a problem to solve. She had spent most of her life trying to figure out who she was.

Her hybrid nature. Eris. Luka. Gabriel.

Nothing had ever felt like a choice. But maybe now, for the first time, what came next could be.

Mira stood and moved to the center of the room. "Come to standing."

The flow quickened, each movement stacking on the next with little time to rest. Muscles trembled. Breath deepened. Heat slicked her spine, soaking through the fabric of her clothes. She wasn't the only one—beside her, Alex's silver hair clung to her neck, and even Brisa's smirk had faded into focus. The room pulsed with collective effort, bodies burning through the tension they carried.

Gabriel tugged his shirt off and tossed it aside. Luka followed a moment later.

Ophelia didn't mean to stare. But gods, she stared.

Fuck me.

Brisa's voice cut in, perfectly timed to interrupt her thoughts. "I think either would."

Ophelia nearly lost her balance and toppled sideways out of Tree Pose, arms flailing, before she caught herself with a muttered curse.

Alex groaned. "Can we not do this during yoga?" she asked.

"I'm just saying what she's thinking," Brisa said, smug.

Ophelia flushed. "I hate you," she said.

"You love me," Brisa responded with a wink.

They moved through the rest of the sequence—bodies glistening, air sharp in their lungs. Finally, Mira guided them down into stillness. "Savasana," she said. "Let the body absorb what it's learned."

Ophelia lay back, arms at her sides, palms open to receive. Her breathing slowed. The air in the tower room grew quiet, thick with the scent of salt, wax, and bodies worked to the edge. Outside, waves crashed in a steady rhythm—nature's own heartbeat.

The bond hummed beneath her skin—not painful now, but undeniably present. A pulse that didn't belong to her alone.

She focused on the rise and fall of her chest.

In. Out.

In. Out.

The silence stretched, time blurring at the edges. Her muscles sank into the mat, and her heartbeat softened.

Mira's voice returned, no louder than a whisper. "Stay for as long as you need."

Ophelia didn't move. But the clarity came anyway—not like a thunderclap, but a quiet truth settling in her bones.

She couldn't break the bond on her own.

But maybe Sofija could.

And she was done waiting.

Somewhere beside her, she heard Brisa stretch with a groan and Alex exhale a quiet sigh. Mats shifted. The soft rustle of movement signaled the end of class.

Then—

A sharp buzz shattered the calm.

Ophelia's phone vibrated against the mat beside her. The sound cut through the fading stillness like a blade.

She blinked up at the ceiling, surprised by the interruption. Then she turned her head toward the screen. A name flashed there.

Her chest constricted, heart suddenly pounding.

It had been months since he'd walked away.

She nearly let it go to voicemail.

Her fingers trembled as she picked up the phone, dread curling in her stomach. The man who had raised her as his own was on the other end.

She pressed it to her ear. "Elijah?"

A fragile inhale answered. Then his voice, raw and frayed.

"Ophelia...I need you."

THREE

The silence in the room was thick—the kind that felt alive, breathing and waiting.

Elijah's voice still echoed in her mind, frayed and fragile, like a man clinging to the edge of something he didn't understand.

Ophelia...I need you.

She rose from the floor too fast, the mat slipping slightly beneath her feet. Her heart thudded painfully in her chest, a dull ache beneath the sharp edge of adrenaline. Her breath came in shallow bursts, her body already reacting even before her mind could catch up.

Gabriel appeared at her side in an instant, steady hands brushing against her arm. Luka moved, as well, standing just behind her, his posture taut. With their vampire hearing, they hadn't missed a word.

Of course, they hadn't.

She didn't look at either of them. She couldn't.

Because all she could see was Elijah. Her Elijah—her

guardian, her anchor, the man who had raised her when no one else could. Or would. Who had once refused to believe in magic, in fate, in her. And now, he knew everything.

Alex and Mira watched her from across the room, concern written across their faces, but it was Brisa who spoke first, arms crossed and jaw locked. "What did he say?" she asked.

Ophelia's throat felt like it had been scraped raw. She shook her head once, trying to steady the tremor in her voice. "He said a woman took him," she murmured, the words tasting like ash. "She looked like me. Exactly like me. And she told him…she told him she was my sister."

Brisa's expression darkened, lips pressing into a grim line.

Ophelia kept going, her voice barely above a whisper. "She showed him magic. Elijah didn't understand it, but he couldn't deny what he saw. She told him Sebastian was a witch. That he hadn't died on a work trip. Told him I'd lied to him about Sebastian's death."

She blinked hard, her hands trembling. "She told him I was powerful. More powerful than he could imagine. That I'd lied to him about everything. And then she…she left him. Dumped him in a place that looked like something out of the medieval ages. Surrounded by people with fangs, who—who acted like vampires."

Her voice splintered. "He sounded terrified. Not just confused—terrified. Like he didn't know what was real anymore. Like the world he thought he understood had turned inside out."

She wrapped her arms around herself. "And I wasn't there. I let him stay in the dark because I thought I was protecting him. And now he's caught in something he was never meant to be part of."

Her voice dropped, thick with guilt. "He left that letter

earlier this year—said he was stepping away. Said he needed space. And I let him go. I didn't try to find him. Or check on him. I barely even thought about him." Her throat tightened, a bitter taste rising in her mouth. "I told myself I was giving him peace. But I think I was just protecting myself. And now he's paying the price for that. For me." He had walked away months ago, broken and adrift, convinced she didn't need him anymore now that Celeste was back. He'd said it gently. But the words had cut just the same.

Luka spoke up from the shadows, where he'd moved to lean against a stone wall. "Based on the description, I think he's in San Marino, at the Concilium headquarters...or what remains of it," he said. The Concilium was traditionally composed of three elder members who governed the vampires. Their headquarters sat in San Marino, protected by a fortified wall and anchored by three ancient castles—one for each council member. But now, only two of the fortresses remained. Ophelia had destroyed the third after the Concilium kidnapped Alex and Sebastian. And then murdered Sebastian. They'd underestimated her once. They wouldn't make that mistake again.

Brisa's gaze sharpened. "Then he's in trouble," she said, tone flat.

"If Eris told him everything..." Ophelia's voice trailed off, shaking her head. "He's not safe. Not from her. Or any other supernatural, for that matter. If they think he knows too much..." She stopped herself again.

She'd told herself she was protecting him. Elijah hadn't understood what was happening to Ophelia when her magic first manifested as a child, just after Celeste disappeared. She tried to explain the warnings—her ability to sense danger—but at the time, they called them "episodes." Determined to find a cure, Elijah became a child psychologist, searching for a scientific explanation. Neither of them had known anything about the supernatural world. Celeste had left them in the dark. Ophelia had been fine leaving him there. At least one of them could lead a normal life. She should have known better. He was a human connected to her. And in a world like theirs, that made him vulnerable in every way that mattered.

And she hadn't heard Elijah sound like that since...since Sebastian died. It had all spilled out of him. She could hear the panic in his voice, the disbelief. He was broken. Or maybe Eris had broken him. Eris, in her cruel, calculated way, had unspooled the truth like a weapon. That Sebastian's death had been preventable. That the supernatural world wasn't some distant mythology but an empire of secrets that Ophelia had been born into. That she had lied to Elijah—about her power, about Luka, about what really happened to Sebastian.

He must have felt like the ground had vanished beneath him—just as it had for her, once. When the truth of the supernatural world shattered the life she thought she knew. When she was just a child, fumbling to explain the magic that surged inside her while he scoured textbooks, desperate for a diagnosis that never came. And again, years later, when she realized that no name, no label, would ever make her normal.

Mira stepped forward, her gaze soft but solemn. "You'll need to be careful." Her voice was gentle, but it carried a warning beneath the calm, and it cut through Ophelia's spiraling thoughts. As a moira, Mira could glimpse visions of a person's destiny.

Then Mira hesitated. Just slightly. "I need to return to Nivara," she said quietly.

Ophelia's head snapped toward her. "Now?"

Mira gave a small smile. Not sad but resigned. "It's time..." She trailed off, eyes locking on Ophelia's.

Ophelia stepped forward, searching Mira's face. "You've seen something."

"I always see something," Mira said, her voice dipping low. "But not everything. Still—I know this much. My part in your path is ending. For now."

A lump rose in Ophelia's throat. "Be careful," she whispered, echoing Mira's words from moments ago.

They embraced, and for a second, Ophelia let herself lean into it—the steadiness Mira always offered, the gravity she never abused. Mira's arms wrapped around her like protection and prophecy in one.

"I love you, Ophelia," Mira murmured, brushing a hand over the hair trailing down Ophelia's back. "You were always meant to burn brighter than the rest of us. Just make sure you don't burn alone."

Ophelia swallowed the ache rising in her chest. She nodded once and stepped back. "Take care of yourself."

Mira gave a last nod, her expression unreadable. "Be careful," she said again.

Ophelia watched her go, knowing she wouldn't see her again for a long time, maybe ever. Then she bent to the boots she'd discarded before yoga, jerking them on one at a time, yanking the laces snug, the rhythm steadying her hands. Her fingers shook anyway.

Brisa scoffed. "Careful? That's an understatement. The vampires are a mess after Ophelia destroyed one of their castles," she said in her typical deadpan. "And we don't know who is taking the empty two seats after Ophelia killed Durante. And after Leander..." Brisa's voice trailed off as she glanced at Ophelia, chastened for once.

Ophelia flinched at the mention of her biological father. Leander had been the oldest known vampire, a figure whispered about in ancient texts and blood-bound legend. She hadn't even known he was her father until it was nearly too late. There had been no time to build anything real between them.

But in the end, he had chosen her. He'd chosen to die at the Kala Ghanta—the Bell of Time—to keep Eris from using the ancient supernatural artifact capable of unraveling time itself. She still wasn't sure whether that had been a father's love or just another thread in the web of fate she'd never agreed to spin.

Ophelia didn't spare her cousin a glance. Her fingers clenched around the phone as she stormed toward the spiral staircase. Boots struck the stone steps with purpose, echoing through the stairwell as Ophelia took them two at a time, each movement fueled by a growing fire in her chest.

Gabriel's footsteps followed, slower but no less certain, his arms crossed over his broad chest like a shield.

"You're not going alone," he said, his voice low—quiet thunder rolling in behind her.

She didn't slow, didn't look back. "I don't need a chaperone," she snapped, breathless but determined, her jaw set like stone.

They spilled into the courtyard, where the sunlight slashed long and sharp across the grounds, painting the cobblestones in lines of light and shadow.

Gabriel's voice dropped again, cool and controlled—but beneath that calm, it thrummed with warning. "This isn't up for discussion, Cinis."

Cinis. Ashes. He'd started calling her that after Luka disappeared. Said it was because she kept rising, no matter what tried to bury her. She'd felt seen in a way that startled her, like he was the only one who didn't just watch her burn but understood why she had to.

Finally, she stopped—so suddenly that Gabriel nearly

collided with her. She whirled, palm landing flat against his chest, holding him in place. Her breath came fast. Her body thrummed with residual fire and something deeper...something older. Longing, bone-deep and maddening.

Since Luka's return, she'd kept Gabriel at a distance, too tangled in confusion to reach for what she truly wanted. The blood bond with Luka slithered through her veins, tightening its grip with every passing day. It whispered with his voice, teased with false heat. She didn't want him—not truly, not wholly—but the bond clawed at her anyway, dragging old shadows into the light and distorting everything it touched.

But this...this was different.

As her palm met the bare heat of Gabriel's chest, that familiar ache surged between them—magnetic and merciless. Months had passed, but her body remembered. The feel of his hands mapping every secret. The rasp of his voice murmuring things meant only for her. The way he saw her, even when she wanted to vanish into smoke.

Gabriel's eyes flicked down, catching the spark in her gaze, and his grin unfurled—slow, feral, devastating. He dipped his head until his breath brushed the shell of her ear, warm and wicked.

"Say the word, Cinis," he murmured, voice like silk pulled taut. "And I'll remind you how good we are together."

A flush bloomed across her skin, chasing heat through her neck and down her spine. Her stomach twisted with want, heat curling low and sharp. A retort rose in her throat—half challenge, half surrender.

But before it could escape, the groan of an ancient door echoed behind her, low and guttural, dragging her pulse to a halt.

She turned, heart stumbling, to find Luka emerging from the tower's shadow. He leaned against the stone like he'd always belonged there, arms folded, face unreadable. Silent. Watching.

Gabriel didn't back off. Luka didn't blink. The air between them thickened, charged with something volatile. The tension cracked—hot and electric, like the space between lightning and thunder.

Ophelia rolled her eyes and flicked a lazy ember toward Gabriel's chest. It flared bright, sparked, and fizzled against his skin.

He didn't so much as flinch.

Of course, he didn't.

With a muttered curse, Ophelia stepped back, the soles of her boots scuffing against the worn stone. Heat clung to her like a second skin, fire ghosting in her wake no matter how fast she walked. She strode toward the long wooden table where Mo sat buried in ancient texts, trying and failing not to let the swirl of panic overtake her.

Mo glanced up, the flickering candlelight catching on the rims of his glasses. His gaze narrowed instantly. "Something happened?" he asked.

Ophelia nodded once, sharp and grim. "Elijah's in San Marino," she said.

Mo set his pen down slowly, as though anchoring his thoughts. "That's not a coincidence."

Ophelia's grip tightened around the phone, the metal groaning under the strain. "Eris left him there. I don't know why. But I'm going to find out," she said.

A heavy silence unfurled around them, broken only by the low hiss of the fire behind them and the song of birds overhead.

Then Mo exhaled, rubbing a hand down his face, smudging ink across his cheek. "The Council won't make this easy for you," he said.

Gabriel's voice sliced through the quiet, firm and low. "She's not going alone," he said.

Ophelia turned to him, irritation flaring in her chest like a struck match. "I can handle this," she said.

Gabriel didn't flinch. His brown eyes locked on hers, unwavering. "That's not the point. You know how the Council operates. If you walk in alone, they'll see it as weakness. Because you're only a hybrid," he said, his voice dripping, dark and deliberate. "You need backup from a true vampire."

Brisa snorted from across the room. "Let's make sure the ancient, all-male vampire ruling class isn't too threatened by a woman doing things on her own," she muttered, sarcasm curling around her words like smoke.

Gabriel didn't so much as blink. His attention was solely on Ophelia, his presence a wall she couldn't walk through. "I'm coming with you," he said.

Mo leaned back in his chair, fingers steepled, his expression unreadable. "You'll need someone who understands vampire politics. But your absence from Luka…" His gaze flicked to the side, where Luka waited, posture perfect, every line of him composed. "It complicates things," Mo said.

Ophelia stiffened as Luka joined them at the table, his movement nearly silent, yet impossible to ignore. Where Gabriel burned, Luka simmered. He was control incarnate— cold, coiled, calculating. Once, she thought she knew every layer of him.

She'd been wrong.

"I don't see what that has to do with getting Elijah back," she said, voice clipped with resentment. The mention of their bond still scraped at her like broken glass.

Mo gestured to the open tomes in front of him, ink bleeding into the edges of yellowed parchment. "From what I can tell, the stronger the bond, the more volatile distance becomes. I don't know how your magic will respond while you're apart."

That was when she felt it—a faint tug beneath her skin, subtle as breath, persistent as a heartbeat. The bond. Still there. Still threading her to him. When she looked up, Luka was already watching her.

"I'll go with you," Luka said, calm as ever.

"You will not," she replied instantly, the words sharp enough to draw blood.

"Two powerful vampires at your side will be a clear show of force," Luka said, unbothered by the venom in her tone. "Especially after what happened the last time you were there."

To her surprise, Gabriel gave a terse nod. "It's a good idea," he admitted, though his voice held gravel and steel.

Ophelia closed her eyes for half a second, drawing in a breath. "Fine. But I'm leading this. We get in, we get out. It'll be fastest if I thread," she said.

A ripple of tension ran through them. Threading wasn't just rare. It was dangerous—a volatile blend of blood, instinct, and willpower that allowed her to slip between magical veins, following invisible currents that carved through space. Few witches could do it. Fewer survived it unscathed.

Mo's gaze darkened, his voice quieter now. "Just be careful. If the vampires know what Eris told him, they'll demand a price. They won't give him up for free."

Ophelia didn't answer. Because deep down, she already knew. This wasn't just about Elijah anymore.

"How about we meet at the Trieste apartment?" she said, referring to the Alliance's so-called neutral territory for all supernaturals. The Alleanza or Alliance was formed centuries ago as a tenuous pact between witches, vampires, and other supernatural factions. They claimed to preserve balance, protect secrecy, and prevent another supernatural war. On paper, it was peace. In practice, it was fractured. Politics soaked in old blood and older grudges. Held together not by trust, but by fear.

Brisa's fingers drummed a restless rhythm against her thigh. "This is bullshit, and you know it's a trap," she snapped.

Ophelia turned, meeting her cousin's gaze with steel. "I don't have a choice," she said.

Brisa snorted, eyes flashing. "There's always a choice. But sure, let's stroll into vamp territory and pretend destroying a castle and killing a Council member didn't scorch the damn welcome mat," she said.

"I'm not walking away," Ophelia said, her voice low. "It's Elijah."

That name hit home. The irritation in Brisa's expression cracked, replaced by an understanding as her gaze flicked to her own father and then back to Ophelia. "I know," she muttered, dragging a hand through her short hair. Her voice dropped, rough around the edges. "I just don't like seeing you walk straight into someone else's power play."

Then, after a beat, she added, without looking at Ophelia, because Brisa never softened with eye contact, "There's something you need to do before you go."

Ophelia sighed and turned toward the house without another word. She made her way to the dim room, lit only by the low flicker of a nearby candle. The air smelled faintly of salt and iron, like old magic and blood that hadn't yet been washed clean.

Celeste lay in the center of the room, her skin ghost-pale against the deep linen sheets, her breath shallow but steady. Her hair fanned out across the pillow like spilled ink, strands tangled.

Alex sat at her bedside, her eyes narrowed in concentration as she pressed her hands gently over Celeste's ribcage. A soft pulse of golden light flickered from her palms, casting faint, shifting patterns across the sheets. She winced slightly, as if the magic stung to wield, too wild or too deep to be painless. She'd retreated here after Elijah's call and still wore yoga clothes damp with sweat, silver hair twisted hastily into a knot at the crown of her head.

"It's as if her power has gone into hiding," Alex murmured. "Like it's afraid to come back."

Ophelia knew Alex spent every spare moment here, studying, pushing her fae magic to its limits in the hope it might be enough to bring Celeste back.

Ophelia stepped forward quietly, her boots making no sound on the cold stone floor. "Thank you," she whispered. "You should rest."

Alex didn't argue. She nodded once, slow and solemn, and rose without another word, slipping from the room like a ghost, leaving Ophelia alone with her mother.

For a long moment, Ophelia just stood there, watching. The rise and fall of Celeste's chest. The furrow still etched faintly between her brows. Finally, she sat beside her carefully, taking one of Celeste's hands in both of her own. The skin was cold. Too cold. Like something caught halfway between the living and the dead.

"You don't have to wake up for this," Ophelia said softly. "But I need you to hear me." She paused, brushing her thumb along the edge of her mother's knuckles. The gesture was gentle, reverent, almost childlike. "I'm going to get Elijah back. No matter what Eris did to him. No matter what it costs," she said.

She swallowed hard, but the ache stayed lodged there like a stone. "But I need you to fight, too. You hear me?" Her grip clenched slightly, just enough to ground her. "I know things between us have been...broken," she said, voice cracking despite the fight to keep it steady. "But I still believe we can fix it. If you come back. If you stay."

The candle beside them sputtered, the flame twitching as if stirred by breath or magic. Shadows danced across the stone walls like watchful spirits. "We can't lose you," she whispered. "Not now. Not like this." There was no answer. No flicker behind her eyelids. No twitch of a finger. No whisper from beyond.

But the pulse beneath Ophelia's fingers fluttered once. It was faint. But stronger than before. Hope sparked in her chest—small, stubborn, and aching to be believed.

She let go slowly, brushing a thumb across her mother's hand one final time, then rose to her feet, the weight of what she couldn't say pressing harder than what she had.

She closed the door quietly behind her, sealing in the silence. When she stepped into the corridor, Luka and Gabriel were already there, waiting in silence, braced like sentinels. One carved from ice, the other from fire.

Gabriel's gaze swept over her, searching for fractures. Luka's gave nothing away.

Neither spoke. The tension between the three of them gathered like storm pressure—dense and electric. Too many things left unsaid, too much history tucked behind guarded expressions.

Ophelia stopped between them, her shoulders squaring as she extended her hands. "Let's go," she said.

She took Luka's hand in her right, Gabriel's in her left. Their fingers closed around hers—Gabriel's callused, Luka's cold as stone.

Ophelia let her magic reach. It slipped beneath the skin of the world, searching for the thread. There—thin, invisible, unmistakable. A shimmer in the fabric of reality. A line etched in blood and memory. Threading wasn't like stepping through a door. It was like being unraveled—every bone, every breath —then sewn back together with something older than time.

The thread pulsed.

Ophelia exhaled and pulled.

The world constricted. Sound collapsed. Light twisted.

And then it snapped.

CHAPTER

FOUR

They slammed into existence with a crack of air.

Ophelia landed hard on cold stone, knees bending beneath her to absorb the impact. The courtyard unfolded around them, vast and shadowed, carved into the mountain with brutal elegance. The air was too thick, like something dead had exhaled and never drawn breath again, and the scent of ancient blood clung to everything. Above them, one of the three remaining castles that formed the Council headquarters clawed at the sky. Its black iron balconies and hollowed-out windows loomed like watchful eyes.

Ophelia's breath caught. The air here was overwhelming. Thick and ancient, it pressed against her skin like humidity laced with static. A witch would feel it as a warning. A vampire would feel it as power.

She was both. And it made her stomach twist.

Two guards stepped into the archway ahead. Gabriel immediately moved in front of her, instinctive and silent. The guards were statuesque—pale, smooth-faced, their symmetry unnatural. They wore black embroidered uniforms trimmed in crimson, with swords sheathed at their hips.

"Remain still," one said. His voice was smooth and flat, the kind of tone that had been trained into obedience, stripped of personality.

Ophelia felt her magic tug in her chest, a ripple of alarm humming beneath her skin. But she held it back.

Luka raised his hand slowly. "We're here by request. Let Zeon know," he said.

The second guard inclined his head once and disappeared down the corridor. The other turned on his heel. "Follow," he said.

They moved through winding stone corridors lit by flickering torches. Ophelia could feel eyes in the dark. Watching. Measuring.

They rounded the final bend and stepped into the Council chamber, a cathedral of shadow and silence carved deep into the mountain. Vaulted ceilings arched high above, lost to darkness. Pale sunlight slanted through narrow stained-glass windows, painting the obsidian floor in streaks of blood red and cobalt. At the center of the room stood a wide hearth, embers glowing faintly beneath soot-blackened stone.

And beside it—

Elijah. Shoulders hunched, arms folded tightly across his chest. He looked thinner than she remembered, like something had been hollowed out. His glasses were smudged. His shoes— he always polished his shoes—were scuffed and unevenly laced. It wasn't just that he looked smaller; it was the way he held himself, like he was trying to fold into the stone. This was someone who didn't know what to believe anymore.

Her heart stuttered because part of her had imagined him safe, untouched, whole. "Elijah," she whispered, the words catching in her throat like glass.

He turned slowly, and when their eyes met, it hit her like a blow: the grief, the betrayal, the exhaustion etched into every line of his face.

"You lied to me," he said, voice low and full of pain.

Her heart cracked. It wasn't the words; it was the way he said them. Like she'd broken something sacred. Her breath caught in her throat, the apology dying behind her teeth. Because no truth she gave him now would undo the damage. "I never wanted to," she said.

"But you did," he said.

Before she could answer, a voice slid in from the shadows, cold and precise. "How touching."

Zeon's presence soaked into the room like a creeping fog—cold, deliberate, impossible to ignore. He emerged from the far end of the chamber, silver-eyed and slow-moving, as though he had all the time in the world to decide their fates.

Three thrones stood behind him, carved from obsidian and bone. Zeon lowered himself into the central seat, his body lounging with the kind of practiced indifference that made Ophelia's skin crawl. The other two seats sat cloaked in dust. One had belonged to Leander, lost to time, the other to Durante, now ash, thanks to her.

As if summoned by his presence, vampires began to file into the chamber, surrounding them in a wide semicircle. Silent. Watching.

Zeon didn't acknowledge them. His gaze was fixed on Elijah.

"This one," he said, gesturing lazily, "truly had no idea. His mind is...loud. Confused. He still believes in logic and reason. Adorable." He shifted his eyes to Ophelia, gaze sharpening. "But you, Miss Wildes...I see you've learned how to shield your thoughts. Much improved from the last time we met."

Her jaw tightened.

Zeon smiled. He was one of the rare vampires who could read memories without tasting blood. His fangs extended—not in hunger, but in warning. "The offer still stands to find your secrets the old-fashioned way," he said.

Gabriel stepped closer to her, the warmth of his hand settling at the small of her back. Protective. Possessive. A low growl vibrated in his throat.

Ophelia's body leaned without permission. A reflex. A betrayal. Because love didn't erase the bond's pull—it just made it more dangerous.

Luka, ever the strategist, bowed slightly. "As you know, Zeon, Miss Wildes is bound to a vampire. She cannot be tasted by another," he said.

Ophelia stiffened. The fact that he'd used the bond here, announcing it like a political shield, made her stomach turn. She refused to look at him.

Zeon's amusement deepened as his smile curved. "Such a conundrum you find yourself in, Miss Wildes. Bound to one vampire. In love with another. And the man who raised you now knows far too much. What's a hybrid to do?" he asked.

The words hit Ophelia like a slap. She didn't deny it. Couldn't. Not with both of them standing beside her like two parts of a war she hadn't chosen.

She stepped forward, voice cold. "Let's get on with it," she said.

Zeon tilted his head, studying her. "So eager. You never inherited your mother's patience."

"You know Elijah was brought here without consent. And you know who orchestrated it," she said. "I'm not in the mood for games."

Zeon's expression didn't waver. "Everything is a game, Miss Wildes."

She took another step, fists clenched. "Say what you want. But he doesn't belong here," she said.

Zeon leaned back into the throne, lacing his fingers together. "Let us be clear. Elijah Chandler is a human with knowledge that endangers the supernatural world. His very existence poses a threat to the balance we've so carefully maintained. The fact that he's still breathing is...inconvenient," he said.

"He didn't ask for any of this," Ophelia said.

"No," Zeon agreed. "But neither did we."

Ophelia's mind spun. There had to be another way. She could try threading out, take Elijah and vanish before anyone stopped her. She could offer something else. Her own blood. A binding oath. Anything but this.

Zeon stood, slow and deliberate. "If you want him released, you will accept the terms."

"What are your terms?" Luka asked evenly.

Zeon's voice dropped, rich with finality. "You will find Eris. Alive, preferably. Dead, if necessary. In return, consider Mr. Chandler's knowledge forgiven."

Ophelia's chest tightened, her breath catching like she'd been punched. She'd only recently met her sister. Barely knew her. But despite everything Eris had done—despite the chaos, the death, the war she'd nearly unleashed—Ophelia couldn't stop asking the question that clawed at her ribs: *What if she could be saved?*

It was a cruel conundrum. Agree to kill her sister, and Elijah would be safe. But what would it cost? Would it break her mother to lose a daughter again? Would it break her to become the executioner of someone who shared her blood?

She could feel Luka watching her. Felt Gabriel's presence tighten beside her.

Everyone waited. Everyone expected her to be decisive. Ruthless.

She wasn't sure she could be.

"That's not your call to make," she said quietly, her voice taut with the strain of everything she wasn't saying.

"But it is yours," Zeon said. "You may refuse, of course. But Elijah will remain our...guest."

"I came to get Elijah, not to negotiate," she said, voice even.

Zeon tilted his head. "Then you misunderstood your role in this," he said, voice like frost.

Ophelia clenched her jaw. "He's human. He doesn't belong here," she said, repeating herself.

"No," Zeon agreed. "But you do. And that is where our concerns lie."

Gabriel shifted beside her, his presence a silent warning. Be careful.

Zeon's gaze flicked lazily between them, amusement dancing behind his silver eyes. Then he turned to Luka with a predator's smile.

"Do you understand yet how the blood bond works?" he asked Ophelia, voice slick with condescension.

Ophelia clenched her jaw. She didn't want the truth. Not here. Not from Zeon's smug mouth. Not with Luka watching and Gabriel listening. But it pulsed beneath her skin anyway—this need to know. Because how could she fight a bond she didn't understand?

Zeon sighed, the sound exaggerated and theatrical. "Fine," he said, rising to his full height. "I'll give you this one for free."

He descended the steps of the dais, slow and instructive, his voice dropping into the register of someone who knew he held the room. "Vampire blood magic—like all great power— is layered. Tiered."

He began circling them like a lecturer before a captive class.

"First—blood healing," he said, gesturing loosely toward Ophelia. "A vampire gives blood to a mortal or a witch. Temporary. Useful. Intimate, yes, but nothing binding. It fades unless repeated or ritualized."

He stopped beside Luka, who stood still and silent. "Second—blood tasting. Deeper. A vampire takes blood and gains truth. Sees memories. Emotion. Power. Origins. Still not binding, unless reciprocated. But oh, the temptation."

Zeon's gaze slid back to Ophelia, gleaming now. "And then there's the third—blood binding. The soul-deep tether. The kind that can form in rituals...or in moments of madness. Sex. Grief. Death. You don't even need to mean it. All it takes is reciprocal exchange when the magic is high and the heart is open."

His smile sharpened. "And that is what you did. Accidentally. Or instinctively. Either way, you and Luka are blood bound."

Her breath hitched, and she fought the instinct to recoil—from the truth, from Luka, from her own body's traitorous heat.

Zeon chuckled. "You didn't even realize, did you? That's the best part. So many witches think they understand blood. But vampire blood is older. Trickier. You let it in—and it stays."

Then his expression turned almost pitying. "But you're not just a witch, are you?" he asked, pacing a slow circle around her, voice lowering.

"No one truly understands how blood bonds behave in a hybrid. Your kind shouldn't exist, and so the rules bend—or break entirely. A witch's magic amplified by vampire blood becomes unstable. Potent, yes. But volatile. You're a conduit that was never meant to carry that current."

He stopped behind her. "That's what Eris has figured out. That's why she's stronger. She's feeding off vampire blood to amplify her power. It makes her unstoppable...and uncontrollable."

He moved in front of her again, tone almost academic now. "Vampire blood doesn't just empower witches. It distorts them. Twists magic into something unpredictable. And when the blood is bound—like yours is—it doesn't just enhance. It consumes," he said.

His gaze sharpened, predatory as he continued. "You feel it, don't you? The way your power pulses differently now. Not just stronger. But hungrier."

Gabriel stepped closer to her again, jaw tight. "That's enough," he said, voice low but steel-edged. "We're leaving with Elijah. Now."

Zeon's smile didn't falter, but the air seemed to shift, colder and heavier.

"You are," he said smoothly. "But not without one final condition."

Ophelia didn't speak. But her fists curled until her nails bit into her palms. Her magic coiled like a snared animal beneath her skin. Because she couldn't scream. Couldn't fight. Not here. Not yet.

Zeon's eyes gleamed like distant moons. "Elijah walks free today because of you. His memories remain intact. His life remains untouched. But understand this, Miss Wildes—if you fail to bring Eris to justice, his protection is revoked."

He let the words hang, savoring them.

"His knowledge is a liability," Zeon continued. "And liabilities are only tolerated when they're useful—or when they're yours to pay for."

Ophelia's heart pounded in her chest.

"And a final condition," he added, almost like an afterthought. "You will not go alone. You'll be escorted by a vampire to ensure Eris is destroyed."

"I don't need—" Ophelia started to say, before Zeon cut her off.

"You misunderstand. This isn't about need. This is about accountability. Luka, unfortunately, is disqualified. The blood bond renders him compromised. He cannot report on your progress objectively," he said.

Ophelia's stomach dropped.

Zeon turned to Gabriel. "Which leaves you. You will accompany her. And if she fails to contain her sister—if the risk to our world worsens—you will answer for her failure. Directly. To us."

Gabriel's voice was steady. "Understood." As a vampire, Gabriel was required to consent to the Concilium's demands—his allegiance, however reluctant, was enforced by ancient law.

Ophelia, as a hybrid, had never been bound by those rules. But she was bound in other ways now: by promises, by love, by blood.

Ophelia looked between them. "So that's it? You use him as leverage, too?"

"No," Zeon said, amused. "You are the leverage. He's just the insurance."

The words struck like a backhand. She was tired of being used. And now she was both weapon and wager, and the people she loved were collateral.

"You think I'm a risk," Ophelia said.

Zeon met her gaze. "I think you're a variable. And I dislike variables."

Gabriel finally spoke, voice low but unwavering. "I'm not here for the Council. I'm here for her."

Zeon gave a slow, satisfied nod. "Then we have an accord."

Gabriel didn't wait.

In a blur of motion, he vanished from her side and reappeared beside Elijah. Before anyone else could react, he had an arm around Elijah's waist and was guiding him—nearly carrying him—across the chamber.

Elijah stumbled, dazed, but didn't resist.

Gabriel brought him to Ophelia's side, eyes sharp and waiting.

She didn't speak. Didn't nod. Didn't flinch. Her silence was not surrender—it was steel being drawn. Because agreeing and complying were never the same thing. And no vampire on this mountain could mistake her stillness for peace.

She had one chance. One thread. One move that was still hers. She reached for Elijah's hand with her left, Gabriel's with her right. Just as the thread of her magic began to hum beneath her skin, she felt Luka's hand close around her shoulder. Steady, anchoring, silent. She didn't shake him off. And that terrified her more than anything Zeon had said.

She let the thread snap into place.

And then they were gone, before anyone else could claim the next move.

CHAPTER
FIVE

The world snapped back into place with a violent twist of sensation—not quite pain, but the memory of it. Threading always felt like being unraveled at the seams and hurriedly stitched back together. Like her bones remembered where they belonged before her skin did. Sound collapsed. Light flickered. And then—

Her boots struck hardwood.

Ophelia staggered forward a step, grounding herself with a sharp exhale as the hum of protective wards whispered around her. The magic here was different—anchored, old, deliberate. Layers of it pressed gently against her senses, like invisible hands checking credentials at the door. They were in neutral territory now. Trieste. A coastal city steeped in ancient lines of power and older grudges, home to one of the Alliance's only "safe zones." Here, all supernaturals were expected to play nice.

Expected. Not guaranteed.

She straightened slowly and let her eyes adjust. Luka's apartment was just as she remembered it, suffused with the kind of stillness that made your skin crawl if you stood still too long. The walls were whitewashed stone, the floors dark polished wood. Wards shimmered faintly at the corners of the room, their magic humming in frequencies only witches could feel.

The air here was cleaner, cooler—salt-touched and unpolluted—but it still carried a scent she hadn't expected to hit so hard: night-blooming jasmine. Faint, but sharp enough to pull memory to the surface. Luka's scent.

She'd only set foot in here once since his supposed death. No one had touched a thing. The books on the shelves remained perfectly aligned. The blanket still draped over the arm of the couch hadn't been disturbed. Even the half-burned candle near the window—black wax, spicy clove-scented—sat unlit, a frozen echo of something that used to mean comfort.

And yet, as her magic spread through the room, testing the edges, she swore she felt the space recognize her. Like the very air bent around her in acknowledgment. Or warning.

Despite the Alliance's treaties, no one here trusted neutrality to last forever. Trieste had been chosen for its long-standing magical convergence and its resistance to supernatural dominance. It was neither witch territory nor vampire-controlled. And so the Alliance—the Alleanza—claimed it as their prize. A symbol of balance. A place where enemies shared space. But the protections were enforced not by trust, but by fear and very old magic.

Wards were laced into the walls, the doors, the very bones of the building. No one could enter Luka's apartment uninvited —not vampire, witch, fae, or otherwise. Which meant they were safe, for now.

Behind her, a soft gasp escaped Elijah's lips.

He stumbled forward, clutching at the wall with one hand, the other pressed to his chest like he was trying to hold himself together. "Okay," he wheezed, voice hoarse. "That was not normal. Definitely not airline-approved."

A strained laugh almost escaped her, but it came out more like a sigh. "It's called threading," she murmured, stepping closer to steady him. "It lets me move through the magical currents that run through the world. You'll get used to it."

But her tone betrayed her. No one ever really got used to threading. Not even her.

Gabriel stood near, his stance alert, every line of his body poised like a coiled spring. His dark eyes swept the room in a slow arc, taking in the doorways, windows, and shadowed corners. Always assessing. Always ready to kill if it came to that.

Luka stood in practiced stillness, hands tucked in the pockets of his black slacks, the barest tilt of his head betraying mild interest. He stared at his home like he was trespassing in someone else's life, even though echoes of him remained. His books lined the shelves.

Luka's gaze flicked briefly to her, then to Gabriel. It was nothing more than a glance, but the air between them grew heavier. Not aggressive. Not yet. But dense with old tension, the kind that didn't need words. Just proximity. Gabriel arched a brow but didn't speak. He didn't need to. The tension crackled without it.

Luka broke the silence first, moving toward the bar cart tucked neatly beneath the window. He walked like he didn't belong in his own skin, like the space had changed while he was gone and hadn't remembered to invite him back.

Ophelia's breath caught. She remembered the first time he brought her here. That night, they'd shared a bed. Not for sex, but for comfort. For quiet. For trust.

It had felt like safety.

And now?

Now it felt like a mausoleum.

Luka poured a drink with steady hands and passed a glass to Elijah without a word. Elijah didn't hesitate. He downed it in one swallow, then a second when Luka handed him another. Luka raised a brow but said nothing, only poured a third and handed it over.

Elijah took it, retreated to the couch, and sat with the glass nestled between his hands, his head hanging.

When Luka offered Ophelia a glass, she paused. The scent of it hit her like memory—warm, biting, familiar. For a heartbeat, she almost said yes. But she shook her head. She wouldn't take that path again, even if forgetting sounded very, very good tonight.

Luka didn't push. Just took a sip of his own and leaned against the edge of the window, one leg crossed over the other like he had all the time in the world. He didn't look at her again. But he didn't have to. The weight of him in the room was enough.

Elijah finally looked up, his eyes scanning the apartment as if waiting for the next illusion to drop. "We're really safe here?" he asked.

Ophelia nodded. "No one gets in without an invitation. Not even the Alliance. Wards on the windows. Triple-locks on the magical protections. And this whole building falls under treaty law. That means no supernatural is allowed to make a move on another here. Even the Council can't touch you," she said.

Elijah's jaw twitched. "And how often do people actually follow those rules?" he asked.

Gabriel let out a soft grunt. "Not often. But it's enough to make them think twice," he said.

That didn't comfort Elijah much. His shoulders sagged, and he sank deeper into the couch, still gripping the glass like it might keep him anchored.

Ophelia took a step back, her limbs heavy with the kind of fatigue that lived deep in the bones. "I need a minute," she said. She didn't wait for a response—just turned and slipped down the hall, heart pounding like she hadn't stopped threading at all.

She slipped into the bathroom and shut the door behind her, the click of the lock echoing louder than she meant. Her breath caught in her chest as she leaned heavily over the marble sink, palms braced against the cold surface. Her reflection stared back, pale and drawn, eyes rimmed in red.

Her hair clung to the back of her neck, still damp with sweat from training, from threading, from the near-collapse of everything she was barely holding together. The glow of the vanity light was too warm, too soft—it made her look fragile. Human.

Her fingers curled against the porcelain, knuckles bone-white. The bond pulsed. Not violently. But present. Unwelcome.

What the hell am I doing?

She was just starting to steady herself when she heard the door unlatch behind her. She didn't have to look. She knew it was him.

The scent hit her first—cedarwood and sea salt, wild and grounding. It curled through her like memory and muscle ache, wrapping around her like a storm-slick cloak. Gabriel stepped inside, silent as a shadow. He closed the door with deliberate quiet, but his presence filled the small room instantly.

She didn't turn. Just met his gaze in the mirror.

"You're not supposed to be in here," she said, voice flat but fraying at the edges.

"I know," he said, low and rough, almost like it hurt to admit it.

She stayed where she was, watching him over her shoulder. He was close, and her body noticed before her mind could catch up. Her magic flared at his proximity, not in warning, but in recognition. Heat skated beneath her skin.

"Gabriel—" she started, trying to give him an out, trying to give herself one.

He didn't let her finish. His fingers brushed her arm—just once, barely a graze—and her entire body seized. Her heart thudded painfully against her ribs. She turned, ready to shove him back, to tell him this wasn't fair. That she was broken, bound, and too confused to make anything that resembled a choice.

But the moment her fists met his chest, he caught her wrists gently. Steadying her. Anchoring her. And then—gods— he leaned in. He kissed her forehead first. Then each cheek, slow and reverent, like he was trying to memorize her. Like he didn't trust he'd ever get this close again.

Her fists dropped. And he reached up, his hand closing lightly around her throat—not hard, not possessive, just claiming space that already felt like his.

He kissed her. It wasn't soft. It was hungry. Desperate. Like he was pouring months of silence, tension, loss into that single collision of mouths. Like he'd waited long enough and couldn't anymore.

And Ophelia kissed him back.

Her fingers twisted into his shirt, dragging him closer. For one breathless, furious second, she let herself fall. Let herself forget the bond, the blood, the betrayal.

Then she pulled back, panting.

"I shouldn't," she whispered. Her forehead pressed against his. "Because of the bond. Because I don't know what's real."

Gabriel's hands stayed firm at her waist. He didn't pull back. His gaze searched hers—dark, shining, heartbreakingly honest. "Yes, you do," he said. "You know exactly what's real. You just don't want to risk believing it."

Her breath caught.

"I want to be enough," he said, voice raw. "I want to be the one you choose. But I'm not going to push. It's your decision entirely."

It was the most open, vulnerable thing he'd ever said to her. And it cracked something in her chest.

She kissed him again—slower this time, softer, but just as deep. And when his hands slid to her hips, lifting her effort-lessly onto the counter, she didn't stop him. She spread her legs to let him step between them, her thighs bracketing his hips, her pulse fluttering wildly beneath her skin.

His hands trailed down her sides, over the thin fabric of her yoga pants, fingers grazing the edge of her waistband. His breath skimmed her ear.

"I know this is what you need," he whispered, his voice all gravel and promise. "I can feel it. You're soaked through those pants, Cinis. But I'm not going to fuck you right now."

She whimpered—barely—but he caught it.

"Not unless you say the word," he said, mouth brushing the edge of her jaw. "It's been too long. And I want to hear you say it."

Her body answered before her mind could. Her hips shifted against him, seeking contact. Her fingers knotted in his shirt again.

But then the bond surged. Hot. Sharp. Invasive. Luka. It sliced through her like a jagged blade. Not memory. Not want. But presence. Distant, watching. She felt it coil like smoke in her chest.

Ophelia gasped, pulling back as if burned. Her body still ached for Gabriel, every nerve ending tingling, but the magic said otherwise. "I'm sorry," she said, pressing trembling fingers to her lips.

Gabriel didn't move. Didn't argue. Just looked down at her with something that might have been pain, or perhaps resignation. "Don't be," he said softly. Then he stepped away, giving her space, and walked out.

Leaving her breathless and shaking in front of a mirror that showed too much—swollen lips, mussed hair, flushed skin— she stared at herself for a long moment. Then she reached for the sink again, ran cold water over her wrists, and tried to breathe.

She pulled a towel from the rack, dabbed at her neck and face, and fixed her hair. Practiced what she might say to Elijah.

I'm sorry I lied.

I thought I was protecting you.

I never stopped loving you for trying to help me, even when you didn't understand.

But when she opened the door, the words fell away. Luka was there, leaning against the wall across the hall. Watching her. She froze. His expression was unreadable—no anger, no jealousy, no judgment. Just silence.

She stared back for a long heartbeat, guilt forming fast in her chest. Then it twisted into something colder: remembrance. Of the bond. Of his lies. Of what he'd done to her without consent.

She walked away, looking for Elijah. She found him on the terrace, leaning over the railing as he stared out at the crashing Adriatic Sea. The lights of Trieste glowed in the distance, golden pinpricks against the endless dark.

He stood silent as she approached. "Were you ever going to tell me about all of this?" he asked, sorrow woven into his voice as he gestured, eyes fixed on the horizon.

She stepped beside him, resting her forearms on the cool

iron railing. She knew he was talking about the supernatural world. "I should have told you sooner. I thought I was protecting you," she said.

"From the truth?" he asked, voice flat.

She hesitated. "From everything. From what it would do to you," she said.

He turned, finally meeting her eyes. "You thought it would break me?" he asked.

"I thought if I showed you what I'd become, you wouldn't recognize me anymore," she said.

He held her gaze. "Bullshit," he said.

The word stung more than she expected. He didn't raise his voice, didn't need to.

"You should've given me more credit," he added.

"I know." Her voice was a whisper. "I hated being lied to. And then I became someone who lied. Someone who hid," she said.

The silence that followed was as vast as the ocean.

"I'm angry at myself," he admitted. "I didn't believe you when you were a kid. I thought the visions, the instincts...were trauma. That I could fix you with therapy. With time. With enough love," he said.

She blinked fast, pushing back the sting behind her eyes. "I was broken. But not because of the magic. Because no one told me the truth," she said. Another beat passed before she continued. "I have a sister," she said. "Eris."

Elijah turned slowly. "We met," he said flatly. "She looks like you. Same eyes. Same mouth. But everything about her is... wrong."

"She's a mirror twisted sideways," Ophelia said softly. "Same roots, different rot."

He exhaled hard, running a hand across his face. "I had gone back to New York to find you, but you weren't there. I hadn't been there long when she kidnapped me from our townhome. And I woke up in Italy, and I didn't know if I was dreaming or drugged. She told me magic was real. Said you were powerful. That you'd lied to protect me. I didn't believe her," he said, pausing and jaw tightening. "So she showed me. Lifted a glass from across the room without touching it. Snapped her fingers and made the fire light. I couldn't explain it. I still can't. Then she said now that I knew too much, the vampires could decide what to do with me."

Ophelia's throat tightened. "She knew exactly where to cut," she said. And taking a deep breath, she told him everything. Not just what was necessary, but all of it. Her hybrid nature. Vampires. Witches. Fae. The blood bond. The Lunula Amulet. The Bell of Time. Leander. Her voice faltered occasionally, but Elijah didn't interrupt.

By the time she was done, hours had slipped away. They'd migrated to chairs on the terrace, the sea wind curling around them, and the moon shone bright and silent overhead.

"She's dangerous," Ophelia said finally, referring to Eris. "More powerful than we thought. And reckless. The blood magic she's using...it's not just ancient. It's forbidden. Forgotten for a reason."

Elijah ran a hand through his curls and let out a long breath. "She's hurting people?"

Ophelia nodded in response.

He went quiet for a long beat.

"And you have to stop her," Elijah said. It wasn't a question; he knew.

Ophelia met his eyes. "I'm the only one who can," she said.

The silence that followed felt heavier than before, no longer empty. But it was filled with grief and things neither of them wanted to say aloud.

Then Elijah asked the one thing she'd been bracing for.

"What about Celeste?"

Ophelia's breath hitched. "She's alive. Barely. Eris nearly killed her. She's...in some kind of magical coma. No one knows if she'll ever wake up."

Elijah's jaw clenched. "Of course, she is," he muttered, his voice rough with old hurt. "That woman spent her whole life keeping secrets. Why should death be any different?"

Ophelia blinked. "You're angry," she said.

"I've been angry for a long time," he said. "At her. At you. At myself," he admitted.

They sat in it: grief, guilt, resentment. All of it, tangled and unsaid.

And then, quietly, Elijah reached across the space between them and took her hand. His large palm was rough, familiar. Steady.

"I'm here now," he said. "And I'm not going anywhere. Just...no more secrets. Not between us."

Ophelia looked down at their joined hands and nodded. "No more secrets."

She turned her gaze to the horizon. A cloud moved across the moon, casting a long shadow over the sea.

Something was coming.

And this time, she wasn't facing it alone.

CHAPTER
SIX

The morning came too soon. Pale light spilled across the floor, catching in the dust motes that floated lazily in the air. Ophelia sat at the kitchen table, cradling a mug of coffee like it might anchor her to the waking world. The exhaustion hadn't faded overnight. It had sunk deeper. A bone-deep kind of weariness clung to her, threaded through her limbs and thoughts.

Confessing everything to Elijah had gutted her in ways she hadn't anticipated. The kiss with Gabriel lingered on her lips, just as the memory of Celeste's still form lingered behind her eyes. She wasn't ready for this morning. But she rarely had the luxury of being ready.

The front door creaked open. Mo and Brisa stepped inside without knocking.

"So, no one thought to thread us in," Brisa yelled from the foyer. "We had to travel the old-fashioned way."

Ophelia rolled her eyes.

Mo entered the kitchen without a word, a thick leather-bound book tucked under one arm. He set it down with a solid thud that made her flinch. "You need to go to Slovenia," he said.

Ophelia looked up, her voice dry. "Sofija. I know," she said, dropping her head in her hands, the ceramic mug warming her face. A flicker of unease moved through her. Mt. Slivnica, a place she was tied to by blood and birthright, but where she did not feel fully welcome. Going there meant confronting not just Sofija, but her own place in a legacy she wasn't sure she wanted.

Elijah appeared in the doorway, rubbing sleep from his eyes. He gave a half wave to Mo and Brisa. They'd met after Luka disappeared, but Elijah hadn't known then who—or what—they really were. Now he did. "What's in Slovenia?" he asked.

Mo glanced at Ophelia, and she gave a small nod. The era of keeping Elijah in the dark was over.

"Mt. Slivnica," Mo said. "It's where the witches gather in communion with their high priestess. The ancestral home of the Coven. That's where Sofija resides."

Elijah's brow furrowed. "And why does Ophelia need to meet with this...Sofija?" he asked.

"Because she might know how to break the blood bond," Ophelia answered, lifting her head. "And she might be the only one who understands what Eris is becoming."

Elijah followed her gaze into the living room, where Gabriel and Luka occupied opposite ends of the couch like rival statues carved from opposing forces. Both broad-shouldered and impossibly tall, they seemed to take up more space than the room should allow. Gabriel's fingers tapped against his knee. Luka, on the other hand, didn't move at all, composed and predatory. He could have been carved from obsidian, watching the room with cold detachment. They were opposites in every sense, yet both radiated a kind of power that thickened the air.

Arms folded, jaws set like stone, they didn't speak or look at each other, but the tension between them vibrated like a live wire strung across the space. Even in silence, they dominated the room.

"Can one of those meat sacks go with you for protection?" Elijah asked, gesturing to them.

Brisa breezed into the kitchen, a devilish grin spreading across her face. "Oh, I knew I liked him," she said, pointing at Elijah with an approving nod. Leaning against the doorway, she cast a glance toward the living room. "Honestly, it's like someone stuffed a football team into a shoebox. Too much jawline. Not enough oxygen," she said.

Mo, as usual, ignored the banter entirely and returned to Elijah's question like nothing else had been said. "Wards prevent other supernaturals from entering our lands. No vampire has been permitted to set foot on Mount Slivnica in hundreds of years," he said, flipping open the worn leather book. He hesitated, then added, "Well, except for Ophelia. Her hybrid nature makes her the exception."

Gabriel entered quietly, his presence as deliberate as his silence. He leaned against the wall, arms crossed, expression unreadable. "I think I should go with you," he said. "At least to the base of the mountain. I don't trust the Coven to keep their end of any agreement. Not with you walking in alone."

Luka appeared a moment later, shoving past Gabriel and moving like the room already belonged to him. Technically, it did. Or had. He poured himself a glass of water, casual as if the tension weren't thick enough to slice.

"I think," Luka said, voice smooth and annoyingly self-assured, "that the stronger vampire should be with Ophelia.

And that is clearly the one with the ancient bloodline. The one who can shift," he said.

He didn't look at Gabriel when he said it, but he didn't have to.

Gabriel didn't so much as blink. "You mean the one who's been healing on a couch for weeks?" he asked.

Luka took a measured sip, then offered a tight smile. "Even at half-strength, I'm more lethal than you've ever been," he said.

Ophelia rolled her eyes so hard it almost gave her a headache. The entirety of Trieste wasn't big enough for these egos, let alone the square footage of Luka's apartment. "If you two are done measuring fangs," she muttered, "I have a high priestess to face."

"What does he mean, shift?" Elijah asked, one eyebrow arched as he stared at Luka.

Shit. Ophelia had forgotten that little detail.

"Gatto nero here," Gabriel said, gesturing lazily toward Luka, "can shift into almost anything." Despite his disdain for the other vampire, something flickered, perhaps reluctant respect. For all Luka's arrogance, that power was real.

"He's got a flair for the rare black jaguar," Brisa added with a grin, "but I've seen him rock dragon scales once when he was feeling dramatic."

Elijah blinked. "And...can all vampires do that?"

He sounded more curious than terrified. Which, honestly, was a shame, Ophelia thought. A little fear might've been healthy.

Luka didn't look at Elijah or Brisa. He simply stepped forward and answered with his usual elegant detachment.

"Vampires have gone by many names," he said. "But we refer to ourselves—those of true lineage—as empusae. Most cannot shift. Only a rare few."

Elijah frowned slightly, absorbing the word.

"The empusae," Luka continued, "descend from the goddess Hecate and the spirit Mormo. When Zeus discovered that Hecate had fallen in love with Mormo—another female spirit—he was enraged. Hecate refused to bend to him, and from that defiance, Empusa was born."

Ophelia watched him as he spoke, the reverence in his voice unmistakable, as if he were reciting scripture burned into his bones. She remembered the first time she'd seen him shift—how the air had stirred, how his bones had seemed to melt into shadow. It had terrified her. And thrilled her. Even now, with all the hurt between them, that memory stirred something deep and unwelcome.

Across from her, Elijah leaned forward slightly, fascinated despite himself. She could see the tension in his brow as myth collided with reality, breaking apart the last of his old worldview.

"As punishment," he went on, "Zeus cursed Empusa and her descendants. To survive, we would need blood. Thus, the first vampires were born—not turned, but born. We are the remnants of divine rebellion," Luka said.

He glanced at Elijah now, eyes cold but gleaming. "Only those descended from Empusa's line carry the shapeshifting gift. It's rare. Ancient. Most haven't used it in centuries," he said.

Elijah opened his mouth, the shape of his next question already forming. But Luka cut him off with a sigh, like he'd heard these questions a thousand times. "And before you ask: no, we don't sparkle in sunlight. The sun doesn't hurt us. We still breathe, our hearts still beat—just slower. We can survive on animal or human blood. Our bodies are efficient—optimized for speed, strength, and lethality. Everything about us is designed to make us better hunters. We can only be killed by shattering the heart or severing the head. Any other questions?"

There was a pause.

Elijah's mouth opened. Closed. Opened again. Then finally: "Not that I can think of right now," he said.

Brisa snorted, flipping her freshly painted orange nails toward the ceiling. "I'm honestly shocked you didn't ask if he sleeps in a coffin. To which the answer," she said, with mock seriousness, "is absolutely yes."

Luka's glare flicked to her like a knife. Brisa just wiggled her fingers and grinned wider.

Elijah stared at Brisa for a long moment, clearly trying to decide whether she was joking.

Mo, however, didn't linger on the banter. He dropped a thick stack of parchment onto the table and turned serious. "Elijah will be safest here in Trieste. Neutral territory protects him—for now. Brisa, you'll go with Ophelia to Mt. Slivnica. But behave," he added, giving his daughter a pointed look. "Ophelia needs answers, not distractions."

Brisa didn't even look up from her nails. "Who do you think I am?" she asked, with the kind of deadpan sincerity only she could pull off.

Ophelia shot Mo a look that clearly translated to: You know exactly who she is.

Elijah cleared his throat. "I'd like to do more than just be… protected," he said, quietly but with intent. "I want to help. Really help." A pause followed. He didn't look like a kid anymore—not just wide-eyed and overwhelmed. There was something solid in his voice. A steadiness Ophelia hadn't heard in a long time.

Ophelia bit the inside of her cheek as she considered. His world had been ripped apart in twenty-four hours. He was lost, unsure of where he fit in this new reality. He needed purpose—something concrete. Something his.

Then it clicked.

"Mo," she said, turning to him, "are any of the texts you're studying written in English?"

Mo adjusted his glasses. "Some of the more recent ones are, yes. Why?"

Ophelia glanced at Elijah, then back to Mo. "Why don't you use Elijah as a research assistant? He's done years of academic work, and he's more organized than the rest of us combined. If there's something buried in those texts—anything about Eris, the bond, or the Bell—he might be able to find it."

Mo looked skeptical, but when he saw Elijah's face—hopeful, eager, ready—his expression softened.

"Your help would be most appreciated, Elijah," he said. "I'll show you where I've left off."

Elijah beamed and immediately rolled up his sleeves, ready to dive in.

As Mo spread ancient tomes and handwritten translations across the table, Ophelia reached for her bag and turned to Brisa. The energy around them began to shift—threading always pulled at her in strange ways, but this time, it felt focused. Grounded.

She offered Elijah a small, encouraging smile. "We'll be back soon. Find something brilliant."

Ophelia stepped away and moved down the hall toward the study. The room felt unchanged—same polished mahogany desk, same worn armchair tucked beside the fireplace. It was here when she'd first uncovered Luka's betrayal, the weight of that truth still echoing in the air like a ghost she hadn't quite exorcised.

She inhaled deeply, then exhaled it all. There wasn't time for ghosts now.

Gabriel appeared in the doorway, eyes shadowed but steady. "Be careful," he said, his voice low enough that only she could hear. He looked like he wanted to say more—final, maybe. Reckless, probably. But whatever it was, he swallowed it, locking it behind that guarded stare that always gave too little and too much at once.

"I always am," she replied, but the corner of her mouth curved, just slightly. She wished it were truer than it felt. And she hated that he didn't kiss her. Hated that part of her wished he had.

He didn't step closer, but the intensity in his gaze lingered. There was more he wanted to say—she could feel it—but the moment passed, and he let it.

From behind him, Luka stood at the edge of the hallway, watching. He said nothing, but his presence pressed against her magic like a pulse. Familiar. Dangerous. Not unwelcome.

Their eyes met for a single breath too long.

Then Brisa strolled in with her usual timing, twirling a silver dagger between her fingers.

"All right, kids," she said, grinning. "Time to find ourselves a cranky old witch in a mountain cave. What could possibly go wrong?"

Ophelia rolled her eyes but stepped forward, brushing her fingers against Brisa's arm. The thread sparked instantly beneath her skin—ready and waiting. The air around her thickened, charged with the hum of unseen energy. Her blood hummed with it, tugged by the invisible seam only she could sense.

She looked back once, catching Gabriel's eyes. Then Luka's.

Whatever they were, whatever they weren't, it would have to wait.

The thread surged beneath her skin, and the world tore open.

Then they were gone.

CHAPTER

SEVEN

Daylight broke silver and sharp across the mountain. Even in the sun, Mt. Slivnica held a quiet kind of cold—the kind that clung to the bones and sank beneath clothes. The wind whispered through the pine boughs like it carried old secrets, and frost still laced the roots of trees that curled along the base of the trail.

The scent of damp earth, pine resin, and ancient stone hung thick in the air as Ophelia and Brisa threaded to the warded boundary.

The moment they arrived, the weight hit them both.

Ophelia staggered forward, bending at the waist as if the air had been knocked out of her. Her magic, usually a steady current beneath her skin, dimmed to a flicker. It wasn't gone, but the connection felt distant, like a voice calling through water. Muted.

Brisa hissed through her teeth and swore under her breath. She flexed her fingers, as though trying to shake the numbness from her power. "It doesn't feel right to be disconnected," she muttered.

Ophelia forced her focus forward, grounding herself in the rhythm of their boots crunching over snow-dusted stone. Each step echoed like a reminder: this place didn't want them here. Not really.

And yet, they climbed.

About an hour into the hike, just as the trail narrowed into a crooked bend, a small clearing opened before them. A dilapidated cabin stood near the edge, its roof sagging with age and shutters hanging askew. Moss climbed the stone walls like a second skin, and the chimney leaned as if it had been exhaling smoke for centuries.

But Ophelia knew immediately: the witches weren't there.

There was no hum of presence. No sense of magic stirred from within. The air near it felt hollow, like a breath that had long since been released.

"I'm sure they're at Coprniška Jama," Brisa said, brushing a pine needle from her shoulder. "They'll want to be close to the source. The cave amplifies everything—spells, wards, illusions. And if they want to impress you, they'll want to do it from the shadows..." She shot Ophelia a knowing look.

Coprniška Jama. The Witches' Cave.

It was the place where witches had convened for millennia, an ancestral site so ancient even the oldest among them didn't remember its beginning. Some said the mountain had been carved around the cave, not the other way around. Others whispered that the cave had once been a mouth of the underworld.

Whatever the truth, it was holy ground for the witches.

The climb steepened, each step pulling them higher into thinner, colder air. The trail snaked between craggy outcroppings and dense stands of fir and spruce, branches clawing at their sleeves. Ophelia adjusted the strap of her bag across her chest, fingers tingling from the cold. She paused, breath curling visibly in the air, and looked back over the slope below.

Lake Cerknica stretched like a mirror in the distance, eerily still. Swollen for now and full to the brim, but she knew that would change. The lake always disappeared when the witches left, vanishing into the porous limestone beneath it. A breathing thing. A secret-keeper.

They pressed on, ducking beneath gnarled branches and squeezing through a thicket of beech and pine. The bark scratched at their arms, but the view on the other side stole the breath from Ophelia's lungs.

A wide, lush meadow spread before them like a spell in bloom.

Blanketed in wildflowers—sun-drenched yellows, vivid purples, and crimson reds—the clearing pulsed with quiet life. The blooms shouldn't have survived this high, or in this cold, but they thrived year-round. Magic lived in the soil here, old and patient, coaxing color from rock and frost.

"This place always creeps me out," Brisa murmured, glancing around. "It's too...alive."

Across the meadow, half-veiled by shadow and root, the mouth of the cave emerged from the side of the mountain. Carved from ancient limestone, it was wide and smooth, the surface weathered pale as bone.

A pair of witches stood guard at the entrance, their silhouettes barely discernible through the mist that clung to the mountainside like breath. They wore heavy robes the color of midnight, lined with silver embroidery that shimmered faintly, symbols of the moon in all its phases winding down their sleeves and across their collars.

Their faces were expressionless, eyes unblinking as Ophelia and Brisa approached. Their presence didn't flare like an aura; it pressed. Quiet, cold, calculating.

The entrance to the cave stopped just one inch above Ophelia's head, narrow enough that only one person could enter at a time. Ivy draped from the stone like a veil, curling over the arch and down its edges in dense green waves. It looked soft, almost inviting, but the magic woven into the vines told another story. Protective. Ancient. Alive.

Beyond the entrance, the mountain rose sharply, its jagged ridgeline biting into the pale sky. The wind up here was colder. Harsher. And everything smelled of stone, snow, and magic.

One of the witches stepped forward, a tall woman with severe cheekbones and sharp brown eyes that gave nothing away.

"The high priestess is expecting you," she said, voice like polished flint.

Ophelia nodded once, resisting the urge to clear her throat. Tension pressed against her ribs like a warning. She wasn't here to kneel. She was here to demand answers.

The guards stepped aside in eerie unison, parting the mist with them as they moved. As Ophelia stepped over the narrow threshold, the air shifted.

The second her boots touched the stone pathway inside, the magic around her pulsed.

The cave unfolded.

What had seemed from the outside like a cramped cavern bloomed open into a vast hall—shaped by magic, not nature. The walls stretched far beyond what should have been possible, veined with glowing crystals and carved sigils that pulsed in rhythm with the earth's slow heartbeat. The floor beneath her feet was smooth stone, warm and dry despite the cold outside. The air thrummed with energy: old, sacred, and watchful.

Torches burned along the walls without flame, their light cast from floating orbs that hovered like stars held in orbit.

Threads of silver mist slithered along the edges of the chamber, clinging to the floor like fog reluctant to leave.

At the far end of the hall, Sofija sat on an ornate throne carved from dark wood so polished it reflected the flicker of the lights. The throne's arms were etched with ancient sigils—symbols of fire, earth, air, and water—and the back rose into an arch carved with every phase of the moon. The stone dais beneath her seemed grown rather than built, like the mountain itself had lifted her there.

She didn't rise. She didn't need to.

Flanking her, six neophytes stood in silent formation, three to each side. Their robes were lighter than the guards', deep indigo trimmed with gold thread, and their expressions were unreadable. But their eyes were sharp, locked on Ophelia like a pack of wolves sizing up a threat.

Brisa let out a low breath beside her, barely audible.

Ophelia didn't blink.

She stepped forward, spine straight, letting the hush of the chamber fall over her like a challenge.

Sofija's eyes found her the moment she stepped into the chamber. Aqua-blue, they were unnervingly clear, like glacial water before the thaw. They were ancient eyes, set deep beneath weathered lines that carved across her face like cracked porcelain. Her thin white hair spilled in silken sheets down to her waist, gleaming against the ink-black fabric of her robes. Her frame appeared almost frail, the bones delicate beneath the folds of cloth.

But her presence filled the chamber like a spell already cast.

Even without moving, Sofija radiated power, restrained only by choice.

To her right stood Ingrid.

The warrior-jawed witch held herself with rigid precision,

spine straight, hands clasped behind her back like she was preparing to stand trial or lead one. Her cropped black hair brushed against her sharp cheekbones, and her brown eyes narrowed slightly as they landed on Ophelia, first measuring and then hardening with familiar distrust.

Brisa leaned in just enough to murmur near Ophelia's ear. "Fun fact: I used to date her," she said.

Ophelia's brow twitched upward, surprised. "You dated Ingrid?" she asked.

Brisa shrugged, grinning without shame. "Briefly. Before I realized you shouldn't shit where you eat. Especially not in arm's reach of combat spells."

Ingrid's gaze snapped toward them like she'd heard every word. She probably had.

Brisa just flashed her a wicked smile.

"The hybrid returns," Sofija murmured, her voice rasping like dry leaves scattered across stone.

Ophelia forced herself to meet those glacial blue eyes. "I never belonged to you in the first place."

A ripple of murmurs swept through the gathered witches, a whisper of scandal or amusement—Ophelia couldn't tell which. The neophytes exchanged glances, some wide-eyed, others smirking. But Sofija? She only smiled.

A slow, knowing curl of the lips. A predator baring its teeth.

"Come forward, girl," she said, her voice reverberating with power. "We have much to discuss." She stood and walked away without waiting, her robes trailing behind like dark ink bleeding into stone.

The chamber where she led Ophelia was smaller than the grand hall, but no less imposing. It was dimly lit by floating orbs of soft blue light that drifted near the ceiling like captive moons. Shadows clung to the corners of the room, and the scent of burning herbs and aged parchment filled the air—

sharp, earthy, and grounding. It smelled like history. Like secrets.

Sofija moved to a long, curved table made of ancient wood, covered in weathered scrolls and cracked-spined books, their pages inked with sigils, diagrams, and blood-toned annotations.

"You seek answers about the bond," she said, running her gnarled fingers across a yellowed parchment as she took a seat at the head of the table.

Ophelia remained standing. She didn't care if it was rude. She folded her arms across her chest, magic still prickling uncomfortably under her skin. "I already know Luka tied me to him. I want to know how to break it."

Sofija looked up slowly. Her eyes gleamed in the pale blue light. "And yet, you hesitate."

Ophelia's shoulders tensed. "I didn't have a choice."

"No," Sofija agreed, tilting her head. "But now, you do."

She tapped her finger against an open page, the sound sharp in the silence. "Blood bonds are not simple, hybrid. They are layered. And they are rarely clean."

Ophelia's throat tightened. "What Luka did to me—" The words caught. Even speaking his name made the bond flare inside her, hot and aching like a reopened wound. Her soul missed him. Craved him. But was that real? Or was it just the magic? How could she ever trust herself again?

Sofija studied her with something between pity and intrigue.

"He didn't just bind your blood," she said. "He tied your souls. It's a ritual older than most can remember. A tether meant to last through lifetimes."

Ophelia's hands curled into fists. The air in the room felt tighter. The pressure behind her eyes, sharp.

"You didn't feel it before," Sofija continued, her voice softening just enough to slice deeper, "because he was hidden. Shielded deep in the underworld of Marisante, behind barriers even this bond couldn't penetrate. But now that he walks freely aboveground again?" She gestured vaguely, as if brushing back a curtain. "The bond is reawakening. In full. It will only grow stronger."

Ophelia staggered a step back before she caught herself. The hollow in her chest hadn't been grief. Or uncertainty. It had been him.

And now it was rising again.

Ophelia narrowed her eyes. "How do you know so much about this?"

Sofija didn't answer at first. She turned one of the old pages with deliberate care, as if the parchment itself demanded reverence. When she finally looked up, her gaze was steady, unreadable.

"Because we all come from the same origin...Hecate," she said. "In the beginning," Sofija continued, "blood bonds were not exclusive to vampires. All supernaturals once used them— to protect their lineages, to connect covens, to seal sacred unions. It was a sacred magic. But witches...we chose to evolve."

"Why abandon it?" Ophelia asked.

"Because it corrupted us," Sofija said, her voice cool and sharp. "Blood magic is powerful, yes—but it's possessive. It doesn't ask. It claims. Witches began to lose themselves. Love turned to obsession. Protection to control. The cost grew too high."

She leaned in just slightly. "So we severed it from our practice. We learned restraint. We relied on choice, not binding."

Her eyes pierced Ophelia's like a challenge.

"But vampires never let it go. For them, the cost was acceptable. It still is."

The chamber felt smaller now, the air dense and charged. The floating lights dimmed, as if reacting to the rise of Ophelia's magic—or her dread.

Ophelia's fingers curled into fists at her sides. "Can it be undone?" she asked, her voice low.

Sofija exhaled, the sound more amused than sympathetic. "I'm not sure," she admitted at last. "Death, perhaps."

Ophelia's stomach twisted. Silence unfurled between them, heavy and unsparing.

But Sofija wasn't finished. Her gaze sharpened, eyes glittering like frozen sea glass. "But that is not the only reason you're here, is it?"

"No," Ophelia said, voice steadier than she expected. "I need to know if my sister can be stopped."

That got Sofija's full attention. "She can be stopped, but only by you," she said.

Ophelia's heart beat louder in her ears.

"Blood magic is not a tool," Sofija continued. "It is a door. It opens the deepest parts of us—our pain, our hunger, our power. What Eris has done is awaken a part of herself that was never meant to be fully unbound."

She turned to face Ophelia again, her expression unflinching.

"It gives her strength, yes. Terrifying strength. But it also strips her of control. Her emotions will be amplified. Her focus will fracture. She may spiral between delusions of invincibility and crushing despair. Her power will shift without warning, her grip on reality unsteady."

Ophelia swallowed. The words rang too familiar: flashes of Eris's brilliance and rage in battle.

"She will not break quietly," Sofija said. "And if you wait too long, she will not be broken at all."

Ophelia felt her pulse in her throat. "So you'll help me?"

Sofija gave a single deliberate nod. "I will help you if you agree to find her. To confront her. To fight her. To kill her, if it comes to that," she said, stepping closer, her presence humming just under the surface. "Eris is not just a threat to you. She is a threat to all of us. The witches, the vampires, the balance we've held for centuries. She may already be wielding powers we don't understand. Powers no one has seen in generations."

Ophelia stayed silent, her hands still curled tight. Her blood pounded with a rhythm that didn't feel entirely her own.

Sofija's voice softened, but it carried weight. "First, you must find your sister. Eris is too powerful. Too volatile. If I am to find a way to break your bond with Luka, I must ensure you are strong enough to withstand the consequences."

"And if I'm not?" Ophelia asked, though she already feared the answer.

Sofija's lips curved into something that wasn't quite a smile. "Then you will remain bound to him for as long as you live, hybrid," she said.

The silence that followed wasn't empty.

Then, Sofija rose from her chair.

"I will train you, Ophelia Wildes," she said, her voice echoing slightly in the stone chamber. "But you are not only a witch. You are part vampire. Your training must reflect that."

Ophelia's chest tightened. "What?" she asked.

Sofija's expression remained maddeningly calm, as if she had expected the resistance and already moved past it.

"Your magic is tied to your bloodline," she said. "And your bloodline is not purely ours. A witch alone cannot prepare you for what is coming. You need someone who will push you beyond your comfort zone. Someone who can challenge your instincts—your magic, your body, your control. A vampire."

Ophelia's teeth clenched. Her emotions tangled together

like brambles—resentment, disbelief, something dangerously close to understanding. She hated that it made sense.

"And where, exactly, do you plan for this to happen?" she asked warily. "Last time I checked, vampires weren't exactly welcome here."

Sofija met her gaze; her voice carried the edge of humor—bone-dry and almost imperceptible. "True. But, of course, hybrids are a loophole."

Sofija paused before continuing. "Trieste," she said, smoothing her robes with a flick of her fingers. "Neutral ground. Miramare Castle will be secure, and it will be watched. You'll be surrounded by magic, but not shielded from danger. A perfect balance."

Ophelia's pulse thundered in her ears. She wanted to argue. To stall. But there was no stalling this.

Sofija's eyes narrowed. "This is not cruelty, child. It is preparation. I am ensuring your survival."

Ophelia lifted her chin, trying not to let the weight of it crush her. "Fine. We train in Trieste."

Sofija's sharp smile deepened, all satisfaction and shadow. "Then it is decided."

Ophelia turned before she could change her mind.

The familiar pull of the thread curled through her gut, wrapping around her like a vise. She grabbed Brisa's hand, stepped into the thread, and vanished.

She landed on the terrace, boots striking with a muted thud.

And there they were.

The moment her magic aligned with the space, they turned. Neither spoke. Both watched her with something unreadable in their eyes: wariness, longing, something in between.

Gabriel waited on her left, Luka on her right.

She stood there for a breath too long, caught in the silence between them.

Then she stepped forward, not toward either of them. Just forward.

But as she passed Luka, something shifted inside her. A low, invisible tug—not pain, not yearning exactly, but a sensation like part of her had been restored. She hated how right it felt. How easy. How much of her still wanted him—even now, even after everything. Relief flooded her like warmth in winter. And that terrified her most of all.

EIGHT

Ophelia gasped, caught between breath and fire, as her back arched into someone's mouth. Gabriel's, she thought; his lips were soft, reverent, tasting her like she was something holy. Every brush of his tongue felt like a prayer. Like he was worshipping her with every kiss, mapping her pulse with something more than hunger.

But Luka's hand tightened around her hip at the same time, grounding her with the unrelenting certainty of someone who had already claimed her. His touch didn't ask. It reminded. His palm branded her through the fabric of her shorts, possessive and absolute.

She couldn't move fast enough to separate them. But she didn't want to. There was no place in her mind for guilt or fear, only sensation. Only heat.

Gabriel trailed kisses down her throat, his breath cool against the fire blooming beneath her skin. His fangs grazed the edge of her pulse, not piercing, just enough to make her tremble. Tease. Threaten. Tempt. His hand slid beneath the hem of her shirt, fingertips dragging along the curve of her ribs like he was tracing something only he could see. Her skin ignited under the touch, alive and electric.

Behind her, Luka's mouth ghosted over the slope of her shoulder. His lips were firmer. Deliberate. He wasn't tasting her...he was committing her to memory. Every freckle, every scar, every shiver cataloged with clinical reverence. He kissed like he was documenting evidence, claiming territory.

Her breath hitched. Her body suspended between worship and domination.

The bond between them pulsed violently, a rhythm that didn't match her heartbeat but ran parallel to it, deeper. Beneath it, something older stirred. Not just the bond. Not just the blood. Older magic. Wild, coiled magic that lived in marrow and moonlight, snapping awake beneath her skin. It laced between all three of them like silk pulled taut, humming with tension.

She wasn't standing. She wasn't even floating. She was suspended, held between them like a cord between two anchors, breathless and burning, unraveling with every touch.

A rough palm tilted her jaw. Fingers slid into her hair, gripping gently but firmly, tipping her head back. Gabriel's mouth found hers. His kiss was deep, slow, unyielding. It was designed to wreck her, to sink into her like ink through paper. She moaned into it, her knees going weak, spine bowing between the press of their bodies.

At the same time, Luka's hand slid lower, trailing down her stomach with maddening control. His palm flattened over her pelvis, slow and deliberate. As her legs buckled from Gabriel's kiss, Luka caught her with his free arm, drawing her flush against him. His forearm locked across her torso, anchoring her while his fingers slipped lower, parting her thighs with devastating ease. He held her like a weapon he knew too well: familiar, dangerous, never left unattended.

Her magic jolted. A wave of heat rolled through her core as Luka's teeth grazed the back of her neck. Her moan turned raw, her head thrown back, hair spilling over Gabriel's wrist, body alight with a need so consuming it blurred the edges of who she was.

She wanted them. Gods, she wanted them. Both of them. Equal hunger, equal ache.

Gabriel kissed like he was unraveling her soul, like her mouth was a secret he'd waited centuries to unlock.

Luka touched her like she was his to own, his to defend, his to destroy—if necessary.

Neither was careful. Neither was cruel.

Her hips rolled instinctively toward every touch, chasing friction, desperate for more. Her magic burned wild between them—untethered, glowing like coals under her skin. It flared and fused with the bond, binding and biting, ancient threads tugging tighter.

A mouth brushed the inside of her thigh.

She gasped, a choked sound torn from her throat. Her hips tilted toward the heat, desperate and instinctive. A cry escaped her lips, wordless and primal.

The air shimmered around them, vibrating with magic. Light flickered at the edges of her vision, like the world itself couldn't decide whether it was real or not. The pressure in her chest built and built, her skin tight with sensation, every nerve ending singing.

She blinked, and time fractured. Luka's mouth was at her neck. No, someone else was behind her. Someone was inside her.

She tried to reach, to speak, to scream.

A name passed her lips. Low, breathless, half-formed.

She wasn't sure whose it was.

And then—

Two sets of fangs.

A whisper at her ear: mine.

Another whisper, deeper: always.

Her body twisted, caught between ecstasy and panic. The magic surged, flared, too hot and sharp. Too much.

And then—

The heat was gone.

The touch, the weight, the mouths, the hands.

Gone.

Everything fractured. The warmth vanished from her skin as if ripped away by unseen hands.

She sat bolt upright, a gasp tearing from her throat like a drowning woman breaking the surface.

The couch beneath her was real, solid and unmoving. So was the cool, warded air of Luka's apartment. It pressed gently against her skin like a hand trying to soothe, but failing. Somewhere outside, a bell tower tolled in the dark, its chime hollow, disconnected, as if calling out across dimensions and finding no one.

Ophelia blinked hard, eyes struggling to adjust to the dark. Her chest heaved.

Sweat clung to her skin in a sheen, cold now, her shirt damp and twisted beneath her arms. The blanket had been kicked down to her ankles, a tangle of fabric like the aftermath of something broken. Her thighs clenched instinctively, still aching. Still throbbing. Still hungry.

"Oh, gods," she muttered, dragging a shaking hand down her face. Her fingers trembled with something half-magic, half-desperation.

Her heart thundered. Her neck was flushed. Her shirt had ridden up over her stomach, baring the skin Gabriel's hand had touched—or dreamed of touching. She couldn't tell where the dream ended and the craving began.

She'd had sex with both of them. Not just sex. That word didn't touch it. Devouring, blinding, ruinous sex. Magic and want and memory tangled so tight she could barely see through it.

And now? She couldn't so much as look at them without her bond surging, without her magic trying to claw through her skin to get to them.

She pressed her palms to the couch cushions, grounding herself against the velvet, knuckles turning white with the effort.

What the hell was happening to her?

Her body didn't care about alliances or bloodlines or what the hell Sofija would say about consequences. It didn't care that one of them had tethered her soul without permission, or that the other had held her in silence when everything else fell apart. Her body only knew want.

And worse, what if it wasn't even her want anymore? What if the bond was bleeding into her subconscious? What if it was rewriting her desire? Was this lust? Longing? Or was it just a carefully arranged illusion built from blood and proximity and pain?

What if none of it was real?

She let out a strangled noise and dropped back onto the cushions, arm flung over her eyes. "This is getting out of hand," she whispered to no one, voice cracking.

The couch creaked beneath her, too soft, too quiet. The silence wasn't comforting; it was accusatory.

Her eyes burned, but there were no tears. Just the ache. Just the rage. Just the bone-deep resentment that she had no say in what her body remembered or craved anymore.

She sat up slowly. The blanket slid from her lap, forgotten. Her skin still prickled, magic crawling just beneath the surface like a thousand threads twitching for connection. There was no going back to sleep. Not like this.

She needed movement. Air. Anything to separate herself from the dream and the reality that was getting harder to tell apart.

She padded to the hall, bare feet cold against the floor. Her shoes waited by the coat rack, and she slipped them on quickly without turning on a light. Her tank top was still twisted from sleep, her shorts wrinkled and askew. She didn't fix them. She didn't care.

She just needed to run.

The door opened with a quiet click. The air in the stairwell was cooler, more real somehow. She slipped out, let the door close behind her, and started down the stairs two at a time, her legs already aching for release.

Halfway down the second flight, a shadow shifted. But she'd sensed him before she saw him.

Gabriel.

He was leaning against the rail just outside the stairwell door, shirtless in a pair of black joggers, a towel draped around his neck. His chest rose and fell with slow, measured breaths, like he'd just returned from a run, or like he was trying not to move too fast. Not toward her. Not away. His skin gleamed faintly in the low light, and his dark hair was damp at the edges and sticking to his temples.

He looked up the second she stepped into view. His dark eyes met hers and held.

For a breath, neither of them moved. The stairwell was too quiet. Too charged. The scent of cool night air threaded with something warmer—sweat, cedar, the barest edge of salt from his skin. It should've grounded her. Instead, it made her dizzy. And she couldn't stop staring at him. She was so hungry for him.

He tilted his head slightly, as if trying to read what haunted her. A shadow passed behind his gaze. And for just a blink, she wondered if he'd dreamed, too. Then one corner of his mouth lifted, slow and tired. "Couldn't sleep either?"

Ophelia shifted her weight and rested her hands on the railing, feigning nonchalance. "Something like that," she said.

Gabriel's gaze dipped to her bare legs, her flushed cheeks, the way her tank top clung damp to her chest. And then he found her face again.

She swallowed hard, throat dry.

"You going for a run?" he asked, voice low, a whisper that felt too intimate in the hush of the stairwell.

"I was. I am," she said, clearing her throat. "Need to clear my mind."

He nodded once. "Mind if I come with you?" he asked.

Her first instinct was to say no. A pause stretched between them. She could say no. She could keep her distance. She should. The dream had scrambled her, left her skin too raw, her thoughts a tangle of heat and guilt and ache. But Gabriel wasn't Luka. He didn't take. He waited.

"Sure," she said. "Just don't expect me to keep your pace."

Gabriel's grin deepened just slightly, the barest flash of teeth. "You never do."

They stepped into the night together and began their run in silence, feet hitting the cobblestone streets with soft, rhythmic thuds. Gabriel ran beside her easily, his body all grace and shadow. Every step was silent, fluid. The moon caught the curve of his shoulders, the taut stretch of his back, and the lingering tension in his shoulders. The city wrapped around them like a half-cast spell, narrow streets heavy with ivy and shuttered windows above wrought-iron balconies. A cat darted across an alley. A breeze stirred laundry lines that had nothing to dry.

Ophelia fell into her stride quickly, letting the cold kiss her cheeks. She hoped it would freeze out the fire still coiling low in her belly, but it didn't. The dream hadn't faded. It pulsed in the curve of her breath, in the way Gabriel's presence made her magic stir like something just barely contained beneath her skin.

They veered onto a broader street, and the incline steepened. San Giusto. The road narrowed again, winding between moss-covered walls and trees bent like sentries. The shadows thickened. The scent of rosemary and woodsmoke drifted on the air.

She pushed herself harder. Her thighs burned, and her lungs screamed. Still, he kept pace without breaking a sweat.

"Of course, you'd take us uphill," she muttered.

He smirked. "You said you needed out. I'm just making sure you get there."

The castle loomed ahead, sharp and dark against the stars. Old lanterns flickered along the trail, casting long shadows across uneven stone.

They reached the overlook and slowed. Their footsteps softened, breath catching in the hush.

Below them, Trieste shimmered. The Adriatic stretched out, silver and endless. Wind curled around them, cool and biting, full of stories.

Ophelia bent forward, bracing her hands on her thighs. Her chest rose and fell in jagged rhythm. Sweat ran between her shoulder blades.

Gabriel stood beside her. Still. Silent. His eyes weren't on the view. They were on her.

"Did the run help?" he asked, voice low, laced with something too sharp to be casual. "Did it clear your...mind?"

She straightened slowly, heart still racing, but for reasons that had little to do with the climb. The burn in her legs was nothing compared to the ache curling deep in her belly. "I don't know," she said, brushing hair from her damp face. "Maybe."

Gabriel stepped in closer, just enough to make the space between them crackle. "Because I know what you really need-ed," he murmured, eyes roaming over her.

She didn't speak. Couldn't.

"I could smell it on you the second you stepped into the stairwell. Still wet with it," he said.

Her pulse stuttered. "You're imagining things," she said.

"Am I?" His voice dipped, the barest edge of hunger slipping through. "Your magic was still humming. You were flushed. And you looked at me like I'd already touched you," he said.

"I was running," she snapped, even though she hadn't started until she saw him.

Gabriel gave a soft, humorless laugh. "Sure."

The air between them thickened. The lights of Trieste blurred behind him, golden and flickering in the mist, but all she saw was him, bare-chested, damp hair clinging to his temples, the scent of heat and salt and something distinctly his.

"You think you know what I need?" she asked, voice low.

He stepped even closer, not touching her, but close enough that his words brushed her lips like a kiss. "I *do*. Because I've missed *us*. What we were. What we still are," he said.

Her jaw tensed. "You don't get to say that. You know things are complicated," she said.

"Don't I?" he asked softly, no real bite in his voice, just a threadbare ache. "Tell me you haven't thought about it. About us. About what it would feel like to stop fighting for one gods-damned second. To take what you want. Not what the bond tells you. What *you* want," he said.

She hesitated. And there it was. That split-second where the decision tilted. Where her restraint cracked wide open. She should've walked away. She should've reminded herself of Luka, of the bond still tangled around her soul like a net. She should've.

But Gabriel wasn't a complication. He was a need.

"I'm tired of fighting," she whispered. "I want to feel *something* that doesn't make me question myself."

His jaw tightened. He didn't say it, but she felt it anyway: *Then let it be me.*

She stepped into him, fingers catching the towel at his neck, yanking him forward. Their mouths collided.

Not gentle. Not slow.

She kissed him like she wanted to erase everything else. The dream. The guilt. The bond. Like she wanted to taste something real. Gabriel's hands flew to her hips, dragging her up against him, and gods, he was already hard—already ready —like he'd been teetering on the edge of this moment forever.

He growled against her mouth, and the sound lit her nerves on fire.

He backed her against the stone stairs, his mouth sliding down her throat, across her collarbone, his breath hot and ragged. She tilted her head back and gave him access to *everything.*

And the magic didn't fight it. It didn't flare in warning. It *sang.*

Her nails dug into his shoulders, and her legs nearly gave out. Gabriel caught her with both arms, lifting her effortlessly. Her back hit the cool stone with a muffled thud, and his body followed, pinning her like he meant to hold her there forever.

He pulled back just enough to look at her, eyes dark and wild, gleaming with something starved.

"I want to ravish you," he said, voice rough. "Slow. Deep. Until you forget anyone else has ever touched you."

Ophelia gripped his face, her breath hot against his mouth. "Not tonight."

He stilled.

"I don't need slow. I need you to fuck me, Gabriel."

His gaze flared with surprise, with heat—and then he moved.

His hands gripped her thighs, dragging her hips forward as she wrapped her legs around him. He worked fast, dragging his joggers low, shoving her shorts aside in one practiced motion.

He didn't hesitate.

With one sharp, claiming thrust, he drove into her.

Hard.

Deep.

She cried out, clutching his shoulders, burying her face in his neck as he held her there—one hand behind her head, the other gripping her ass as he began to move.

Fast. Brutal. *Perfect.*

She moved with him, grinding down, her body catching every stroke like it had been made for this. For him.

There was no pretense. No patience.

Just friction. Just need. Just them.

The wind howled across the Adriatic Sea as Ophelia stepped onto the castle grounds, her boots crunching against the gravel path. Waves crashed far below, restless and cold, as if the sea itself resented her return.

Miramare Castle loomed above them like a specter from another age, its white limestone towers jagged against the storm-darkened sky. It felt more like a monument to expectation, a cage carved from marble and history. Here, the Alliance met when the stakes were highest. Vampires, witches, and fae cloaked themselves in old rules and fragile truces. And she had no patience for it. Ophelia wasn't built for courtrooms or councils or any table where you had to pretend politics weren't just power with better manners.

She didn't belong here.

The air reeked of salt and storm and barely leashed power. A faint hum rose from the wards stitched into the castle's bones, old enchantments embedded so deep they vibrated in her chest. Each step closer to the perimeter made her stomach twist. The wards didn't reject her, but they didn't exactly welcome her either. Not witch. Not vampire. The magic pulsed against her like it couldn't decide what to do with her.

Gabriel walked beside her, silent. His eyes swept over the battlements, tracking movement even where there was none. His jaw was set, his expression unreadable to anyone else, but she saw it. The friction simmering beneath the surface. He was all control and calculation, until he wasn't. And after last night, she could still feel the pressure of his mouth against hers.

But he didn't touch her. Didn't look at her. Just walked with lethal grace, eyes always scanning. A protector. A shadow.

Luka followed a few paces behind, inscrutable as ever. The wind tugged at the edges of his jacket like it was trying to peel him open, but he didn't stir. Didn't even shift. There was something magnetic about his stillness, like gravity didn't apply to him the way it did to everyone else. And yet, she could feel him with every step. The bond thrummed louder the closer they came to the threshold, like it recognized this place and didn't approve. It flared through her ribs and spine, lacing tight and wrong, pulling her back toward him even when she refused to turn.

She didn't need to look to know his eyes were on her.

Brisa and Alex walked hand in hand behind Luka. Mo and Elijah brought up the rear, their arms full of ancient tomes and cracked leather-bound texts that probably hadn't seen daylight since the last major supernatural war.

"Careful with that one. It's older than your country," Mo muttered, shifting a heavy grimoire in his arms.

"I was valedictorian," Elijah said, beaming. "I can carry some books without collapsing."

"Sure, scholar. Until one of them leaks binding dust and curses you with ghost boils," Mo said.

"Ghost boils aren't real. Right?" Elijah asked, only slight worry showing between his eyes.

"Says the guy carrying a necromancer's field journal," Mo said.

Ophelia's lips twitched, just slightly. It helped, hearing them banter like none of this was about to end in blood and ruin.

She glanced at Gabriel from the corner of her eye. "You're tense," she said under her breath.

His reply came low and deliberate, just for her. "So are you. But for what it's worth, I slept like a goddamn saint after last night." He looked down at her then, and the gleam in his eyes made something stutter in her chest. "We should repeat that sleep aid sometime," he added, mouth curling into a slow, knowing smile. "Call it...therapeutic."

She inhaled sharply, thrown for just a second. But she didn't answer, because her bond with Luka surged the moment Gabriel said it. Like it knew. Like it resented the intrusion.

And Miramare's wards pulsed harder in response. They closed around her with invisible fingers, probing, as if the castle itself sensed the chaos inside her and wanted to press it into order. But she didn't bow. She just kept walking, toward a place she didn't want to be, with two men she couldn't untangle, under a sky that looked ready to break.

A figure stood at the entrance of the east wing, arms locked across her chest, every inch of her radiating don't-fuck-with-me energy. Ingrid. The witch's cheekbones caught the light like a blade, and her dark eyes swept over them with a look that could gut a man at twenty paces. That cold, assessing gaze landed on Ophelia and lingered, sharp and unimpressed.

"You took your time," she said, voice flat as stone.

Of course, they were expected. Sofija had made it clear: training would happen here. And not just training: residency. Every last one of them was to remain within the walls of Miramare Castle until Eris was dealt with or they were strong enough to fight her. Whatever came first. It was half protection, half captivity.

Ophelia understood the logic. Luka's apartment had been too small, too exposed. And after last night's dream—after Gabriel—far too charged. At least here, there was room to breathe. Room to avoid. For now.

Brisa stepped slightly in front of Ophelia, arms swinging loosely at her sides. "Aw, Ingrid," she said sweetly. "Miss us already?" she asked.

Ingrid's expression didn't shift, but her shoulders went just a shade tenser. "I'm thrilled to be your glorified chaperone," she said. "Really. It's the highlight of my year."

Brisa grinned. "Don't worry, I'll make it fun for you," she said.

"I doubt that," Ingrid responded without blinking. She didn't even twitch. Just stood there like a statue carved from midnight and weaponry.

Ophelia rolled her shoulders, ignoring the knot forming at the base of her neck. "I wasn't in a hurry," she said coolly.

Ingrid's lips twitched, something like a smirk, but colder. "Sofija has already outlined the terms of your training," she said. "She expects discipline."

Ophelia bit back a laugh. Discipline. Control. Like that was even an option anymore. The bond inside her wasn't a polite guest to be managed. It was a feral thing clawing at the inside of her ribs. Every hour, it grew stronger, hungrier. Now someone else wanted to put a leash on it?

Gabriel shifted beside her. Calm on the surface, but she

could feel the unrest crackling through him. "Where are we staying?" he asked.

Ingrid jerked her chin toward the eastern wing. "Rooms have been prepared. You'll begin immediately."

Mo stepped forward, frowning, the books in his arms tilting dangerously. "This many supernaturals under one roof? Miramare's neutrality won't hold if someone decides to test it," he said.

Ingrid's eyes flicked to him. "Sofija has reinforced the wards. No one enters without permission. If something goes wrong inside..." Her gaze slid deliberately to Ophelia. "That's your problem," she said.

Ophelia's stomach churned. The air felt heavier. The castle, once distant and monolithic, suddenly pressed closer on all sides. No way out. No way forward but through.

She nodded once. As she passed Ingrid and stepped over the threshold, the castle doors groaned open with a sound that wasn't quite natural. Like the structure itself resented her entrance.

The moment she crossed inside, the pressure hit. The wards slammed against her skin—not aggressively, but densely. Claustrophobically. Like stepping into too-hot water and trying not to flinch. Her hybrid magic recoiled, then surged. It didn't know how to settle here. The wards recognized her as witch—but something else curled beneath that recognition, and the castle wasn't sure what to do with it.

The air was thick with layered enchantment. It smelled of damp stone and oiled wood and spells that had been cast and recast over centuries. Dust and age. Power, old and unmoved. And beneath it all, that gnawing sensation she couldn't shake —like the bond inside her was already trying to unravel what the castle had locked down.

Gabriel silently followed close behind. She could feel the heat of him at her back, steady and watchful. Luka came next. She didn't turn, but she felt him enter; the bond flared the moment his foot crossed the threshold, and her body tightened in response.

Welcome home, it whispered. Or maybe: welcome to your cage.

THE TRAINING COURTYARD behind Miramare's eastern wing was carved directly into the cliffside, open to the wind and sea below. The stone floor was etched with faintly glowing runes —marks of containment and focus. Here, and only here, the castle's suppressive wards had been deliberately lifted. Magic was allowed to flow freely within this space, not to protect but to test. The air crackled with unleashed energy, wild and waiting. It smelled of salt, sweat, and old power, the kind that remembered old wars.

Sofija stood near the outer wall, her robes whipping in the wind like storm flags. She didn't raise her voice. She didn't need to.

"Ingrid. Brisa," she called. "Show me what you've retained."

Brisa stretched like she'd just rolled out of bed. "Retained?" she echoed, glancing sideways at Ingrid. "Is that her subtle way of saying we've gotten soft?"

"I don't do subtle," Ingrid said, already stepping into the ring, expression flat, eyes gleaming like flint. Her shoulders rolled back with precise efficiency, every movement controlled, lethal.

"Oh, I know. You do repressed. And terrifyingly competent.

It's your whole thing." Brisa grinned and cracked her knuckles. "Fine. Let's play." She summoned her daggers with a flick of her wrist. Air magic shimmered around her fingers, lifting the blades from the sheaths at her thighs and spinning them lazily in the air before catching them cleanly.

Ingrid didn't respond. She simply drew her own blades from the holster at her back. Her grip was loose, but her stance was ready. Impossibly still. Like she was waiting for a reason to tear something open.

"Begin," Sofija said.

They collided in a blur, blades flashing and magic snapping the air between them. Brisa went low, fast, grinning as she swept toward Ingrid's side. Ingrid met her easily, parrying with brutal precision. Their movements were a language unto themselves: familiar, intimate, haunted by history.

Ophelia stood at the edge of the circle, lungs seizing for a beat. "They've done this before," she murmured.

"Dozens of times," Luka said beside her, neutral. But his arms were crossed tightly, and his jaw had locked a little too hard.

Gabriel didn't speak, but his attention didn't waver.

Inside the ring, Brisa feinted left, flipped backward, and landed with a flourish. "Come on, Ingrid. Try to hit me like you mean it," she said.

"I do mean it," Ingrid growled, slashing toward her in a vicious arc.

They met in the center with a hiss of magic, steel clashing and wind howling. The warded runes flared under their feet, reacting to the spike in power.

Ingrid caught one of Brisa's wrists and twisted hard. Brisa yelped and dropped one blade, but ducked out of the hold and slammed her elbow into Ingrid's ribs. Ingrid staggered half a step, eyes narrowing. Her blade traced Brisa's side in a retaliatory swipe that grazed but didn't cut.

"You're slower than last time," Ingrid said. "Too much time flirting, not enough time practicing," she said.

Brisa lunged, driving her shoulder into Ingrid's sternum and knocking her back a step.

They locked again, this time up close, blades crossed between their faces, breath mingling, neither giving ground.

Finally, Sofija raised a hand. "Enough."

They broke apart on command, panting, blades lowered. Brisa flipped one dagger into the air and caught it by the hilt, grinning. Ingrid's expression didn't shift, but her knuckles were white around her blade.

Brisa brushed her hair out of her face, cheeks flushed, a shallow cut blooming across her shoulder. She didn't even wince. Just flicked her blade into its sheath and grinned, breathless and unrepentant.

Ingrid did the same, though more precisely. No flourish. No drama. Just that ever-present restraint, like even her rage had rules. But Ophelia caught it, the fractional hitch in her breath, the twitch in her jaw. Something had cracked beneath that iron surface. And not from the fight.

Neither turned their back on the other as they exited the circle.

Ophelia swallowed hard and looked up, straight into Sofija's waiting gaze. The high priestess didn't blink. Didn't smile. She just lifted her hand and pointed at Ophelia and Luka. "You're next," she said.

The air snapped taut. The ground felt suddenly smaller, like it might close in around her. Luka stepped forward without hesitation, shadows at his heels, expression a mask.

Ophelia's spine straightened. She'd burned for Gabriel the night before. She'd dreamed herself into ruin. And now here she was, about to spar with the vampire who'd bound her soul without asking. She flexed her fingers. Felt the spark of fire coil at her fingertips.

Luka tilted his head slightly, looking at Ophelia as if assessing her like a puzzle. "Ready?" he asked.

No, she wasn't. Not even close. But she would be.

CHAPTER
TEN

The wind died as Ophelia stepped into the circle. She could still hear it screaming over the cliffside, battering the castle walls. But inside the training ring, the world felt vacuum-sealed. No breath. No sound. Just the rhythmic thump of her heartbeat and the scuff of Luka's boots on worn stone.

Ophelia flexed her fingers at her sides, magic coiling low in her belly. Not rage. Not fear. Something else. Anticipation. Like her body already knew this wasn't just a spar. It was a reckoning.

Sofija raised one hand. The runes etched into the stone floor flared, glowing brighter as the surrounding air warped and thickened. Shadows spilled inward, curling at the edges like smoke drawn toward a flame. The scent of sea salt and old wards rose, sharp and clean and cold.

With a flick of her wrist, the high priestess transformed the space. The courtyard cleared itself, distractions vanishing in a gust of wind that stung Ophelia's cheeks. The magic that normally suppressed and silenced now pulled back, lifted like the release of a dam. Magic was allowed here. Unleashed. And it rose to meet her like a summoned tide.

She inhaled sharply, fire flickering beneath her skin, air magic ghosting along her shoulders like invisible wings bracing for flight. The bond pulsed once, twice. A warning. A dare.

Across the circle, Luka watched her with that same unreadable stillness. Unmoving. Unbothered. But the bond between them thrummed like a wire drawn too tight. Something had shifted since Trieste. Since Gabriel. Since the dream. Ophelia felt it in her gut, in the hot press of magic licking up her spine.

This wasn't just training. This was a test. And she didn't plan to fail.

They circled.

Not fast. Not yet. Just two bodies slowly orbiting, testing the air between them.

Ophelia could feel every molecule of space: charged, restless, waiting. Her magic shimmered just beneath her skin, eager to burn. The wind tugged at her hair, curling it around her cheekbones like a taunt. Luka's eyes never left her.

He moved with that same unbearable control: shoulders relaxed, spine loose, as if he didn't care. But she knew him now. Knew that behind that cool stillness was a fuse ready to burn. And she was tired of pretending it didn't call to her.

The bond pulsed again. Not gently. Her lip curled. She hated how it made her ache and hunger in the same breath. With a snap of motion, she struck first.

A blade of air sliced from her fingertips, fast and precise. It whipped toward Luka's side. But he was already gone, shifting like smoke just out of reach. She didn't give him time to breathe. Her fire followed: a spiral of heat meant to disorient, not destroy.

Luka ducked, rolled, and came up in a crouch. "More than last time," he murmured, just loud enough for her to hear.

She didn't answer. She was already moving again.

Magic flared hot beneath her ribs. The air thickened, pressing out in waves as she summoned more. Threads of wind wrapped around her body, lifting her slightly off the ground with every leap. She struck again, with fire this time, curling from her palm in a stream that lit the circle in molten gold.

He dodged—barely—and lunged for her.

They collided with a shuddering impact that cracked the runes beneath them. Ophelia stumbled, grit scraping her palms, and Luka caught her wrist mid-fall, only to twist her momentum and send her skidding sideways. She rolled, came up on one knee, and flung a burst of wind at his feet.

It sent him sliding, but not far. He planted a hand and used the motion to pivot, his boot catching on the edge of a glowing sigil. In two strides, he was behind her again.

Ophelia whirled, fire surging. But this time, he didn't block. He moved through it.

She gasped as Luka's hands closed around her wrists and forced them down. Her flames sputtered against the warded ground, contained but wild. His breath hit her neck, and his body pressed hers into the curve of a rune-carved stone.

He was too close. "Get off," she said, voice low and sharp. But he didn't move.

His chest rose and fell in ragged rhythm. And still, those dark eyes didn't leave hers. There was no triumph in them. No mockery.

Only want.

"Why do you always fight it?" he asked, voice low.

"I fight you," she spat. "There's a difference."

He leaned in, barely a breath away. "Not tonight, there isn't," he said.

She shoved him hard.

Luka let her go, but not fast enough. His fingertips dragged across her hips like he couldn't help it. The contact sent a pulse of magic ricocheting through her ribs. Her knees nearly buckled. She growled.

"Fuck you," she said, breathing hard.

"Later," he murmured. "When we're not in front of an audience."

Her cheeks burned.

Around them, the air fractured. Sofija hadn't called a stop. The others still watched in silence, though the tension had thickened into something tangible.

Ophelia raised her hands again. Magic surged. If this was going to be a spectacle, she was going to give them something to see. She struck again, this time combining two of her elements. Wind and flame twisted into a spiraling column that cracked across the courtyard. They clashed at the center of the ring. It was brutal. Fast. Beautiful in its fury.

Her magic met his partially shifted form, teeth bared and claws unsheathed in the form of a black jaguar. There were no flourishes now, no restraint. Just need and frustration and heat so thick it turned the courtyard into a furnace. Ophelia pushed harder. Harder than she ever had.

And for one brilliant moment, she had him. She felt it. The shift. The break. His balance faltered. She surged forward, her body crackling with energy. The light beneath her skin flared white-gold as her fingers curled toward his chest.

Then her boot slipped. The world tilted. Luka moved. And suddenly, she was on the ground, the breath knocked from her lungs, pinned beneath the weight of him.

He wasn't gloating. He wasn't smiling. He was just there—solid and inescapable—his hands on her wrists, his hips locking hers against the stone. Their magic fizzed and snapped where they touched, like the contact alone was too much for the world to hold. Raw charge radiated off him as he maintained his hold, his head hovering just above hers.

Ophelia's breath came shallow and rapid. Despite the strain of the fight and the splintering tension in her muscles, she felt the unyielding pull of the ancient bond tugging at her, coaxing her closer to him. It was as if the very magic that had once made her shudder now offered a magnetic, unbidden solace.

Her heart pounded in her ears, each beat resonating with both defiance and a forbidden longing. Part of her rebelled; this was not how she intended to feel. But another part, hidden deep within the tangled network of blood and magic, was drawn irresistibly to him. Amidst the chaos of combat, the bond whispered its seduction. The unspoken language of their forged connection murmured its forbidden song.

Luka's grip tightened as he maintained his dominance over her. The force of their struggle left no room for words, only the fierce physical conversation between their bodies. And in that heated, desperate moment, as his presence reigned over her and the remaining sparks of her magic sputtered, her body was caught in the inertia of the bond. Ophelia felt it pull her toward him with a power as undeniable as it was dangerous.

They didn't hear Sofija's next command. Didn't see the others standing at the edges of the courtyard. Didn't feel anything but the weight of breath and proximity.

Ophelia's eyes widened.

His mouth was close enough to make her shiver. And gods help her, she wanted it. Not just the kiss. The chaos. The bond. The madness of it all.

But before she could speak, before she could do something reckless and irreversible—

A low growl cut through the air.

Dark. Animalistic. Gabriel.

Ophelia's head jerked toward the edge of the circle, too late.

Gabriel was already moving, backing away, jaw locked so tight she could see the muscle twitch along his cheek. His eyes burned—not with jealousy, but something older, darker. Not bloodlust. Rage. Possession. Hurt. A sound ripped from his chest. Low. Animal.

And then he turned on his heel and stalked away, fast and furious, as if he didn't leave now, something inside him would break open.

Ophelia's chest caved in around the sound of his retreat. She blinked and really saw the courtyard for the first time. Brisa stood frozen nearby, her mouth parted in disbelief. Ingrid's expression had gone blank, but her eyes darted away the second Ophelia met them.

Heat rushed up her throat. "Shit," she whispered.

She shoved Luka off her with both hands. He let go, but not before his fingers skimmed down her arm, reluctant to release her. She didn't take the hand he offered. Didn't look back.

She ran.

The corridor was colder, quieter, but it didn't help. Her breath came fast, too shallow. Magic sparked against her skin like it hadn't settled from the fight. Or the touch.

"Gabriel—" she called, her voice cracking on his name.

He didn't stop.

"Gabriel, please," she said, desperate now, half running to catch him.

He spun around, and she almost collided with him. He grabbed her wrist midair as if he'd known she would reach for him. He twisted it gently, too gently, behind her back, pressing her against the wall before she could breathe. Her heart stuttered.

His face was inches from hers. Every part of him shook—from anger or restraint, she didn't know. "I don't share," he growled. His voice was low. Brutal. His pupils were blown wide, drowning out the brown in his irises. He looked feral. Not just jealous: wounded and betrayed.

"Gabriel, it wasn't—" she started, but he cut her off.

"I can smell you." He stepped closer. His mouth ghosted her jaw. "You want him. You're wet for him. Right now." He didn't ask like he wanted confirmation. He said it like it had gutted him.

His voice dropped, breaking into something like disbelief. "You still want me, too, don't you?"

Her breath caught. She hated that he could read her like this and that her body gave her away.

"Don't do this," she whispered.

But he wasn't listening. Or maybe he couldn't. "Do you want to clench around his cock right now, Cinis?" he asked, voice sharp as broken glass. "The way you did mine last night?"

She gasped—furious, embarrassed, something in between—and shoved at him with her free hand. He caught that, too, pinning both wrists with one hand and holding her there. His forehead pressed to hers for a second, as if he could burn the truth out of her skin.

"You think you can fuck us both and stay neutral?" he rasped. "You're mine, Ophelia. You always have been."

And then he kissed her. It wasn't soft. Wasn't kind. It was a collision of need and fury. A claim. A breaking point.

She kissed him back like second nature. Like she didn't know how not to.

And then...he pulled away. He turned without another word and stalked down the corridor, movements jagged, shoulders taut. He didn't look back.

Ophelia stayed pressed against the wall, breathless, reeling. The silence he left behind wasn't empty—it was aching. Loud.

She didn't move. Couldn't. Because the worst part wasn't that he'd walked away. It was that some part of her didn't want to run after him.

ELEVEN

The corridor felt colder in Gabriel's absence.

Ophelia pressed her back to the wall, arms cinched tightly around her middle as the echo of his footsteps faded into silence. The kiss still branded her lips, marked from need and everything unsaid. It hadn't been gentle. It hadn't been kind. And maybe that was what scared her most.

She closed her eyes. Tried to slow her breathing. But everything inside her kept spiraling: the pulse of the bond with Luka, the taste of Gabriel on her tongue, the smell of stone and magic lingering on her skin from the training circle.

The wall at her back was cold. Unforgiving. Her knees gave a little, and she slid down until she was sitting on the floor, arms still wrapped around herself like a shield she hadn't realized she'd raised. The stone bit through her leggings, but she welcomed the discomfort. It gave her something to hold on to.

Gabriel had walked away.

Not just with fury. Not just with possessiveness. But with pain. That gutted her, because somewhere beneath the tangled mess of the bond, he was hers. He always would be. Even when he broke her heart. Even when she broke his.

And Luka—

Gods, Luka. She hated how her body still remembered the heat of him. The way her magic had sparked at his touch, familiar and consuming. How he'd looked at her, not like a rival or an enemy or even a lover, but like something inevitable. She hated that she didn't hate it.

The ache in her chest stretched wide, threatening to hollow her out. Her magic was still simmering under her skin, a chaos she didn't know how to soothe.

She didn't look up when she heard footsteps approach. Not at first. But when the steps stopped beside her and didn't move, she blinked and tilted her head up. Elijah stood there, hands in his pockets, gaze soft but sharp. "You okay?"

Ophelia opened her mouth. Closed it. Then shook her head. "I don't know."

He didn't flinch. Just nodded like he understood something she didn't know how to explain. "That honest now, huh?" he said, sinking down beside her.

A soft sound escaped her, part laugh and part sigh. "I'm too tired to pretend," she said.

He bumped her elbow lightly with his. "Good. Pretending never suited you."

And they sat like that, shoulder to shoulder in the dim hallway, while the wildfire inside her finally quieted enough to let her find herself again.

"I saw Gabriel storm off," Elijah said eventually.

Ophelia didn't answer.

"And Luka looked like he'd just swallowed a dagger," Elijah continued.

Still, she said nothing.

Elijah sighed and leaned back against the wall. "You don't have to pick right now, you know," she said.

Her head jerked up. "What?" she asked, confused that he saw so much.

He gave her a tired look. "You're trying to stop your sister from destroying everything we know. Maybe give yourself a damn break on the love triangle drama."

Ophelia snorted. "It's not a triangle. It's a slow-motion explosion."

Elijah chuckled. "Then don't stand in the blast radius. Not yet."

She stared at the floor for a long moment. "I just...I don't know how to feel. I don't know what's me and what's the bond."

"Then don't make a final decision until you do," Elijah said.

She looked at him, really looked at him, and for the first time in days felt a thread of solid ground beneath her feet.

"Thanks," she said quietly.

He bumped her shoulder. "That's what uncles are for."

Ophelia sat frozen in the hallway long after Gabriel disappeared into the shadows, her arms still wrapped tight across her ribs like they could hold her together. Elijah didn't push; he just stayed with her, solid and warm. But the quiet couldn't last forever. She inhaled sharply and stood. No more stalling. No more indulgence.

The corridor stretched ahead like a gauntlet, long and cold and dimly lit. Her boots struck the stone with a deliberate rhythm, every step echoing louder than it should. A reminder of everything she carried. Of how much had changed and how little she still understood.

As she turned the corner near the east wing's end, she heard it: a voice. Muffled. Familiar. Her breath caught. Not a hallucination. Not a memory. Alive.

She moved faster, heart suddenly thudding in her chest. Elijah kept pace behind her, silent but alert. When she reached the room Sofija had designated as hers, she paused with her hand on the door. The scent of magic drifted through the crack: warm, herbal, laced with something gently electric.

Ophelia swallowed hard and pushed the door open. The sitting room was dim, the air thick with warded stillness. But across the room, in the cocoon of a low-slung couch, the faint shimmer of healing magic glowed soft and steady. Amber and green light arced gently through the air like fireflies moving in time.

Alex knelt beside the couch, her posture slumped with exhaustion, one hand hovering over Celeste's chest, the other pressed lightly to Celeste's temple, sweat trailing down her brow as she whispered. The air around her pulsed like lungs inhaling and exhaling. Living magic.

And Celeste was awake. Propped against a pillow, her silver-streaked curls tumbled across her shoulders. Her skin still looked too pale, her energy too thin, but her eyes were luminous and present.

Ophelia stopped cold. Elijah came up behind her and froze, too, his breath catching beside hers.

Alex looked up first. Her face was drawn, cheeks flushed from the exertion of the healing energy, but her eyes lit with quiet relief.

"She's stable," Alex said, her voice rough from magic and effort. "Stronger than she's been in days."

Celeste turned her head slowly, as if the movement itself cost energy. Her gaze met Ophelia's, and a tired smile curved her lips. "It's good to see you," Celeste whispered.

Ophelia took a single step inside, then another, unable to breathe around the pressure behind her ribs. "I thought—I wasn't sure you'd wake up," she whispered, her voice cracking.

Celeste's smile grew, faint but full of the fire Ophelia had thought lost forever. "Surprise," she rasped. "I never did have good timing."

Elijah's hand settled gently on Ophelia's back, grounding her as the moment spun too large to hold. She blinked rapidly, swallowing down the heat in her throat. "How?" she asked, stepping closer.

Alex let out a soft sound and slowly lowered her hands. "She threaded us here. On her own."

"What?" Ophelia's voice went sharp with shock.

"I tried to stop her," Alex said. "I told her she wasn't ready. But she reached for me, linked the spell before I could block it, and...here we are."

Celeste coughed lightly. "Not my best landing," she admitted. "But I've had worse."

Ophelia dropped to her knees beside the couch and reached for her mother's hand. It was warm and real. She gripped it like it was the only thing anchoring her to the ground. "You stubborn woman," Ophelia whispered. "You should be unconscious."

"I was. Then I got bored," Celeste said sardonically.

Alex made a sound that was half laugh, half sob. "She nearly collapsed. I've been keeping the healing spell active ever since."

Elijah crouched beside Ophelia, eyes bright with relief and something more fragile beneath it. "You scared the hell out of us," he said softly.

Ophelia didn't look away from her mother. "I thought I lost you," she whispered.

Celeste's fingers curled around hers, weak but deliberate. "You almost did," she murmured. "But not yet. There's more to do."

A voice rang from the doorway, cutting through the

emotion like a gust of fresh air. "You could've mentioned you were planning a magical jailbreak," Brisa said, stepping inside. Her tone was sharp, but the relief behind it was unmistakable. "You scared the hell out of me." She strode across the room and dropped to her knees beside Alex, wrapping her in a fierce hug.

"You're lucky I'm in love with you," she muttered against Alex's shoulder. "Otherwise I'd hex your ass for coming to this place."

Alex let out a shaky laugh. "Noted," she said.

Brisa pulled back slightly but didn't let go. Her gaze shifted to Celeste. "You good here for a bit?"

Celeste nodded, her voice still quiet but sure. "Go. She looks like she needs something besides crisis response," she said.

Alex hesitated, glancing at Ophelia like she wasn't sure stepping away was allowed.

Ophelia gave her a small, exhausted smile. "Go," she said. "You've earned a break. Both of you."

Brisa took Alex's hand, weaving their fingers together with the kind of ease that made something ache behind Ophelia's ribs. They slipped out quietly, Alex leaning slightly into Brisa as they disappeared into the corridor.

Silence settled again. Ophelia reached for the blanket draped over the armrest and gently pulled it up over Celeste's shoulders.

Celeste's hand caught hers mid-motion. "I owe you both the truth," she said, her voice raw but steady. "I made a mistake. A long time ago."

Ophelia stilled.

Celeste turned her gaze to Elijah. "I sent Sebastian," she said.

The words landed like a stone in still water, rippling and sinking. Ophelia's lungs seized. Elijah didn't move.

"I didn't tell anyone who you were. Not even him, at first," Celeste continued, her voice barely above a whisper. She stared past them, as if watching it all unfold on some invisible screen. "But when I realized Eris was slipping—when I saw that darkness beginning to take root in her—I panicked."

She paused, swallowing hard. "I thought if I couldn't save one daughter, maybe I could protect the other. Even if it meant doing something I'd have to live with for the rest of my life," she said.

Her gaze flicked to Elijah again, full of raw regret. "You were always Ophelia's constant. Her anchor. But you were only one person. And I was afraid—so afraid—that if Eris found Ophelia, Ophelia wouldn't survive it. I needed someone else. Someone she could trust. Someone who could protect her when I couldn't."

Her fingers trembled in her lap. "Sebastian wasn't tied to any of the old alliances. He didn't care about court politics or bloodlines. No one would've looked twice at him. That made him safe. And useful. I told myself it was enough," she said.

She let out a hollow laugh. "And maybe...maybe I hoped the two of you would fall in love. Not because it was strategic. But because I thought if you did, she'd have something real. Something that could hold," she said to Elijah.

Ophelia blinked, her voice brittle. "You sent him to spy on us?" she asked.

Celeste winced. "No. To protect you. But I didn't give him the full truth. Not even close. He knew you were a witch. But he didn't know about your hybrid nature or what that would mean down the line. He didn't know what you could become," she said, turning her face slightly, as if ashamed. "That was my failure. Not his."

Elijah lowered himself onto the edge of the couch beside Celeste, elbows on his knees, hands clasped tight. He didn't speak right away. When he finally did, his voice was low and even. "I loved him," he said. "Even when some things didn't quite add up. Even when he deflected questions. I still loved him. We built a life together, even if some of it rested on omissions," he said.

He paused and then looked at Celeste, eyes glassy. "I won't pretend I'm not hurt. But I don't hate you for it," he said.

Celeste blinked quickly, holding herself together. "I thought I had more time. More chances to make it right," she said.

Her gaze flicked to Ophelia. "But we don't have time, do we?" she asked softly. "Not anymore. Eris has to be stopped. Whatever it takes."

Ophelia didn't speak. She couldn't.

Celeste leaned her head back against the pillow, her strength clearly fraying. "I just wanted you safe," she whispered. "Both of you."

No one answered. There wasn't anything left to say. Eventually, Celeste's breathing evened, her body softening into sleep. The shimmer of Alex's healing magic had faded completely, but the warmth it left behind clung to the air like a memory.

Ophelia sat there in the stillness, Elijah beside her. The truth sat between them—not gentle, not easy—but it was something solid. And for the first time in days, she didn't feel like she was falling. She looked down at her mother's sleeping form, then over at Elijah, and realized: the past had come for them. But they were still here. And they weren't done yet.

CHAPTER

TWELVE

ERIS

They always think madness looks like chaos. But true madness is quiet. Polished. Patient. It's the silence between heartbeats. The smile before the scream. The stillness of water before it boils.

And beneath that silence: something listening back.

I stand at the edge of the Eye of the Earth and watch the surface ripple without wind. The Cetina shimmers in shades no human eye was meant to hold: turquoise and azure so deep it devours light. I used to think this place was sacred.

Now I know better. It's mine.

The wind brushes my cheek like a lover's apology. Behind me, the ruins of the old church stretch like bones beneath a silk sheet of moss. Galla's wards still linger here, nearly spent, but I can feel them. Whispering. Clinging. Regretful.

They tried to bury me in this place. But I am not earth. I am fire and fury and memory. The stones remember me. Every scream buried beneath this chapel, every spell unspoken—etched in silence now. I can taste the iron in the air, thick with old blood and older betrayal. I am not the girl they left behind. I am what she became when no one came back. I am every prayer unanswered, every mercy withheld. They wanted me to vanish. Instead, I became inevitable.

I kneel and trace a hand through the gravel path, feeling for the pulse beneath. There. A faint hum, metallic and ancient. The amulet calls, even in pieces. I gather them like relics, one fragment at a time. The curve of a golden crescent. A shard still slick with old magic. They tremble in my palm, humming with heat and memory. Holding them hurts. Like a kiss with teeth.

"You remember her," I murmur. "Don't you?"

The amulet doesn't answer, but I feel the truth in my blood. Ophelia touched these stones once. Her magic left fingerprints. She was always meant to kneel beside me. She just doesn't know that yet. But I'll teach her.

I rise, cradling the fragments in both hands, and walk the narrow path that circles the spring. My footsteps are soundless. The world dares not interrupt me when I'm composing fate.

High above, the clouds shift. No birds. No breeze. Even the trees bow inward.

In the chapel ruins, my scrying bowl waits. I pour moonwater over the stone rim, my fingers bleeding from ritual cuts that sting like kisses. The water stills, then dances. Images bloom in the depths—Trieste. Miramare. Her.

Ophelia. Hair damp with salt, magic flaring under her skin like fire beneath glass. She doesn't see me. But I see her.

"Look at you," I whisper. "Shining. Unmoored. Perfect."

My voice is calm. Sweet. I'm proud of her, really. She's grown so much.

"She's waiting for you," the voice hums. Mine. Not mine. It doesn't matter.

"She loves you," it says. "You're her sister."

And yet—

"She dreams of them," I hiss, tone snapping sharp. "Even now.

Gabriel. Luka. Parasites. They feed on her power. They pretend it's love."

The water ripples as my breath hitches. I press a palm flat over the surface. "You should have come to me. You should have known I'd never hurt you. I was made to protect you."

She called me sister once. Her voice was honey and salt. I remember. Or dreamed it. Does it matter?

My fingers drip with blood, and I paint the rim of the bowl like a lover's mouth—slow, reverent. The spell purrs beneath my skin. For a moment, I feel divine. Then, a sudden spike of energy cracks through the bowl. The image warps. The spell breaks.

No.

"No," I say again, louder. "Don't look away."

I shove the bowl off the altar. It shatters against the stone, water mixing with blood. I stare at the wreckage. At my trembling hands. At the pieces that no longer hold her face.

Why would she hurt me like this?

Why would she choose them?

They kept us apart. Hid me. Lied to her. Twisted her against me. And she believes them.

No. No, no, no, no—

Why would she—

They lied. Lied. LIED.

My knees hit the ground.

She is my mirror. My missing name.

I can't breathe.

I rock back, hands in my hair. The world tilts. A sound keens from my throat—thin, animal, too old for human understanding.

Then silence.

Long. Deep. Drowning.

The Eye watches.

And slowly, slowly, I begin to breathe again.

"She'll come to me," I murmur, voice ragged. "She always does."

I rise, hair matted to my temples, hands wet with blood and magic and something older. I gather the Lunula Amulet fragments once more, kissing each one before placing them in a velvet pouch inked with binding runes.

"She's confused. I'll rebuild what they broke. What I broke." *There is no version of the future where she is not with me. I have seen it in the bones. In the fire. In the scream beneath the thread. She was forged for me. She belongs beside me. If the world won't make room for that truth, I will carve one open. With teeth. With flame. With love.*

And if she won't come?

I'll burn down whatever she hides behind.

I press the pouch to my chest and close my eyes.

Sister.

Come home.

"She'll come back to me," *I whisper.*

THIRTEEN

The scent of healing magic still clung to Ophelia's skin as she stepped into the gray light.

She had barely slept. The truth about Sebastian still churned in her gut, not sharp like betrayal but dull and aching—like a wound stitched too snugly. And beneath it all, the thread of the bond pulled taut. Luka. Gabriel. Eris. Her mother alive but fragile. The world waiting. No space left to unravel.

She needed focus. Purpose. Control.

The training grounds behind Miramare were thick with tension. Even the sea seemed to hold its breath, the usual crashing rhythm of the Adriatic muffled beneath a sky gone heavy and sullen. A low mist clung to the cliffside, wrapping around the carved stones of the courtyard like a veil. Ophelia descended the steps slowly and stopped short.

Brisa was warming up with a series of precise kicks, her short braid swinging like a metronome. Alex stood beside her, stretching her arms across her chest, but her focus kept drifting. Every few seconds, her gaze flicked toward Ingrid, then away, uneasy.

"Oh, come on," Brisa muttered, twisting at the waist and cracking her neck. "She's still glaring at me?" she asked.

"She's glaring at me," Alex whispered, voice uncertain. "Like I've betrayed her in some deep way I don't know about."

"She's glaring at both of us," Brisa said breezily, then smirked. "Must sting, watching me trade up."

Alex's cheeks flushed. "You dated her?" she asked, confusion laced with something quieter and close to hurt.

Brisa shrugged, casual to the point of cruelty. "Briefly. Sparring led to kissing. Kissing led to bad decisions. Classic coven romance. It ended when I realized she liked power more than people."

Across the courtyard, Ingrid's jaw flexed. Her narrowed eyes sharpened to slits. If magic could eavesdrop, hers was doing it now, and it didn't like what it heard.

Alex blinked, glancing between Brisa and Ingrid. "And you didn't think to mention this before today?" she asked.

Brisa rolled her shoulders in a lazy arc. "Sorry, I was distracted by the apocalypse," she said with her usual disinterest. But something flickered, barely. A twitch at the corner of her mouth. The slightest crease between her brows. Not regret, but not indifference either.

Alex caught it, her mouth pinched. "Right," she said.

Brisa didn't respond. Her arms dropped to her sides, loose and limber, but her gaze lingered on Ingrid just a moment too long. Not defiant. Not amused. Just...watching.

Ophelia cringed inwardly. Brisa's flippancy was predictable, as reliable as it was infuriating. But this wasn't the time for armor or games, not with the air strung tight and the courtyard charged like a fuse already lit. And if Ingrid's magic was a language, then right now, it was speaking in warnings.

But before Ophelia could step in, a new ripple of energy disturbed the air, cold and sudden. Someone else had arrived.

Luka stepped onto the stone floor, dressed in black from neck to boot. His movements were precise and practiced. He was the picture of vampiric restraint. But that restraint was stretched thin, and his control was fraying. His gaze flicked to Gabriel, standing a few paces away, and a muscle twitched in his jaw.

Gabriel was already watching him, arms crossed over his chest. He hadn't said a word since arriving. But the tension between them crackled like a frayed nerve exposed to air.

Ophelia sighed and stepped closer to the edge of the circle. "I swear to the gods," she muttered to Mo, who had appeared beside her with a notebook and a mug of tea, "if they combust, I'm not cleaning up the ashes."

Mo didn't look up as he scribbled something in the margins of his page. "I don't think there'll be ashes," he replied dryly. "Just shattered egos and a trail of cracked bones." He paused, squinting toward the center of the training circle, where Gabriel and Luka were stalking each other like rival predators.

"They look like ancient mythic beasts," he added, almost to himself. "Not men. Titans. Seconds from tearing the world in half just to prove a point," he said.

Ophelia blinked. "Well. That's...ominous."

Mo sipped his tea. "I've read worse epics. But rarely with this much sexual tension," he said.

A slow breath escaped Ophelia, somewhere between a laugh and a groan as she pinched the bridge of her nose. "I need to reevaluate my life," she said.

Mo arched an eyebrow. "Start with one that doesn't involve dueling vampires with unresolved feelings," he said.

She gave him a sideways glance, then looked back at the

circle where Gabriel and Luka were still posturing like the world was watching. Her lips twitched, half embarrassed, half amused. And entirely unsurprised.

Sofija's voice sliced through the courtyard, sharp and cold. "Enough posturing. If you're going to fight, then fight." She gestured toward the center. "Burn the resentment out of your bones. All of you are useless like this," she said.

Gabriel didn't hesitate. He stripped off his shirt in one smooth motion, revealing a body built like a weapon: broad shoulders, carved muscle, every inch of him honed and hard. Black tattoos inked their way across his chest and arms in sweeping lines and ancient symbols, some protective, some dangerous, all earned. They looked like they belonged to an old god. Or a curse. He stepped into the circle like it was already his.

Luka followed a beat later. Silent. Still. Then, with deliberate slowness, he tugged his shirt over his head to reveal lean, rippling strength. His body was lithe—built for speed and precision rather than brute force—but no less lethal. Scars marred his skin like ghost-written histories and whispers of wars survived. No ink adorned him, but the magic that allowed him to shift shimmered faintly beneath his skin.

Gabriel was bigger. More imposing.

Luka was leaner. Sharper.

And neither looked willing to walk away without blood.

Ophelia tried not to look. But it was impossible to ignore the sheer force of them. Gabriel, all chiseled muscle and ancient ink, radiated heat like a forge. Luka, sleek and sinuous, moved like a blade drawn in slow motion. It wasn't just their bodies; it was the way they filled the space, two forces of nature circling the inevitable and humming with tension.

Brisa let out a low whistle. "You know," she said, eyes locked on the two shirtless vampires, "I've always liked women. But the fact that you've had both of those? Honestly, it's enough to make a girl reconsider. That's just greedy, O."

Alex choked on a laugh.

Ophelia groaned. "Not helping," she said.

"They're going to kill each other," Alex said.

"No," Brisa replied. "But they're going to try."

Sofija lifted a hand, and magic shimmered across the edge of the circle, anchoring the warded boundary that would keep the worst of their powers contained.

"Begin," she said. The word had barely left her mouth before they exploded into motion.

Luka struck first, a blur of black cleaving through the air, his hand closing around Gabriel's throat with unnatural speed. The sudden violence made Ophelia's heart stutter, but Gabriel didn't flinch. With a grunt and a twist of his torso, he broke the hold and slammed an elbow into Luka's ribs. The sound cracked across the courtyard like a gunshot.

Luka staggered but caught himself, pivoting on the balls of his feet. Gabriel was already on him again, boots scraping stone, a brutal right hook aimed straight for Luka's jaw.

Luka ducked, sleek and low. The punch sliced through empty air.

Their rhythm was pure chaos: bone against bone, boot against stone, breath tearing ragged through clenched teeth. Gabriel's blows came like wrecking balls: heavy, punishing, relentless. A man forged in war, shaped by heartbreak. Everything about him screamed *end it*.

But Luka didn't fight the same way. He slipped where Gabriel struck. Redirected instead of resisted. He was exacting and deliberate, like every movement had already played out in his mind.

And he didn't shift. That, Ophelia understood with bone-deep certainty, was the point. He could have used claws. Fangs.

The jaguar sleeping beneath his skin. But he didn't. He wanted this fight as a man. To feel every hit. To bleed with his own hands. Not a monster. Just him.

Gabriel lunged again, landing a blow to Luka's ribs that made him stumble. But Luka twisted midair, caught the momentum, and slammed his knee into Gabriel's abdomen.

Gabriel let out a growl—low, guttural, more beast than man—as he caught Luka's forearm and hurled him backward.

They broke apart, panting, circling. Blood slicked their mouths. Sweat glistened across bare skin, streaked with dirt and thin cuts. The runes beneath them pulsed faintly, as if absorbing every ounce of fury.

No words passed between them.

This wasn't a spar.

This was territory.

Luka moved first, a vicious uppercut aimed for Gabriel's ribs. Gabriel caught it and retaliated with a savage headbutt. Blood sprayed from Luka's nose, but he didn't fall. He spat crimson to the side and grinned—a flash of something wild, something dangerous.

They moved like war given flesh. Gabriel: all brute strength, ruthless, and unyielding. Luka: swift and exact, a weapon carved down to its sharpest edge.

Every blow sent tremors through the courtyard. Dust spiraled beneath their feet. Their collisions struck like fault lines fracturing open. Shockwaves of violence shook the air. It wasn't magic. It didn't need to be.

It was domination.

It was rage.

It was history with fists.

Ophelia felt the bond flare inside her. Luka's emotions were bleeding into her bloodstream, raw and volatile. But her gaze stayed locked on Gabriel.

His fury wasn't supernatural. It was old. Human. Real. She saw it in his clenched shoulders, in the rigidity of his jaw, in the tremble in his fists. He was holding back, just barely.

"He's pulling his punches," Brisa muttered, arms crossed loosely.

"Which one?" Ophelia asked, voice barely audible above the pounding in her chest.

Brisa didn't answer right away. Then: "Both," she said.

But not for long.

Luka surged forward, eyes gleaming, fangs flashing. Gabriel snarled and caught him mid-swing, their bodies crashing together in a tangle of rage. With a brutal twist, Gabriel slammed Luka into the stone hard enough to crack the edge of the warded runes.

Luka hit the ground, rolled, and rose in a single motion.

They circled again.

Breathing heavily.

Bodies battered and bloodied.

Neither giving ground.

Neither willing to yield.

And in that moment, they forgot. Forgot the watchers. Forgot the war. Forgot why they'd come here in the first place.

That was their mistake.

Because neither of them saw her.

Ophelia stepped into the circle with quiet, deliberate fury, runes flaring beneath her boots as if the stone itself recognized her presence. Her magic surged from the marrow of her bones: coiled, patient, and now wholly unleashed. The air warped around her with a sudden intake of power, like the world itself had gasped.

They didn't notice.

Luka lunged, his hands half-shifted, claws gleaming under the misty light.

Gabriel met him mid-charge with an explosive roar, muscles bunching for another devastating strike.

And then they hit it. A wall of pure, unfiltered force exploded between them. Ophelia's magic, sharp as flame and cold as lightning.

The impact knocked them both back as if they'd been yanked out of time.

Flame lashed outward, spreading through the air like liquid gold. Wind howled across the training ground, ripping up dust and salt and sweat-soaked tension. The stone beneath their feet cracked in a spiderweb pattern, the fractures glowing faintly at the edges.

Gabriel crashed to the ground with a curse, skidding on his shoulder, air torn from his lungs.

Luka flipped in midair and slammed down on his back, stunned, limbs spread like he'd been struck by divine wrath.

And at the center stood Ophelia.

Her hair whipped around her face, wild and wind-tangled, her eyes lit from within, glowing gold at the edges. Power radiated from her skin in heat waves.

She didn't yell.

She didn't need to.

Her voice was low, controlled, and *deadly*.

"You forgot yourselves," she said. Silence rang louder than any magic. Even the sea seemed to hush. "This isn't about the two of you," she continued, stepping forward, her boots crunching over fractured stone. "This isn't about your pride. Or your pissing match. Or who bleeds better."

The air rippled with her power, oppressive and electric.

Gabriel pushed himself onto one elbow, his chest heaving. "What the hell—" he started.

"You didn't see me," she snapped, cutting him off. "You

didn't *feel* me. I walked into the middle of your fight, and you didn't even register it."

Luka sat up slowly, rubbing his jaw. His gaze was dazed, but wary now. "We were—"

"I don't care," she said. Her voice cracked like a whip, reverberating against the warded boundary around them. She looked between them, and for a split second, the gold in her eyes brightened. Her magic flared, a pulse of heat so sharp she saw the hairs on Gabriel's neck rise.

"You want to prove you're strong? Start by proving you can control yourselves," she said.

Neither of them moved.

Ophelia's lip curled. "Pathetic," she said.

She turned and walked away from them both, crossing the training circle without a backward glance.

Gabriel didn't follow.

Neither did Luka.

Sofija's voice rang out behind her, echoing against the stone. "Well," she said. "At least *one* of you is ready."

Gabriel wiped blood from his mouth, eyes locked on her retreating form. "She's stronger than both of us," he muttered.

Luka said nothing. But he didn't argue.

Brisa folded her arms, eyes skating between the two bruised, breathless vampires. "All that posturing. All that vampire dick-measuring." She let out a low, theatrical sigh. "And in the end? She really doesn't need either of you."

FOURTEEN

The Adriatic shimmered below, silver and indifferent. Waves broke in slow motion against the base of the cliffs, as if the sea itself had grown bored of crashing. Late afternoon draped Miramare's cliffside courtyard in long shadows, the sun slung low on the horizon, bleeding orange and gold across the sky. The light should've been beautiful, turning the salt-washed stone to gold and kissing the air with warmth. But everything felt muted. Blunted. Like the world had been muffled under a spell of waiting.

Ophelia stepped onto the training grounds with the grace of someone walking toward her own execution.

Her boots echoed against the stone, each step a quiet surrender. She hadn't spoken to Gabriel or Luka since the fight. She hadn't needed to; every glance they'd tried to give her was a weight she refused to carry. Her magic still buzzed faintly beneath her skin from the eruption earlier, unpredictable and raw, like a song stuck in the wrong key. Her chest ached with too many unsaid things, each breath a quiet rebellion.

She had eaten alone, if a few grapes and a bite of cheese

could be called eating. Now, Brisa and Alex flanked her as they approached the circle, both dressed in light training clothes, weapons slung lazily at their sides. Brisa kept a running commentary, something about a cursed mirror in the east wing and a ghost who refused to stop monologuing. Ophelia barely listened.

When they reached the circle, Sofija was already there. Ophelia's gaze swept the group as she entered. Gabriel and Luka stood apart, positioned on opposite sides of the courtyard like magnets repelling each other. Neither looked at her, but she could feel them watching anyway. Gabriel's jaw was tight, the dark bruising at his ribs a reminder of just how far things had gone. Luka's hands were clasped behind his back, calm in posture, but his eyes were full of tension.

Mo and Elijah lingered along the edges, both quiet, both wary. Mo had a journal tucked under his arm and a pen twirling absently between his fingers. Elijah just folded his arms across his chest; Ophelia could read the worry in his face, even if he tried to hide it.

Sofija surveyed them all with cool indifference, then settled her gaze on Ophelia. "You've proven yourself physically capable," Sofija said. Her voice was calm, but it cut through the air like honed glass. "But strength of body means little if the mind is weak."

A low ripple moved through the group like a shared intake of breath. Brisa stopped fidgeting. Alex's spine stiffened. Gabriel's gaze sharpened. Luka's expression didn't flicker, but his jaw flexed once.

Sofija's tone did not change. "What's coming will not be won by brute force. You must learn to make decisions when there is no right one. To act when hesitation could cost lives. To suffer without unraveling," she said.

Ophelia's heart thudded harder in her chest.

"This," Sofija continued, her voice silk-wrapped steel as she raised her arms, "is a simulation." The courtyard stilled. The salt-laced wind died mid-breath as Sofija stepped into the center of the training circle. She moved like the high priestess she was, her authority deeper than magic.

Her fingers were spread wide like a conductor calling forth a symphony only stone and air could hear. The atmosphere pulled tight, dense and old. The kind of magic that didn't ask permission. That remembered blood oaths and ancestral bones. Ophelia tasted iron on her tongue and knew it was beginning.

"This kind of spell hasn't been used in centuries," Mo murmured, more to himself than anyone else. He edged closer to the circle, face drained of color. "It was abandoned for a reason. Because of what it demands."

"What does it demand?" Brisa asked, voice low and unusually serious.

Mo didn't answer.

Sofija began to chant. Her voice slipped into a language Ophelia didn't recognize. Each syllable sounded jagged, like bones dragging over stone, soft and wrong all at once. Her words echoed without volume, resonating in the marrow, not the ear. The runes beneath Ophelia's feet responded first: faint pulses of white-blue light bleeding outward like veins awakening in the stone.

The sky dimmed. Shadows stretched and twisted. The sun's warmth vanished from her skin like it had been snuffed out. Beyond the cliffs, the sea darkened to indigo. The stone beneath her boots began to hum, taut with held power.

Ophelia glanced at the edges of the circle.

Gabriel. Luka.

Both watching her.

Neither moved.

Sofija's chant deepened, the cadence shifting. Her voice no longer sounded like her own. It became layered—echoing, hollow, like the earth itself had borrowed her throat to speak through.

Ophelia inhaled once, steady and shallow, then stepped forward.

The instant her foot crossed the warded boundary, the spell seized her. Magic ripped from her body, sharp and commanding. Her knees buckled under the weight of it.

A spike of pain knifed through her skull and behind her eyes, brutal and blinding. Her magic bucked, instinctively resisting, thrashing against the foreign presence like a body rejecting poison. Her vision swam. Her breath hitched. It felt like being peeled open, unmade from the inside.

Sofija whispered one final word. It was a word Ophelia didn't know, but her bones did.

And then she fell. Not forward. Not back. *Inward.*

The world folded around her like paper curling in flame. She reached out on instinct, but her limbs didn't move. Her body was paralyzed, locked in place, her mind spinning in a vacuum of pressure and heat.

It was like being submerged in molten glass: too hot to scream, too bright to see. The training grounds dissolved, smeared away like chalk under water. She could still hear them: voices at the edge of consciousness. Gabriel's command. Luka's breath. Alex's sarcasm, blurred by panic. But all of it was slipping away. Pain bloomed behind her eyes, sharp and relentless.

And then—

Nothing.

No ground beneath her feet. No wind across her skin. No passage of time to anchor her.

Only heat.

Only pressure.

Only magic—ancient, invasive, and precise—splitting her open like a blade through silk.

Ophelia gasped as her eyes snapped open. Except...they didn't open. Not in the way she expected.

The courtyard was gone.

In its place stood something else, a twisted mirror of the world she'd left behind. The stone floor remained beneath her boots, but it was cracked and scorched, as if fire had eaten through it. The sky overhead bled red and purple, streaked with clouds that moved too fast, like smoke trapped in glass. The Adriatic Sea had turned black, no longer moving in waves but churning like molten ink. There was no sun. Only light that pulsed, sickly and unnatural.

And her hands...they were coated in blood.

Ophelia staggered back, staring down at her wrists. A blade hung from her right hand, its hilt charred, its edge glinting with fresh red. Her pulse thundered in her ears. Her arms ached, not from combat, but from something deeper.

She tried to drop the blade.

It didn't move.

Then Sofija's voice drifted through the air, not from in front of her, but from *inside* her. Like thought given form.

"Only one lives," she said.

The words settled like frost across Ophelia's spine. "What?" she asked, her voice cracking and echoing, distorted like she spoke from underwater.

There was a sound behind her. Chains clinking. A groan.

She turned.

Two pillars rose at the edges of the warped courtyard, one to the left, one to the right. Between them, bound and kneeling, were Gabriel and Luka.

Both shirtless. Both broken. Both chained.

"No," Ophelia whispered, stumbling forward a step. "No, no, no—"

Their heads rose slowly, as if awakening from the same nightmare. Gabriel's dark eyes locked onto her instantly, searching, furious and desperate all at once. Luka's gaze was slower—calculated, intense—but when it landed on her, something raw cracked through his stoic expression.

"Ophelia," Gabriel growled. "Get out of here. This isn't real."

"It feels real," Ophelia said, voice hoarse. "It feels *real*."

Sofija's voice again, cold and final. *"You choose. One to live. One to die. The other...vanishes. Forever."*

Ophelia screamed, but no sound escaped.

Gabriel yanked against the chains, fangs bared. "Don't listen to her! Fight this!" he said.

Luka jerked forward as well, metal rattling. "She can't. Not without finishing it. She has to choose," he said, eyes on Ophelia.

"Bullshit," Gabriel spat. "She doesn't owe anyone that choice."

"Your indecision will end them both," Sofija's voice murmured again, like wind in the bones of the earth.

Ophelia's breath came in ragged gasps. Her hands shook. Magic rippled along her fingers *unbidden*, as if her power was trying to make the choice for her.

Her right hand lit with fire. Burning, restless, volatile.

Her left hand shimmered with wind. Cold, slicing, quick.

One for Gabriel. One for Luka.

She backed away, heart hammering. "I won't do it," she said.

"You have to," Luka said. "You think this is just a spell? It's more than that. It's a reflection. Your magic is making it real."

"Look at me," Gabriel said, voice sharp. "Look at me, Ophelia. You don't need to do this."

"Only one lives."

Her knees buckled.

Luka's voice turned soft, dangerous. "You remember what we were. What we still are. I feel it, even now. That connection, that bond. You can't just erase that," he said.

Gabriel shook his head. "You didn't *choose* that bond. It was forced."

Ophelia's magic surged higher.

Her fingers spasmed, energy arcing from both hands. Fire sparked from her right, wind gathered around her left in a keening whistle.

She tried to lower her arms. Couldn't.

"Decide."

Chains rattled again. Both of them struggling, pleading in different ways.

Gabriel: "Don't let them break you," he said.

Luka: "Don't lie to yourself. You still want me," he said.

Fire flared. Wind screamed. Ophelia sobbed. But her body didn't move. Her magic no longer listened to her commands. It fed off her indecision, growing wilder with every breath she wasted.

The blade in her hand lifted of its own accord.

"No. No. No. STOP!" she screamed, but again, no sound emerged.

Her heartbeat thundered. The world spun.

Gabriel's eyes were pleading, sure.

Luka's were haunted, hungry.

"Only one lives."

Something cracked. The wind whipped into a vortex, howling around her. Her hair tore free from its braid. Flames leapt from her skin, catching the ground in streaks of gold and red. The chains holding Gabriel and Luka began to glow.

They were burning.

"No!" she screamed again, fighting the spell, pushing back.

But her magic surged.

Wild. Uncontrolled.

And then—

Everything exploded. In the real world, the training circle erupted. The stone flared white-hot, pulsing like a heartbeat gone berserk. Magic cracked the air and rippled outward in wild, invisible arcs. Energy burst from the circle's center in a radius of force, snapping through the misted courtyard like a shockwave.

Alex was the first to go down. She staggered back with a yelp, flung violently from her feet as a coil of wind magic slammed into her chest. She hit the ground hard, skidding across the stone with a grunt. Brisa cried out and dropped to her knees beside her, shielding her instinctively.

Inside the circle, Ophelia hovered in the air, her feet no longer touching the ground.

Her arms were flung wide, head tilted back, mouth open in a silent scream. Magic spilled from her in twin columns—one of fire, one of wind—shooting into the sky like flares. Her hair whipped around like a banner in a storm. Her body jerked, spasming, fighting something no one else could see.

Gabriel tried to reach her. So did Luka. But the moment they stepped too close, the air screamed, and a blast of force knocked them flat, sending both careening across the court-yard like rag dolls.

Sofija didn't move. Her expression was unreadable, but the muscles in her jaw were tight.

"She's going to destroy herself," Mo yelled. "Or all of us."

"No," Brisa growled. "She's not." And then she was running. Straight into the circle.

"Brisa!" Mo tried to yell, but his voice was drowned out by the magic in the air.

Brisa didn't slow. "Dammit, Ophy," she shouted, eyes bright with panic. "Don't make me be the goddamn hero!"

With a grunt, Brisa launched herself into the circle, using her air power to go airborne, and tackled Ophelia like a linebacker possessed. It was almost comical, if they hadn't been on the brink of magical combustion. Brisa was half a foot shorter and all wiry muscle, and Ophelia went down like a felled tree.

"I'm trying to *grab* you, not move a mountain." Brisa gasped as they hit the ground in a heap of limbs.

And the spell snapped. It didn't fade. It *shattered.*

Light exploded across the courtyard in a brilliant, blinding flash. The wards let out a shriek and collapsed. The runes flickered and burned out. Ophelia cried out as the illusion dissolved around her, and the physical weight of the world came slamming back.

Brisa lay half-sprawled across her, panting hard, a trickle of blood at her temple. "That was the most disturbing version of 'fuck, marry, kill' I've ever seen," she said.

Ophelia blinked up at the gray sky, lungs heaving, body trembling, hands still warm with phantom fire.

"Next time," Brisa rasped, "you're doing the heroic shit."

"I didn't choose," she whispered.

"I know," Brisa said, quieter now but not dismissive.

At the edge of the circle, Gabriel stood frozen. His expression was unreadable, but his eyes were full of wreckage.

Luka hadn't moved. He looked carved from the same stone that cracked beneath them, his mouth parted slightly like he'd forgotten how to breathe. Like the spell hadn't released its grip.

And Sofija? She stepped forward through the fading haze. "Well," she said, glancing once at Gabriel, then at Luka. "Now we know what line she won't cross."

"So," Brisa said, voice too light, "was that the part of training where we all die horribly, or did I miss a memo?"

Ophelia tried to sit up but winced. Her limbs trembled, magic burned raw and useless in her veins, and her ears rang.

Gabriel turned his back on it all. Not a word. Not a glance. He walked away in stiff, furious silence, his broad shoulders tense, fists clenched like he needed something to hit. The sharp sound of his boots on the stone echoed louder than any scream.

"I couldn't choose," Ophelia whispered again, the words barely passing her lips.

Sofija stepped back into view. She surveyed the damage without emotion, eyes lingering on Ophelia for a long, heavy beat. "And that," she said coldly, "is why you're still dangerous."

CHAPTER

FIFTEEN

Ophelia didn't wait. She pushed to her feet, legs still trembling from the spell's collapse, and ran. She barely registered Brisa calling her name or the murmurs that followed in her wake. The shattered training circle, Luka's hollow stare, Sofija's warning. They all blurred into the static roaring in her ears. She shoved through the castle doors, boots slamming against the stone with punishing speed, ignoring the ache in her limbs and the thrum of burnt-out magic in her veins.

She didn't know where she was going, only who she needed to find. Her boots echoed in the silence, each step a drumbeat beneath the roar in her ears. The castle corridors warped, but her body kept moving, muscle memory overriding panic. The scent of stone and ash still clung to her skin, a reminder of the spell that had nearly unmade her. Her palms burned faintly, residual magic dancing across her nerves like static. She didn't know what she would say. Didn't even know what she needed from him. Only that, without this, without him, she wasn't sure who she was trying to save anymore.

Her feet knew the way before her thoughts caught up, up the winding servants' stairwell, down a long, torch-lit corridor humming with ancient wards. His room sat at the far end, heavy wood carved with warding sigils and old battle runes. The door was slightly ajar.

She hesitated for only a second, then pushed it open.

The room was dim, lit only by a low fire smoldering in the hearth. Shadows spilled long across the stone floor, flickering over worn tapestries and cold steel weapons hung with the care of a soldier who never truly stopped preparing for war.

Gabriel stood near the window, shirtless and back turned, his hands braced against the sill. His shoulders rose and fell with measured breath, but tension bled from every line of him.

"Gabriel," she said, hesitantly.

He didn't turn. "Don't," he said, voice low and raw. "Don't say my name like that."

She took a step in. "I needed to see you," she said.

He turned then, slow and deliberate. His expression was a ruin—anger buried beneath hurt, pain dressed in silence. His dark eyes caught hers and didn't. "Why?" he asked. "So you can say sorry for nearly killing us?"

"I didn't mean to—" she started to say, but he interrupted her.

"You didn't choose," he snapped. "That's what you meant."

Ophelia flinched. "It wasn't real. It was an illusion," she said.

"No, it was you." He crossed the room in three long strides, stopping just short of touching her. His voice dropped to a growl. "The spell didn't create your hesitation, Ophelia. It revealed it," he said.

She swallowed hard, the air between them charged and suffocating. "You think I wanted that? To hurt either of you? I was trapped—"

He interrupted her again. "I was chained. Watching you try not to look at me. Watching you wonder if he meant more." He paused, breathing hard. "And still, I'd rather burn than watch you hesitate again," he said. He broke then, not into rage, but into something rawer. "Do you have any idea what it felt like?" he asked, voice splintering. "To watch you, inside that illusion, and know you were choosing him even as you begged yourself not to? It wasn't just the magic, Ophelia. It was real. And it gutted me."

She stared at him, words choking behind her teeth.

"I kept waiting for the moment you'd turn to me. That something in you would remember what we are. But it didn't come."

Her chest ached like she'd been hit again.

"And gods help me," he whispered, "I'd go through it again if it meant I'd still get to hold you like this."

She looked away. "I'm confused. The bond is eating at me. It masks everything," she said.

"I know." His voice cracked. "Gods help me, I know. You're being torn in two. I can feel it. The bond. The pressure. The weight of everyone's need. But I'm still standing here." His hands closed around her upper arms, firm but not cruel. "And I'm still yours."

Her breath hitched. "Gabriel…"

"You are mine," he said, more ragged now. "And I am yours. That's not a bond. It's fate," he said.

His forehead pressed to hers, and she felt him tremble.

"I want to kill anyone who tries to take you from me," he whispered. "Because we're meant for one another. In this lifetime and the next. You don't have to choose, Cinis. Not right now. But don't lie and say this doesn't mean something," he said.

She closed her eyes. She wanted to scream. To sob. To run. Instead, she leaned in.

Their lips collided, a crash of flames and fury that had nowhere else to go. His hands tangled in her hair. Hers clutched at his bare skin like he was the only thing holding her upright. They kissed like they were drowning. Like the world could wait.

There was no finesse. No softness. Only heat.

Only need.

Only them.

It wasn't just lust. It was survival. A reclamation of something stolen. They weren't trying to forget the nightmare. They were trying to remind each other that they'd survived it. That in this tangle of limbs and breath and heat, they were still real. Still here. Every touch carved a line back into her body, back into her name. Gabriel murmured her name between gasps like it was a prayer and an apology in one. And Ophelia clung to it, not because she needed saving, but because it reminded her she still had something left to lose.

She met Gabriel with teeth and tongue, dragging her nails down his back like she wanted to carve herself into him. He growled low, hands everywhere: gripping her hips, her shoulders, the sides of her face as if he couldn't decide whether to worship or ruin her.

She barely registered the sound of furniture crashing aside. He walked her backward with unforgiving grace until the backs of her knees hit the bed. But instead of pushing her down, he dropped to his knees.

Gabriel looked up at her, eyes blazing wild, but clear. "You belong to me," he said, voice raw. "But gods, Ophelia, don't ever forget. I'm yours, too."

She gasped, heat pooling low in her belly.

"I will burn the world to keep you," he said, lips brushing

the flesh just above her navel, "but I'll fall to my knees every damn time to remind you who you are. And what you do to me," he said.

His hands skimmed her thighs, thumbs hooking into her waistband as he pulled her pants down slowly, agonizingly slow. His mouth followed, pressing kisses along the inside of her leg, each one a promise, a surrender, a claim.

When he buried his face between her thighs, she forgot how to breathe.

Gabriel didn't tease. His tongue moved with purpose, coaxing moans from her lips with every stroke, every flick, every slow pull that sent her spiraling. She braced herself on his shoulders, hips rolling against his mouth, her magic crackling beneath her skin like it might combust.

"Gabriel—" Her voice broke on his name.

He looked up briefly, eyes dark and reverent. "Come for me," he said. "Let me taste what's mine."

Her power didn't just flare. It sang. Notes of fire, threads of air, currents of water rolling over her skin as her body surrendered. The orgasm wasn't just physical. It was elemental. Like her power recognized his mouth as worship and answered accordingly. Sparks crackled at her fingertips, lighting up the space between them. She was molten, unmade, every nerve a starburst. And when her cry broke loose, it wasn't just pleasure. It was grief, release, and a reclaiming of every part of herself she'd once given away.

She shattered. The orgasm hit fast and deep, like a wave breaking over her. Her thighs trembled. Her hands fisted in his hair. She cried out his name, half a sob, half a confession. And when she finally opened her eyes, he was already standing, already kissing her again, and the taste of her on his tongue made her dizzy.

"Now," he growled, lifting her effortlessly into his arms, "now I fuck you."

They fell into the bed in a tangle of limbs, a tangle of power and need and something almost too fierce to name. He was all muscle and heat and unrelenting pace. She gave as good as she got: biting, gasping, anchoring herself to his body like he was the only real thing left in the world.

He drove into her, again and again, and it wasn't gentle. It was a claiming, a collision, a plea carved in skin.

"Say it," he rasped, his forehead pressed to hers. "Say you're mine."

"I'm yours," she whispered. "Always have been."

And when she came again—wrung out and shaking beneath him—it was with his name on her lips and her heart in his hands. Gabriel groaned as her body clenched around him, and a moment later, he followed with a curse and a growl, burying himself to the hilt as he spilled into her.

For a long moment, they didn't move.

Only breath.

Only heartbeats.

Only skin against skin.

Gabriel collapsed beside her, dragging her against his chest. Neither spoke. But as Ophelia lay there, chest still heaving, slick with sweat and energy and the remnants of what they'd made between them, one thought threaded through the chaos in her mind. She didn't feel claimed. She felt seen. And gods help her, it scared her more than anything else.

Gabriel shifted beside her and brushed a thumb across her cheek, drawing her gaze back to him. His dark eyes searched hers, not demanding answers, just holding space for them.

"You don't have to choose tonight," he said softly. "But don't pretend you don't feel this."

Ophelia didn't answer right away. She pressed her face

against his chest, just for a moment, and inhaled. He smelled like clove and iron and something wild, familiar and fierce.

"I do," she murmured. "I feel it, Gabriel. I feel everything."

For a while, they didn't speak. His hand traced lazy circles along the curve of her hip, grounding her. She almost forgot how to be still, how to let silence be safety instead of tension.

Then, quieter than before, he said, "I'm not afraid of him."

She lifted her head slightly. "Luka?" she asked.

Gabriel nodded. His jaw was tight, but his voice didn't shake. "He could tear me apart in ten seconds. Maybe five. And I'd still fight him if I thought it would bring you back to me," he said.

Ophelia's throat tightened at the admission.

"But that's not what scares me." He looked at her now, no shields between them. "I can survive losing you. I can survive you loving someone else. But I can't survive watching you destroy yourself."

The words landed like a stone in her heart. Her hand found his cheek. She kissed him then, slow and soft and aching. Like gratitude. Like an apology. Like a thread trying to stitch her back to something she'd forgotten how to hold.

"I'm trying to find my way back," she whispered. "To myself. To you," she said.

Gabriel's eyes fluttered shut for a beat, like the weight of her words physically moved through him. But he didn't cling. He didn't beg.

And maybe that's what undid her.

Ophelia sat up slowly, wrapping the sheet around herself. Her body ached in a way that had nothing to do with the fight. Her legs felt heavy, her chest hollow. She needed air. She needed—

"I have to see Alex," she said.

Gabriel propped himself up on one elbow, watching her as

she moved across the room, gathering her clothes. "Is she awake?" he asked.

"I don't know," Ophelia said, pulling her shirt over her head. "But I need to see her."

He nodded once. "Go. She needs you," he said.

Ophelia paused at the door, her hand resting on the frame. She looked back at him—bare-chested, tousled, still glowing faintly with sweat and heat and everything they hadn't said.

"But, Ophelia, I need you, too," he added.

The words hit lower than she expected. Not desperate, just true. "I know," she said, her voice breaking around it. She didn't look back. But she felt him anyway, in every breath, like the echo of a vow that had no ending.

The infirmary at Miramare wasn't a place for rest; it was a place of reckoning.

The scent hit her first. A strange blend of iron and crushed herbs, laced with something older: lavender, sage, and the bitter trace of blood. It clung to the air like smoke in a burned-out room. Somewhere, a vial clinked against glass. A healer murmured softly in another tongue, the words barely louder than breath. The shadows stretched long across the stone floor, draped over rows of cots like shrouds.

Ophelia walked slowly between them, boots quiet against the tile, every step like walking into a confession. The faint blue glow of a warded sigil pulsed underfoot, flickering slightly as she passed. Her magic—still frayed from the explosion—responded dully, buzzing at her fingertips like a warning she didn't want to hear.

Alex lay on the far cot, surrounded by low candlelight. The blankets were tucked tight, as if they were afraid she'd vanish if they let her breathe too deeply.

Ophelia sat beside her, sinking into a too-small chair that

groaned beneath her weight. The wood was old. The legs uneven. Fitting, she thought. Everything felt tilted now.

Her hands rested in her lap. Trembling, burning. The skin beneath her nails still darkened from the magical surge, raw and ragged. Her veins hummed like they didn't know how to be still. But it wasn't pain she felt. It was absence, as if something essential had been hollowed out.

She looked at Alex's face and nearly broke. There was a blood smudge trailing from one ear, dried and dark against too-pale skin. A thin cut split her bottom lip. Her lashes fluttered now and then, but her body didn't stir.

This was her fault. Ophelia reached forward, fingers trembling as they hovered over Alex's hand. For a moment, she couldn't quite bring herself to touch. But then her hand closed gently, her thumb brushing against knuckles that had once punched a werewolf out cold for grabbing Ophelia's arm too hard.

"I'm sorry," she whispered. The words scraped out, brittle and broken. Her throat tightened. Her vision blurred.

"Gods, I didn't mean to—" Her voice cracked, disappearing into the hum of candlelight and silence.

She bowed her head. Let her hair fall like a curtain around her face. Let herself sit there in that quiet, aching moment, where nothing moved and everything hurt.

For just a moment, she let herself be as wrecked as she felt.

Then Alex stirred. It was subtle at first, just the twitch of her fingers beneath Ophelia's. But to Ophelia, it felt like a thunderclap. She leaned forward so fast the chair squeaked beneath her. "Alex?"

A low groan escaped from the bed. Eyelids fluttered, then cracked open, revealing glassy green eyes that immediately narrowed. "Don't yell," she rasped.

Relief hit Ophelia like a blow. Her body sagged forward,

laughter breaking from her in a half sob, half hiccup. She pressed her forehead to the blanket beside Alex's hip and let the sound shake loose.

"I wasn't yelling," Ophelia managed, voice raw.

Alex's brow crinkled faintly. "Could've fooled me. I feel like I was hit by a mountain," she said.

"More like a magical tidal wave," Ophelia said. "Sorry about that," she added quietly.

Alex groaned. "That explains the headache," she said.

They both fell quiet again before Alex turned her head slightly on the pillow. Her hair was matted, her lip still split, but her gaze was steady. "You okay?" she asked.

Ophelia opened her mouth. Closed it. Her throat worked around words that refused to come.

"Yeah," Alex said dryly. "Didn't think so."

A silence stretched between them, full of everything they didn't know how to name.

Then Ophelia spoke again. "I couldn't stop it. I couldn't choose. I froze. I lost control," she said.

"I know," Alex said, her voice flat. Not cruel, just honest. She exhaled slowly through her nose. "I felt it. It was like watching your magic tear itself in half. And then tear us all apart with it."

Ophelia winced. "You could've died," she said.

Alex squeezed her hand. "Probably won't be the last time."

"Don't joke," Ophelia responded.

Alex's eyes sharpened. "Then don't lie. You didn't freeze because you're weak or lost control, Ophy. You froze because you still don't know what you want."

Ophelia turned her head away, cheeks burning. Shame knotted in her chest.

Alex didn't let go. Her fingers tightened. "You think I haven't felt it? The way it pulls on you? The blood bond. The guilt. The pressure. It's all feeding into your power and twisting it," she said.

"I wanted to save them both," Ophelia whispered. "I wanted to make the right choice."

Alex closed her eyes. "Then maybe the real problem is thinking you're supposed to make one at all."

Ophelia blinked at her.

"You keep trying to pick a side. But what if you're not meant to? What if you're meant to choose yourself first?" Alex asked.

The words landed heavy. "I don't know who I am anymore," Ophelia admitted. "I keep trying to be what everyone needs, and I don't think I even know what *I* need."

Alex exhaled, eyes closing briefly. "You need time. Space. And probably someone to smack you every time you try to martyr yourself," she said.

Ophelia huffed a watery laugh. "I think Brisa already claimed that job."

Alex cracked a smile. "Of course, she did."

They were interrupted by the unmistakable cadence of someone who rarely waited for permission. Brisa. She stepped toward them without ceremony, arms crossed. "Well," she said, eyes flicking between them, "are we talking about me, or do I just have good timing?"

Alex gave her a ghost of a smirk. "Mostly you. Don't let it go to your head."

Brisa moved to the other side of the bed and perched on the edge, careful not to jostle the blankets. Her expression softened the moment she saw Alex's face, marred and bloodied, but awake.

"I thought I'd lost you," she said, voice barely above a whisper.

Alex blinked slowly. "Not that easy to kill," she said.

Brisa gave a short, brittle laugh. "Yeah, well. I'm not interested in testing that theory again."

Silence laced with old affection and fear stretched between them. Then Brisa looked up at Ophelia, and her voice turned sharper. "And you. You look like hell," she said.

"Thanks," Ophelia muttered, managing a faint smile. "You always know just what to say."

Brisa's grin didn't reach her eyes. "You scared the shit out of me, O," Brisa said, not quite managing her usual smirk. "One minute we're training, next minute you're screaming and lighting up the sky like a goddamn doomsday flare."

"I didn't mean for it to happen," Ophelia said. "I wasn't trying to hurt anyone—"

"But you almost did," Brisa interrupted, not unkindly. "It wasn't just a little flare-up. You nearly lost control. You *did* lose control."

"I know," Ophelia whispered.

Brisa nodded once, then glanced back at Alex, who was watching her with a tired sort of patience. "And I can't lose her."

Alex blinked. "Brisa..."

"No," Brisa said, more fiercely now. "You don't get to play hero and throw yourself into the blast radius. I'm not built to live without you."

Alex opened her mouth—maybe to tease, maybe to argue—but the words didn't come. Her lips pressed into a thin line. Her gaze turned glassy.

Ophelia looked between them, heart knotting. "I don't know what to do," she admitted. "Everything feels like it's fraying all at once. Like I'm being pulled in every direction."

Brisa didn't offer an answer. She just sat there, her fingers brushing lightly against Alex's blanket-wrapped arm. She looked like she wanted to punch something. Or cry. Maybe both.

But Alex looked at her old friend and reached forward to grip her hand. "You have to face what's coming. Or it'll break you before you get the chance."

Suddenly, the air shifted, dark and dangerous.

Ophelia sat up straighter as a pulse rolled through the room, not quite strong yet, but *wrong*. It was the kind of energy that didn't announce itself. It crept toward them, unseen until it was on them. The candles flickered sharply, their flames leaning toward the door like something had exhaled just beyond the threshold.

Her spine locked. "Did you feel that?" she asked.

Alex's fingers tightened around hers. "Yeah. Something just...moved."

Brisa's head snapped toward the window. The wind outside had stopped. Not faded. *Stopped*. The stillness of a world holding its breath.

"I don't like that," Brisa muttered. "That felt like a warning."

Another tremor slid through the air. This time slower. Colder. It coiled around Ophelia's ribs like a ghost brushing bone. She stood, unsteady but alert as her magic rose to meet the pressure. "Something's coming."

"Something bad," Alex agreed. "And close."

Brisa was already on her feet, crossing the room in a few clipped strides. "Time's up," she said, voice low and grim.

Ophelia looked back at Alex. "I should stay with you," she said.

"No," Alex said, shaking her head. "I don't need a babysitter. You need to be ahead of this, not behind it."

At the doorway, Brisa pulled it open. Ophelia hesitated for one breath. Then she gave Alex's hand one final squeeze and turned toward the dark. The door shut behind her with a soft click.

The corridor beyond stretched long and pale, lit only by dim torches. But the magic in the walls no longer hummed in welcome. It *rattled*. Like breath caught in a throat. Like a warning that had come too late. Something had changed. And whatever was waiting, it had already begun to wake.

CHAPTER

SEVENTEEN

The walls of the hallway trembled. It was subtle at first, just the faintest shudder. A low groan followed, stretching through the bones of Miramare Castle. Candles along the walls flickered in sync, their flames bowing to a breeze that shouldn't exist. It wasn't wind from an open window. It came from nowhere, a phantom breeze crawling its way along Ophelia's skin and lifting the fine hairs at the back of her neck.

She stopped walking. Brisa did, too.

Then came the crack. A deep, resonant sound that rolled through the floor like a fault line giving way. Dust fell from the rafters. The air thickened, warped by a pressure that didn't belong to this world.

Brisa's boots scuffed to a stop. "What the hell was that?" she asked, reaching instinctively for the blade at her thigh. Her tone was sharp, but Ophelia didn't miss the thread of unease in it.

Ophelia didn't respond. Her eyes were fixed on the corridor ahead, where the sconces sputtered and guttered as another tremor rolled through the floor. This one was sharper, grating. Like claws dragging through the castle's foundations.

Behind them, a soft sizzle disturbed the quiet. Mo emerged from a side passage, breathless and already brimming with power. Faint sparks licked across his knuckles like miniature lightning.

"I felt it," he said without preamble. "From the eastern tower all the way to the crypts. The wards are failing."

Brisa turned sharply. "They can't fail. Sofija said she reinforced them after the last breach," she said.

"I don't care what she said," Mo said, voice clipped and tighter than Ophelia had ever heard from him. His eyes snapped to her. "Something's pressing against the seams. Something big. Old. And it's not just power. It's pressure," he said.

A beat passed. Then another tremor: a final, rolling quake that made the walls groan in protest. A glass vial shattered somewhere in the infirmary. Pieces scattered across the floor, catching the candlelight in fractured gleams. And then…the flames went out.

The sconces snuffed out in unison, as if the castle itself had exhaled. Darkness rushed in with unnatural speed, and the temperature dropped like a stone. Not the chill of winter air, but the kind of cold that burrowed deep and whispered, *you are no longer alone.*

Brisa's mouth tightened. Her hand curled around her weapon.

Then came the sound: a faint, hissing whisper, like paper burning underwater. Not fast. Slowly. Like it was savoring the undoing.

Ophelia's magic sparked against her skin in warning. Her pulse stuttered.

And then, Sofija stepped from the far end of the corridor

like she'd been conjured from the earth itself. Her gaze—sharp and ancient and terrible—locked directly onto Ophelia.

"Everyone outside," she commanded, voice like ice cleaving granite. "Now."

The group moved.

Mo was already at the door, energy charged faintly around him like a storm waiting for its sky. Ophelia followed close behind, her pulse thrumming in her throat like a second heartbeat. Brisa brought up the rear, throwing one last glance over her shoulder toward Alex, her mouth tight with worry.

The corridor outside glowed faintly as the sconces sputtered, struggling to reignite. The faltering light stammered wildly, casting shadows that stretched and twisted like living things. The warded stones underfoot no longer pulsed in soft welcome. Instead, the magic in them shivered, distorted and off-beat, as if the castle itself was trying to cough up something it couldn't digest.

They moved quickly, boots pounding against uneven rock, breath catching in the thick air.

A sudden gust of wind slammed into them from nowhere, and the doors to the outer courtyard groaned open on their hinges, not pushed by hands but pulled by something deeper. Something that wanted to be seen.

The sky over Miramare had turned the color of steel. Clouds swirled low and tight, unnatural in their rotation, as if a great hand stirred them from above. The sea wind tore through the courtyard in a scream, lashing at hair and clothes, burning salt into skin.

Gabriel and Luka burst through the side passage just as they stepped out. Both armed. Both deadly. They swept the horizon in unison. Luka's eyes were narrow, calculating. Gabriel's were sharp and fierce. They didn't need to speak.

Everyone could feel it. Something was wrong. More wrong than it had ever been.

Then the sea began to retreat.

Ophelia saw it first. The water pulled back from the base of the cliffs, not like a tide, but like the Adriatic itself was recoiling in horror. Rocks that hadn't seen air in centuries glistened slick and black in the sudden exposure. Fish flopped and gasped. Seaweed curled like withered hands.

Brisa sucked in a breath. "That's not normal," she said.

"No," Mo said grimly. "That's a harbinger."

The ground trembled beneath their feet again. Deeper this time. Hungrier.

Sofija's head lifted sharply.

And then, Brisa's voice, low and tight. "Top of the cliffs," she said, pointing.

Ophelia looked up, her stomach dropping.

Eris stood on the craggy ridge above the castle, her silhouette backlit by the churning sky. She looked like a revenant from some half-forgotten nightmare. Her long jacket flared like broken wings, hair whipped to madness by the wind, a dark smear against the angry clouds. The air around her shimmered with unstable energy, the very stone beneath her feet scorched and splintered as if even the earth tried to shrink away.

Ophelia's breath turned to ice in her throat.

Eris didn't just *radiate* power, she radiated *wrongness*. The kind of twisted magic that didn't just break rules. It rewrote them.

And then Ophelia saw what she was holding. And her heart stuttered.

The Lunula Amulet.

Or what remained of it.

Even from afar, it pulsed with grotesque clarity. The crescent half had been reforged, but not with gold or light. With bone. With blood. With madness. The pieces pulsed with a sickly light, bound together by some sinew-like material that looked like it had been spun from nerve and nightmare. The power that bled from it was chaotic and hungry, crawling across the air in tendrils of red and violet.

"That's not possible," Ophelia whispered.

Brisa's jaw tightened. "It was destroyed," she said.

"It *was*," Ophelia said, her voice hollow. "We shattered it into pieces."

A voice floated down from the cliff, sing-song and strange. "Not destroyed, sister mine. Only sleeping." Eris tilted her head, eyes gleaming with fever-bright certainty. "You can't kill a soul like this. Only scatter it. And where do you think the pieces landed?" she asked. Her gaze found Luka and lingered, hungry and knowing. "The Eye of the Earth...leaks such *wonderful* things," she said.

Sofija's weathered hands curled into fists. "The shards," she muttered, voice like crushed glass. "She's rebuilt the Lunula from fragments."

Mo exhaled, the sound tight with dread. "If she can wield it —even fractured—she can override the minds of other supernaturals. Turn them into weapons. Slaves. Puppets."

Sofija's gaze never wavered. "I can shield us. But not everyone. Not at this scale. So stay close," she said.

Brisa's blade spun once in her hand, fast and irritated. "Cool, cool. Great to know we're on the short list for not being mind-controlled meat puppets."

Eris smiled, a terrible, gleaming thing. "The world forgets," she called down to them. "It always forgets. But I remember. I remember what this power *was* before they caged it. Before you tried to shatter it like glass."

She raised the amulet.

Magic lanced outward in a jagged arc of sickened light. It

struck the outer perimeter of the courtyard, slamming into a cluster of witches and vampires stationed along the edge. They dropped as one, screaming without sound, bodies seizing in unison. Their eyes burned red. Their limbs jerked like marionettes tangled in invisible strings.

Ophelia barely had time to register what was happening and throw up a protective shield with her air power.

The blast clipped the edge of her ward, sending a hairline crack through it like fractured glass. "I can't cover the full courtyard!" she shouted.

Another surge came. A second group fell, knees hitting stone. Their eyes were vacant, their power turned against them.

"They're being controlled!" Mo shouted, panic fraying his usually measured tone. "The amulet is overriding their minds!"

Eris tilted her head, as if admiring her handiwork. "Blood remembers. Magic obeys. You think I need armies when I can twist yours against you?" she asked, yelling above the wind now.

Sofija didn't speak, but the air around her turned lethal. Energy flared along her fingertips like frost kissed with fire as she shielded the minds of anyone near her.

The possessed horde began to descend, charging straight through the courtyard. The pounding of feet filled the air like a drumbeat of war. One of the possessed vampires lunged. Brisa flipped him over her shoulder and slammed him down with a gust of wind, teeth gritted. "I'm trying *not* to kill anyone, but it's getting harder by the second!"

Luka ducked away from a vampire's blade that hissed too close to his head, his body already shifting mid-motion. His features sharpened, limbs fluid, muscles coiled tight. "They're not in control," he snapped. "We can't fight them like enemies."

Gabriel's blade rang as it met a possessed witch's dagger. "Then what do you suggest? We *hug* them out of it?"

Another pulse from the amulet. Another wave of allies turned. The courtyard erupted into chaos of friendly fire and blood, the ground slick with water and power.

Mo slammed a pillar of rock between two of the possessed, knocking them back. "We're outnumbered!"

"Seriously, can we stop fighting the possessed? It's exhausting," Brisa said.

Ophelia turned in place, her shield faltering, her vision going hazy. Her magic burned in her palms, her reserves draining too fast. Every defense frayed quicker than the last.

A familiar scream tore through the air. Ophelia's head snapped toward the sound.

Alex stood at the far edge of the courtyard, one arm braced against a marble pillar, body swaying. Her skin was pale, sweat on her brow, but her hands glowed with healing light. She knelt beside one of the witches, trying to pull her out of the spell.

"No!" Ophelia shouted. "Get back—"

The witch shuddered. Her eyes began to clear. It was working.

And then Eris saw her. The amulet flared with unnatural light. A jagged, corrupted spell carved the air and struck Alex in the chest. She was too far for Sofija to reach.

Alex screamed once more and then collapsed.

"*Alex!*" Brisa's voice ripped from her throat, raw and ragged. She was already moving, faster than thought, air whipping into a cyclone around her as she sprinted forward. She vaulted over rubble, lurched across fractured stone, reached with everything she had. "No—no—no—"

But it wasn't fast enough. It was too far. And she was too slow.

Eris lifted her other hand and made a sharp slashing gesture. The air tore open. A seam in space ripped wide, violent with red lightning and the echo of blood magic. She reached through it, threading forward to seize Alex's limp form like a broken doll.

With a smirk, she threaded again, and the seam slammed shut behind her like a mouth swallowing its prey.

Alex was gone. Just gone. Eris had taken her, and no one had been able to stop it. Silence dropped over the courtyard like a thunderclap.

The possessed collapsed where they stood, the force in them snuffed out suddenly. The glow in their eyes vanished. Some wept. Some stared at their own hands, bloodied and confused.

Ophelia fell to her knees.

Brisa didn't scream. She just stood there, trembling, lips parted in a silent, stunned horror that didn't quite make it to sound.

Gabriel's blade slipped from his hand. He didn't flinch when it clattered to the ground.

Luka turned away.

Sofija was the only one who moved.

She stepped into the dead center of the courtyard and spoke with calm, quiet finality.

"She has the amulet," she said. "And now she has your strongest fae healer."

No one answered. Because Eris hadn't just attacked them. She had taken something irreplaceable. And now, finally, they understood. There would be no warning. No time to prepare. Eris wasn't coming. She had already arrived.

CHAPTER

EIGHTEEN

The sun had barely crested the horizon, but the morning haze did nothing to soften the air. It was sharp, brittle, like it knew something had broken. Brisa's fists were raw. Blood streaked her knuckles, the skin split from punching the stone wall behind the training grounds. A jagged crack spiderwebbed through the rock, and her breath came in harsh bursts as she stalked back and forth like a caged animal. Her eyes were wild. Feral.

Mo stood a few paces away, hands raised like he was approaching a wounded predator. "Brisa, please—"

"Don't," she snapped, interrupting him. Her voice cracked like glass underfoot. "Don't tell me to breathe. Don't tell me it's going to be okay," she said.

Ophelia lingered just behind them, her heart clenched tight. Her magic buzzed faintly beneath her skin, a half-healed wound. The training circle still held the scent of scorched air and broken trust. She hadn't slept. Couldn't.

"Tell me this isn't real," Brisa growled. "Tell me you got the report wrong."

Mo didn't speak. He just held up the paper, the envelope already cracked and discarded. His fingers trembled as he read.

Casualty report from Marrakesh Covens. No survivors. Consistent with blood magic and corruption. Victims unrecognizable. Magic residue traced to Lunula Amulet signature. Initial witness accounts report one woman, silver hair, fae-adjacent aura. Controlled.

It was Alex. It had to be her. Brisa made a sound halfway between a sob and a snarl.

"She didn't know what she was doing," she said, gasping and so unlike herself. "She would've never, never..." Her voice fractured. She doubled over, palms braced on her knees, like the weight of what she'd heard had shattered something inside her. The Brisa they all knew—the one who deflected pain with smirks and barbs—was gone.

She straightened, shoulders rigid, but her hands still trembled at her sides. The fury in her gaze struck like a curse. It wasn't loud or theatrical, just deeply and devastatingly real. "You were supposed to protect her," she said to Ophelia.

The words didn't just land. They pierced. Sliced. Lodged somewhere deep in Ophelia's chest, where all her magic and muscle couldn't reach. "I tried—" she said, but her voice cracked like thin ice. Trying hadn't been enough. Not when Alex was gone. Not when Brisa was breaking in front of her.

"Try harder," Brisa hissed. She turned her back, shoulders trembling, and didn't speak again.

Silence fell, thick and strangling. Even the air around them felt still, like the world was listening in.

Gabriel stepped beside Ophelia. He didn't touch her, just

stood close enough that she felt his presence like a shield. "This isn't your fault," he said.

Ophelia stared straight ahead. "Isn't it?" she asked.

"She was taken. You didn't let her go," he said.

She swallowed, but it stuck. The silence between her ribs ached. "I should've been faster."

Gabriel's jaw flexed, but he said nothing more. He just stayed beside her.

Across the courtyard, Luka watched from the shadows of the castle wall. Arms crossed. Face unreadable. But his eyes didn't leave her. Not once.

HOURS HAD PASSED. The blood had crusted on Ophelia's boots, but the ache in her chest was fresh. When the summons came from the Alliance, she didn't ask questions. She just followed the weight in her bones.

The ceremonial chamber at Miramare was woven from ancient stone and silence. Vaulted ceilings arched above the gathered leaders like the ribs of some long-dead god, and the sconces that lined the walls pulsed with faint magical light, more ember than flame. Shadows pooled in the corners like waiting judgments.

Ophelia stood just inside the door, her arms crossed tightly, shoulders stiff. She hadn't changed clothes since the attack. Her boots were still caked in dust and blood, her magic still ragged at the edges. But none of that mattered now. Not with what they were facing.

The Alliance had called a supernatural meeting to discuss how to deal with Eris. Zeon was already there. He stood near the center of the chamber, flanked by two lesser vampires in ceremonial black. His dark coat swept to his heels like spilled ink, and his expression was marble-carved fury. When he turned and spotted Ophelia, his voice cut through the murmurs like a dagger thrown point-first.

"If this is what your sister is capable of," he said, "then I was right to demand your cooperation." His lip curled. "You should've stopped her when you had the chance."

Ophelia didn't flinch. She couldn't afford to. "She wasn't using the Lunula Amulet before," she said coldly. "None of us knew how far she'd gone."

"Then you weren't looking hard enough."

Gabriel stepped in before she could answer, solid and unwavering behind her.

"Now's not the time for blame," he said, his voice low and dangerous. "We need to talk strategy."

Zeon's gaze lingered on him, then flicked to Luka, who leaned silently against a pillar, arms crossed, eyes unreadable. "Interesting that both of your companions are here," he said. "Let's hope they're not liabilities."

Before the tension could crack wider, Sofija's voice cut clean through the room. "Enough," she said.

She stepped into the center, long gray robes whispering around her feet, the runes on her sleeves glowing faintly as if drawn to the current of fear in the room. She lifted her hand, and the doors groaned shut behind them with a soft thrum of magic.

"You were all summoned because this is no longer a question of rogue magic or political fallout," Sofija said. "This is war." The words dropped like a gavel, sealing the silence that followed.

Ophelia scanned the room. The fae stood at the far side, their ethereal features sharp and silver-lit, expressions unreadable. Beside them, a selkie ambassador shifted anxiously in his seal-leather coat. A lone necromancer from

Prague leaned against the back wall, her eyes flicking with uneasy interest.

Sofija continued. "We have confirmed what many of you feared. Ophelia did not destroy the Lunula Amulet as we all thought. She shattered it. And Eris Wildes later reformed it using remnants recovered from the Eye of the Earth. Eris has stabilized it through blood magic. That is why she appears so powerful."

"She controlled over a dozen supernaturals at once," Zeon said. "That's not just power. That's corruption."

"And instability," Sofija snapped. "Blood magic can give you temporary strength, but it doesn't last. It feeds on the user. The more she controls, the more she must sacrifice. Eventually, it will consume her."

"Will she die from it?" someone asked from the circle.

"No," Ophelia said, voice flat. "She'll take the world with her first."

A hush followed.

Sofija nodded solemnly. "Which is why we cannot wait. The coven has determined the next likely step. If Eris has reformed the Lunula Amulet, she will attempt to restore the Kala Ghanta."

Zeon's jaw clenched. "The Bell of Time is inert. Destroyed."

"Not entirely," Sofija said. Her gaze flicked to Ophelia. "It remains dormant. We don't know if it can be resurrected."

Ophelia felt a shiver crawl up her spine.

Then, at last, the fae leader spoke. Their voice was cool, deliberate. "If that's true...then your sister isn't just playing with fate. She's trying to rewrite it," they said, tilting their head as if the entire conversation had been mildly diverting rather than dire.

All eyes shifted toward the fae, standing apart from the rest of the gathering as if the rock beneath their feet belonged to a different realm entirely. They were cloaked in silver-gray, their skin moon-pale, features both youthful and ageless. The lead envoy—tall, silver-eyed, and draped in magic older than language—watched her with the stillness of a creature used to watching civilizations fall.

Ophelia stepped forward. "Alex is one of yours," she said. Her voice didn't tremble, but it burned. "She's using fae magic. You must have felt it when the amulet took her. When she was forced to kill—"

"She is not one of ours," the fae leader interrupted.

The room went still.

Ophelia's lips parted, confusion tightening into disbelief. "What?" she asked.

"She is too far removed from the source," they said smoothly. "Her blood is too diluted. Whatever magic remains in her is wild and fractured. She does not carry the birthright of the fae."

Ophelia flinched like she'd been slapped. "That's not her fault," she said.

"No," the envoy agreed. "But it is a fact. And now, she has been twisted further, aligned with blood magic, and bound to the Lunula Amulet. To Eris."

"She didn't choose this," Ophelia said sharply. "She's being *used*. She's been *taken*. She's still in there—"

"We do not dispute your belief," the envoy said. "But our role in this war is not to rescue those who have already crossed the threshold."

Ophelia's voice rose. "Then what is your role? To stand there in your perfect detachment and watch while the rest of us bleed?" she asked.

A murmur spread through the hall, some bristling with agreement, others stiff with discomfort. But the envoy remained unmoved.

"We do not interfere in supernatural politics," they said, as if it were a tenet etched in the fabric of their existence.

Ophelia stared at them. At their perfect skin. Their glowing veins. Their ageless poise. She thought of Alex. Of Brisa, still shaking with grief. Of the carnage Eris forced onto the world.

And something inside her snapped.

She slammed her hand down on the table with a crack that echoed through the chamber like a lightning strike. "Then what *good* are your gifts if you hoard them while the world burns?" she demanded. "What purpose do your rules serve if they let this happen?" she asked.

The lead envoy blinked once. Not slowly. Not kindly. Like a predator regarding something smaller than itself. "Our gifts are our own to guard," they said. "And we have seen what happens when they are given freely."

Ophelia opened her mouth, but she couldn't find words sharp enough.

"We mourn the loss of your friend," the envoy added with a tilt of their head. "But we will not act." They turned then, as if nothing more needed to be said, the other fae following silently. Their footsteps didn't echo. They left behind no scent, no warmth, not even a whisper of wind.

Just absence.

Sofija let out a breath like a curse. Zeon muttered something in another tongue.

Ophelia stood frozen, her hand still pressed to the table, shoulders heaving. "They could've helped," she whispered.

Brisa's voice came softly from behind her. "They don't help. They just...watch. Collect information," she said.

The flickering sconces dimmed all at once, as if the air itself exhaled. A hush fell over the chamber. And then Celeste appeared in the arched doorway, her figure half-shadowed, half-silvered by the magic that hummed faintly in the Alliance hall walls.

She leaned heavily on a dark wood cane, her skin pale as parchment, her hair loose down her back. Her presence was quieter than before—muted, fragile—but no less commanding.

Brisa moved toward her instinctively, but Celeste lifted a hand. "I'm fine," she said, voice low but steady.

Ophelia stood, chest tight. "You shouldn't be here," she said.

"And yet here I am," Celeste said with a tired smile. "Because you need to hear this."

Even Zeon fell silent.

Celeste stepped forward, pausing every few feet to catch her breath. Sofija conjured a chair with a flick of her wrist, and Celeste sank into it, lips tight with pain. "Eris is drawing power from old blood," she said. "Older than most of you in this room can comprehend. I think...it's why she's stronger than she should be."

Celeste looked at Ophelia then, her expression lined with guilt and inevitability. "If she's revived the amulet, then she'll try to do the same with the Bell of Time."

Ophelia's blood turned to ice. "Because that was always the plan?" she asked.

Celeste gave a near-imperceptible nod. "She's not trying to control the world. She's trying to change it. To rewrite it." Her voice thinned. "To undo the past."

There was no need to say which past. They all knew.

Celeste's eyes went distant, then widened, focus sharpening like a blade. "That's where she'll go. That's where it began."

Mo whispered the answer on all their minds. "Marisante," he said.

Sofija stepped forward, robes whispering against the floor. "Then we act before she does. We retrieve what's left of the Bell of Time, in its dormant state."

Zeon's voice was low and grim. "If she raises the Bell, she won't just shift the past. She'll break the laws that hold our world together."

Ophelia looked at her mother. "Then we stop her."

Celeste's eyes fluttered closed, her hand tightening on the cane. "We'll have to."

And somewhere, beyond stone and sea, the past stirred, restless and unfinished. Because Eris wasn't just reaching for it. She meant to rewrite it.

And this time, the world might not survive the retelling.

CHAPTER

NINETEEN

The library felt colder than usual. Morning light slanted through the tall windows, falling across maps and scrolls spread across the long table. Protective wards hummed faintly, their low thrum usually comforting. Today, it only sharpened the tension coiling in the corners of the room.

Elijah stood near the head of the table, fingers steepled beneath his chin. He didn't pace. He didn't fidget. He simply watched them: Brisa with her arms crossed so tightly her knuckles had gone white, Mo adjusting the edges of the threading chart, Luka staring blankly at nothing. And Ophelia, her jaw clenched so hard it trembled.

Elijah had studied psychology for Ophelia. In the early days, it had been about helping her—understanding her "episodes" and the nightmares, the weight she carried even as a child. He'd read books on trauma, devoured theories on grief and attachment, hoping it might give him a roadmap to reach her when words failed. But now, all that learning—psychology, conflict theory, studies on emotional fracture and moral disintegration—wasn't just helping Ophelia. It was helping him predict her sister.

He'd spent the last few nights rebuilding Eris's psychological profile from memory, from Celeste's accounts, from the pattern of blood and ruin she'd left behind. And disturbingly, it was beginning to make sense. The spiral, the choices, the almost surgical precision of her cruelty. There was a structure to it. All those years spent trying to understand a broken mind weren't being wasted on the wrong sister. For once, all that study was paying off when it came to a Wildes witch.

"She's not ready," Ophelia said for the third time, her voice tight. "She shouldn't go." They'd been circling the same argument for the past hour about whether Celeste was strong enough to make the journey to the Bell of Time, or if bringing her was just another risk they couldn't afford.

Elijah's voice was quiet, calm and measured, the way it always became when he was about to say something that would hurt. "She's the only one who might reach her," he said.

"No one can reach her," Ophelia shot back. "You saw what she did. You saw what she made Alex do."

He nodded slowly. "I did. But that's exactly why this matters." He stepped forward, hands unfolding, voice slipping into the cadence that once soothed her as a child. "This isn't about forgiveness. It's about familiarity. Psychological imprinting runs deep. If there's any humanity left in Eris—any thread of memory, any tether to who she used to be—it's likely tied to Celeste. You said yourself she looked at her differently."

Ophelia's throat tightened. "She also tried to kill her," she said.

Elijah nodded. "She could have—many times over. But she didn't. That matters."

He held Ophelia's gaze, his voice even but weighted with meaning. "If Eris were acting purely on instinct or bloodlust,

Celeste would be dead. But she's not. Somewhere in all that rage and power, something's holding her back. That hesitation is not just restraint. It's memory. Attachment. Maybe even longing for her mother and familial bonds. And if that thread still exists, Celeste might be the only one who can pull on it," he said.

Celeste sat in a worn chair near the window. She looked smaller than usual, shoulders hunched, hands still in her lap. But when she lifted her gaze, something clear and sharp glinted behind her tired eyes. "I want to go," she said softly.

Ophelia turned to her. "You nearly died the last time," she said sharply.

Celeste's smile was faint but steady, the kind worn by someone who'd survived too many things to flinch anymore. "I nearly died a dozen times before breakfast, sweetheart."

"That's not funny," Ophelia snapped, her voice fraying.

"It wasn't meant to be." Celeste shifted forward in her chair and rose slowly, a wince tugging at her features as she stood. "But it's also not untrue."

She met Ophelia's eyes then, something old and unmovable in her expression. "I've been broken and burned and dragged back from the edge more times than I care to count. And maybe I'm slower now, maybe I don't burn as bright, but I'm not as fragile as I look." She paused. "Especially not where she's concerned."

Her voice dropped, quiet and grave. "She was my daughter before she was your nightmare. And if there's even a flicker of her left, I have to try."

Mo looked up from the map, eyes full of quiet warning. "We'll need your strength if things go south," he said.

"Then I'll give it," Celeste said without hesitation. "If I can help, even a little, I will."

Ophelia's shoulders slumped. Her mother's voice was

calm, resolute. And when Celeste decided something, there was no moving her, not by argument, fear, or magic. But that didn't stop the worry curling in Ophelia's gut like smoke.

Gabriel stepped beside her, brushing her fingers lightly. "We'll protect her. All of us."

Ophelia didn't answer. She just nodded once, sharp and bitter. She couldn't stop this. She could only bear witness to it.

Celeste stepped into the center of the room, already drawing a threading circle with a firm hand. Her magic bled into the chalk as she traced it, slow and deliberate, the symbols ancient beyond memory. Ophelia watched her mother's fingers tremble only slightly as she finished the last sigil and pressed her palm to the stone.

"Threading this far isn't just about power," Mo murmured, standing just outside the circle. "It requires harmony."

Celeste offered a hand to Ophelia first, always her first. "Together," she said quietly.

Ophelia hesitated for a breath. Then she took it. Brisa slid into place beside her, fingers warm and grounding. Wordlessly, Gabriel and Luka each offered a palm, avoiding each other's gaze.

The circle closed.

And the magic began.

It moved like breath before a scream: sharp, ancient, inescapable. Not just pulling them through space, but memory. Regret. Bloodlines too tangled to sever. The thread twisted around Ophelia's ribs and heart like frost-laced wire, cold and numbing. By now, she'd threaded more times than she could count. But this was different. This time, it hurt.

The strain of it shivered through Celeste's limbs. Ophelia felt it in their link: her mother's magic unraveling and reforming the world around them, stretching farther than she should. And for a heartbeat, Ophelia almost pulled back. Almost broke the thread.

But Celeste held steady. Even when her breath faltered. Even when the edges of her form blurred in the magic's surge.

The air snapped.

And they were gone.

THE THREADING spell released them at the jungle's edge, where time seemed to pause. Crumbling stone steps led into a moss-covered plaza, swallowed by creeping vines and the slow hunger of the earth. The air hit them like a wall: wet, heavy, choked with heat and something fouler, something spoiled. It wasn't just decay. It was despair, soaked deep into the bones of the place.

They'd come here first out of necessity, not strategy. Isla del Aquelarre, for all its distance from Trieste, was still easier to reach than Marisante. Threading to an underwater city, especially one submerged beneath layers of magical pressure, would have demanded more power than even Celeste could afford to risk. And they couldn't afford to arrive in Marisante exhausted. So they came here, to the island nexus that had once been sacred.

The sun hung high and pitiless overhead, too bright against the stillness below. But no shadows moved. No wind stirred the leaves. Even the jungle, usually alive with birdsong and insects, held its breath.

Ophelia took a careful step forward, boots crunching against scattered gravel. The ruined heart of Aquelarre stretched before them, not just abandoned but desecrated. What had once been a thriving magical sanctuary—a convergence of cultures, spells, and sacred rites—was now a shell, hollow and haunted. Vines strangled archways, cascading over rooftops like spilled entrails. Shattered stained glass winked like teeth from a broken jaw.

Brisa came up beside her, voice hushed but sharp. "This doesn't feel like ruin," she said. "It feels like aftermath."

They moved deeper, slow and wary. Even their steps seemed too loud. Pants brushed tall weeds. Boots caught on fractured mosaics. The deeper they went, the more the silence pressed in, thick with the memory of screams.

Signs of slaughter were everywhere. Charred scorch marks spiraled up marble columns like vines of fire. Burned-out sigils clung to doorways, twisted beyond recognition. The very air shimmered with unstable remnants of power—reds and purples and tar-black shadows, flickering faintly like dying stars. The ground underfoot was slick in places, but not with rain. And then they saw the bodies.

Too many.

Some slumped over crumbling stairs, others frozen mid-motion, caught in death like mannequins posed by horror. Some curled in the fetal position near fountains that had long since run dry. Their eyes were wide. Their mouths were still open, as if the last thing they'd seen had hollowed them from the inside.

But it wasn't the death alone that made Ophelia falter. It was what surrounded it.

Sigils were etched into stone and flesh alike. They were bloody, burned, and wrong, pulsing faintly even now. Corrupted symbols of binding and sacrifice.

"She used them," Mo murmured. His voice was hollow, reverent in the face of what had happened. "As anchors. Blood beacons. To twist the blood magic of this place to her will."

Gabriel crouched beside three figures curled together at the base of a fractured arch, their hands still clasped in a circle.

"They didn't even have time to cast a shield," he said. "They died trying to protect each other."

The path beneath them was blackened with magical fire. A handprint, scorched deep into the center, still glowed faintly. Brisa stepped over a fallen lintel and froze beside a smaller figure, no more than a child. Her hand went to her blade, but she didn't draw. "Gods," she whispered. "There are no survivors."

Ophelia's voice was tight. "She's already been here," she said.

"No," Celeste said behind them, voice brittle. "She's done here." She stepped carefully between the fallen, her cane tapping gently against the earth. The sound echoed like a metronome in a morgue. She paused beneath a warped temple gate, staring up at the sigil burned into the lintel. Ophelia didn't recognize the symbol, but she didn't have to. Every line in it screamed wrongness.

"She used the Lunula Amulet to drain them," Celeste said. "To feed the blood magic."

Luka's voice rasped behind them. "Why here? Why Aquelarre?" he asked.

"Because it was a nexus," Mo answered. "The island sat on a convergence of ley lines—north, south, sea, spirit. It was a bridge between supernaturals. She didn't need to perform a ritual to access its magic. She just needed bodies and their blood."

Gabriel rose, his jaw tight. "She's not hiding any longer," he said.

Ophelia's magic flinched beneath her skin. It didn't want to be here. It recoiled from the corruption around them like a living thing. Her eyes caught on a shattered altar at the center of a blackened plaza, its surface cracked down the middle. "This isn't destruction," she said quietly. "It's preparation."

Celeste nodded grimly. "Which means we're already behind."

A chill raced down Ophelia's back, despite the oppressive heat. She turned slowly in place, taking in the full devastation. The stillness. The absence. The silence so loud it hurt. And still, in the far-off shimmer of the sea, the waves curled gently against the shore. A mocking, peaceful backdrop to the carnage left behind.

Ophelia swallowed hard. "We need to go," she said.

They returned to the broken circle near the edge of the ruins. Their fingers brushed, forming a thread. As the magic pulled tight around them once more, Ophelia breathed a single hope into the air: *Please don't let us be too late.*

TWENTY

The threading spell dropped them into darkness. This wasn't the soft, shimmering place they'd encountered the first time they entered the underwater city of Marisante. This darkness was dense, clinging to the air like mold. The ground beneath their boots wasn't the smooth stone of memory. It was fractured, uneven, webbed with long cracks that pulsed faintly with residual magic. But the pulses weren't random. They beat in a slow, steady rhythm. Too steady.

Ophelia inhaled and nearly gagged. The air, once warm and fresh, now tasted metallic like blood. The hum of magic that had once welcomed them here was gone, replaced by a strained silence that seemed to press against her eardrums, a silence thick with expectation.

"It's changed," she whispered.

"No," Celeste murmured beside her, voice barely audible. "It's dying."

The ruins of Marisante rose ahead, jagged and broken. Once-graceful archways now slumped into piles of rubble.

Columns that had shimmered with enchanted carvings flickered sporadically, their runes stuttering like a candle about to extinguish. But some runes didn't flicker; they pulsed uniformly. A few glowed red instead of blue.

And still, a broken charm lay near Ophelia's foot, cracked in half but still glowing faintly, as if whispering a warning no one could hear.

Brisa stepped cautiously over a loose tile, her hand extended for balance. "This place looks like it's been gutted," she said.

Gabriel scanned the darkness ahead, blade already in hand. "Because it has," he said.

Mo lifted a glowing orb and held it aloft. The light cast long shadows against the warped walls. The stone here hadn't just crumbled; it had been melted and reshaped into strange, unnatural curves. Like scar tissue. Like something had tried to heal the city and failed.

Ophelia walked slowly, fingertips brushing the wall beside her. The carved patterns sparked and then shuddered away. Faint, jittery lines of light recoiled as if remembering her and flinching from it.

"It wasn't like this before," she murmured.

"She took something," Mo said. "Something that was anchoring the magic here. Maybe more than one thing."

A dull clatter echoed in the distance, stone shifting against stone. Or something else moving. No one spoke. They just pushed deeper into the ruins, their footsteps muffled by grit and ash.

Somewhere to their left, a rune flared. Then vanished. Ophelia's magic stirred beneath her skin, unsteady and alert. Her instincts prickled.

And then she glanced back.

Celeste was lagging. At first, Ophelia thought it was

caution, perhaps fatigue. But something in her mother's posture was off. She was leaning hard on her cane, her other hand braced against the wall. Her face had gone even paler than before, her mouth set in a tight, bloodless line.

"Mom—" Ophelia started, stepping toward her.

"I'm fine," Celeste said, her voice low but brittle, cracking with effort. "Just...keep moving. We're almost there." She tried to smile, but it faltered.

Ophelia fell in step beside her anyway. Celeste didn't argue. Not now. But she didn't like the way the air weighed down here. Didn't like the silence. Or the way some of the sigils flared and flickered like dying stars...while others watched. Like eyes.

They entered the long corridor that led to the central chamber. The air grew colder with each step, though no wind stirred. Only the echo of their footfalls followed them—slow, steady, dread-thick. The walls closed in tighter the deeper they went, and even Mo's orb of light seemed to dim, its glow absorbed by the broken magic creeping in from all sides.

Ophelia's chest constricted. Her heartbeat thudded in her ears, matching the rhythm of some remembered horror. She could feel it now, the faint, sickly imprint of the place where they'd once destroyed the Kala Ghanta. It called to her like nerves left too close to the surface.

The memory burned: almost losing Gabriel. Losing Leander when she'd just found him. Gabriel walked near her, and she weaved her fingers through his, wanting to feel him. He glanced at her, almost surprised, but he squeezed her fingers back.

They followed a narrow passage, faint luminescent veins of magic illuminating their path in eerie blues and greens. They emerged into a smaller chamber, with a floor of smooth, polished obsidian that reflected the glowing sigils on the walls.

A shallow pool of water dominated the center of the room, its surface rippling with unseen movement.

The great arch leading to the central chamber yawned before them like a mouth forced open. A thick crack split the ceiling overhead, and the doorless frame radiated a shimmer of displaced power. Inside, the chamber was half-collapsed. The ceiling bowed inward as if it had tried—and failed—to resist whatever power had been unleashed.

Chunks of the dome lay scattered across the floor, blackened as if scorched from within. Dust floated in the air, catching Mo's light in soft spirals. Nothing moved. No wind. No energy. Not even ghosts.

Ophelia stepped through first, her boot brushing a fine scatter of ash. Her eyes found the shallow pool at once. It was empty.

Brisa came to stand beside her. "That's not good," she said, her voice flat but trembling at the edges.

Mo didn't respond right away. When he did, his voice was distant. "We're too late."

Their destruction of the Bell. Leander's sacrifice. It was all... gone.

Celeste arrived last, leaning heavily on her cane, her breathing shallow and uneven. Her gaze found the empty pedestal and locked there, unmoving. For a moment, her expression was frozen in place, no sorrow or rage. Just the terrible stillness of understanding.

Then she exhaled. "She has everything she needs," she said.

Ophelia's throat burned. There should have been screaming. Shouting. Something. But instead, there was only silence. The kind that settled like a grave.

No enemy waited in ambush. No spell burst to strike them down. And somehow, that was worse. This kind of stillness was not peace. It was precision. The aftermath of a knife already drawn across the throat.

Then came the ripple.

Subtle. Soft. Like a sigh under glass.

Ophelia stiffened. Her magic twitched, sensing something she couldn't yet name. She turned slowly, eyes narrowing. The tension in the air wasn't lifting. It was coiling tighter. Compressing. The energy didn't just feel old or broken. It felt wrong. Too slick. Too regular. As if something artificial was mimicking the cadence of Marisante's natural rhythms.

Her gaze caught on a rune embedded in the wall. It was cracked, but faintly glowing, not fading like the rest. It was pulsing.

And then another. This one scratched into the base of a support column. It should have been inert. Instead, it throbbed faintly. Like a heartbeat counting down.

Ophelia turned in a slow circle. "Something's wrong," she said. "We need to get out. Now."

Her stomach twisted. Her power recoiled.

And somewhere beneath her boots, the trap began to breathe.

Brisa took a step toward her, but the air shifted, *tilted*, like the entire chamber exhaled all at once.

Gabriel's voice was steady, grim. "We've been drawn here. She wanted us to come," he said.

Luka moved to the chamber's edge, eyes sweeping the walls. "There are fresh marks," he said tightly, sword already half-drawn. "This wasn't part of the original structure."

Near the pool of water, Celeste swayed. Her skin had gone ghostly pale again, lips tinged with blue. "This magic..." she murmured. "It doesn't belong to the city. It belongs to her."

A pulse trembled through the floor. It was subtle at first, like a breath held too long. But it vibrated through their boots, climbed their bones. Ophelia staggered, catching herself on a column. Her magic flared instinctively, but the air was slick and uncooperative.

Mo swore under his breath. "She's warped the city's magic. Bent it to mimic Marisante's signature. No wonder we didn't feel it until now," he said.

Brisa stepped back from the wall, her breath catching. "We're in a snare," she said.

Gabriel moved in front of Ophelia, eyes scanning the shadows like they were alive.

"She let us come," Ophelia whispered. The realization iced down her spine. "She wanted Celeste here. Me here."

Blood-red light pulsed through the runes carved on the walls. That light began to spread. It threaded into the floor cracks, spidering outward and racing toward the walls. It was a trap, waking.

Luka's voice dropped to a low growl. "Everyone, get ready," he said.

Celeste lifted her head as if drawn toward something none of them could see. "She's close," she said, voice hollow and far away.

Another flare. Stronger. The chamber groaned around them.

Ophelia's magic surged, wild and unfiltered. "We need to move. Now."

But it was already too late.

The first scream didn't come from any of them. It came from the walls.

CHAPTER

TWENTY-ONE

The chamber *splintered* open with a sound like bones breaking under centuries of pressure.

Eris stepped from the darkness like a flame igniting in still air. She was radiant, unsteady, and untouchable. Her hair was wild, curls snapping like whips in the electric energy around her. Her black pupils were pinpricks swallowed by bloodred power. Magic lashed from her body in furious arcs: wild, unfocused, but deadly. It tore through the air like lightning splitting dry wood.

And in her hand, the Lunula Amulet throbbed, whole but twisted. It throbbed with deep-crimson veins, as if it had a heart of its own. Every pulse sent ripples through the air, cracking the already unstable foundations of Marisante.

"*Oh, gods,*" Mo breathed, eyes locked on the artifact. "It's not just restored. It's evolved."

Behind her, someone small and trembling staggered into the chamber. Silver hair hung limp, eyes vacant and glowing faintly. Alex. Limbs moved with rigid grace, as though pulled by unseen strings. Every step was wrong. Too smooth. Too *still.*

Brisa lurched forward, voice breaking. *"Alex!"* she screamed. "It's me!"

No answer.

Alex blinked, but there was no recognition in her gaze, only the flicker of the amulet's magic mirrored in her irises.

"Stop, stop, stop," Brisa whispered, backing away, her breath coming in gasps. "She's not in there. She's not—"

"Your fault," Eris hissed, her voice piercing the stillness. "All of you. You watched. You let them try to tame me." Her head snapped toward Celeste. *"You.* You called me daughter but kept me caged like a beast."

Celeste stood straighter, but the cane quivered in her grip. "You were loved," she said gently.

Eris's laughter tore through the chamber. *"Loved?* You *abandoned* me. Hid my truth. Buried me in silence," she said.

She lifted the Lunula Amulet, her fingers twitching.

For a beat—just one—she didn't move.

The magic flared in her palm, but her gaze flickered, unfocused. Something cracked beneath the fury. Her breath hitched, eyes glassy, as if some small part of her remembered what it felt like to be held, to be known.

And then she blinked it away.

Her jaw tightened. She hissed, *"Too late."*

The amulet flared. The floor fractured beneath her feet. And from it, *they came.* Not just skeletons. Not just ghosts. These were new.

Twisted horrors cobbled from broken bloodlines, beings with insect wings and glowing eyes, their limbs wrong, distorted, echoing things that were once supernatural but no longer belonged to any known species. Shifting shadows crawled across the walls, splitting into fanged mouths and reaching hands. The dead and the unnatural surged as one.

Brisa stumbled back toward Ophelia. "What *are* those things?" she asked.

"Nightmares," Gabriel muttered, his blade sliding free with a hiss of steel. "Made real."

Ophelia raised her hands, channeling every ounce of magic she had left.

A shield bloomed around them: red and gold, flickering and fragile, but enough to buy time. Enough to *think*.

Alex moved first. Faster than anyone should've been able to. One second she was behind Eris, the next she was a blur.

She *slammed* into the barrier. The shield cracked.

Ophelia cried out, knees buckling, the force of the blow hitting her like a freight train of power and grief.

Alex's face was empty. Her hands were wreathed in cold flame. Her magic—normally healing, warm, *gentle*—now rattled with something corrosive and rotting.

"Alex, *please*," Ophelia gasped. "Fight it."

Alex tilted her head. A puppet on strings. A woman made weapon. She attacked again. And again. And again. And again.

Finally, the shield shattered like glass. Chaos descended.

Gabriel was already moving, intercepting one of the winged horrors with a clean, brutal strike. Mo summoned a warding circle with his earth power, but it fizzled against the corruption in the air. Brisa cried Alex's name again—this time not in hope, but in fury—as she conjured a gust of air to deflect a lunging shadow-thing with teeth where its eyes should've been.

Celeste stood frozen at the center of it all, eyes locked on Eris. "I should've told you," she said softly, voice shaking with things too late to say.

Eris bared her teeth. "You're right. And now you'll drown in what you let grow," she said.

Alex moved again, this time toward Ophelia. And Ophelia

didn't have time to think. She raised her arms, magic instinctive and erratic. Fire bloomed in her palms, but it was *sluggish*, reacting to her emotions instead of her command. She wouldn't hurt Alex, but she couldn't let her near either.

"*Stop!*" she cried, not at Alex, but into the ground, erupting in a burst that split the chamber floor and knocked them both off balance.

Ophelia hit the ground hard, the wind knocked from her lungs, her vision fracturing.

Alex stood again, unharmed.

And behind her, Eris smiled, triumphant.

Celeste stepped forward, unsteady but resolute. Her cane slipped from her grasp and struck the floor with a hollow clatter. The sound louder than it should have been, as if the chamber itself held its breath.

She didn't spare a glance for the horrors rising behind Eris. She didn't look at the clawing shadows, the twisted constructs, or the cold silence of her allies drawing weapons. Her gaze never wavered. It was fixed solely on Eris, not as an enemy, but as the child she once swaddled.

"You never wanted to destroy the world," Celeste said, her voice a thread of silk in the darkness. "You just wanted to be loved, completely and without fear. Without condition. And I failed you in that. I take responsibility," she said.

Eris's face contorted, as if the words struck a nerve too raw to bear. "Don't you dare," she said.

"I should've seen it sooner," Celeste whispered, tears gleaming but unshed. "I thought if I hid the truth, if I protected you from yourself, I could save you. But all I did was bury the parts of you that needed healing," she said.

"*Shut up!*" Eris yelled, her magic lashing out like a whip of fire, carving a violent groove in the stone. But there was something behind it, perhaps panic or wounded fury. It was the kind that came not from hatred, but heartbreak.

Ophelia stumbled forward, clutching Gabriel's arm for support. "*Mom, don't—*" she shouted.

Celeste raised a hand, not in defiance or surrender, but in remembrance. Her other hand moved through the air with aching grace, weaving a spell so old it hadn't been spoken in centuries. It was the kind of magic taught from mother to daughter, handed down like lullabies. Golden white light, tinged with blue, coiled around her fingers and stretched toward the thing that had stolen her child.

"I didn't come here to survive," Celeste murmured, as tears welled but didn't fall. "I came to set things right. I came to make peace with the truth. To face what I should have done long ago."

"Celeste—" Mo gasped, stepping forward.

But Brisa grabbed his arm, tears spilling freely now. "Let her," she said.

The magic thickened. The spell took form, weaving around Celeste's frail frame, then spiraling outward toward Eris.

No, not *Eris.* Toward the amulet.

Eris tried to pull away, her hands lifting in defense. But it was too late. The spell was already coiled around the Lunula Amulet.

"*Let it go,*" Celeste said, her voice breaking. "Let me go."

And the amulet cracked.

It didn't explode with fire. It folded *inward*, collapsing on itself with a sound like a thousand whispers suddenly silenced. The light vanished. The power unraveled. Blood magic shrieked as it was *cut* from its source.

Celeste dropped to her knees, the last threads of her magic dissolving with a shudder that echoed through the chamber like a whispered goodbye. Her body trembled, spine bowed, not just from exhaustion but from the cost of what she'd given. Magic bled from her like smoke dissipating in the wind, leaving behind only a flicker of light in the hollow where her strength had been.

Across the room, Alex let out a strangled gasp. It was the sound of freedom wrenched from a prison that had become part of her bones. Her limbs buckled as though gravity had remembered her all at once. She collapsed silently, a marionette with its strings cut. Her eyes fluttered, dull and wet with something that might have been tears if she were fully there.

Brisa broke. A cry tore from her chest, raw and shattering. She dropped beside Alex, cradling her and whispering her name over and over like a spell she wasn't sure would still work.

And Eris *screamed*.

The noise wasn't human. It wasn't *anything* recognizable. It was the cry of something broken and betrayed. Her hands clawed at the air, her body convulsing as the power she'd hoarded tore away from her. She blinked down at the crumbling dust of the Lunula Amulet. And then her eyes snapped to Celeste.

"You," she hissed, a single word steeped in venom.

Ophelia moved, her legs carrying her forward as she ran. But she was too slow.

Eris surged forward with a movement so fast it barely registered as motion, just a blur of red and shadow. Her hand wasn't a hand anymore. It was a blade of living shadow, twisted into something lethal.

It plunged through Celeste's chest before anyone could stop her.

Time froze. The silence was too thick. Too final.

Celeste's breath hitched once. Just once. Her eyes found

Ophelia's across the chaos. No pain in them. Just peace. A mother's love, unwavering, unafraid.

Then she fell.

The sound of her body hitting the stone cracked something in Ophelia she didn't know how to name.

Eris yanked her clawed hand back. Blood followed, arcing through the air like spilled ink, painting the floor with finality.

Then the screams came.

Gabriel was already running. Mo shouted, voice ragged with a fury that made the walls quake. Brisa's sobs turned to wails. But Eris didn't move. She only stood there, shaking, smiling. Her breath came in ragged gasps, wild and uneven.

Eris looked down at Celeste's body like it had been an offering. A sacrifice laid at her feet. The amulet was gone, but she'd taken something else. Something far worse. And then she exhaled. It wasn't grief. It wasn't even rage. It was release.

The scream that followed shattered what was left of the chamber's stillness. Eris's body convulsed, and the magic around her snapped free. It lashed out in all directions, wild and unchecked, cracking the very air. And then she began to *shift*.

It started with her spine. A sickening crack echoed as it lengthened, curved unnaturally. Her arms distorted, bones fracturing, stretching past the limits of any humanoid frame. Black veins rippled beneath her skin like ink poured through glass. One eye went stark white, the other burned with a golden hue too bright and unnatural.

Her skin tore. Her face twisted, muzzle elongating, mouth splitting around sharpened teeth. She was no longer witch nor woman. She was hunger and fury and magic twisted into flesh. A creature born from grief. Forged in vengeance. Stitched together with bone and blood and the worst kind of power.

"She's not a person anymore," Brisa whispered, holding Alex like a shield against the sight.

"She never has been," Mo said hoarsely, his hands already glowing with magic.

Gabriel grabbed Ophelia's arm, yanking her back behind him. "Move," he said.

But she didn't. Couldn't.

Her eyes were locked on Eris.

"This is what she's been building to," Ophelia said softly, voice numb. "This is what she wanted to become."

And Eris—monstrous, magnificent, and full of ruin—looked back and smiled. Ophelia stared, the realization slamming into her like lightning: *Central Park. The black jaguar in the woods. The way it had fought. Protected her.* Eris had been watching her then. Tracking her.

Luka didn't hesitate. Fur erupted from his skin. Bones snapped and realigned like branches under pressure. His body twisted and reformed in the space of a heartbeat, rippling into the black jaguar form Ophelia had seen before: massive, sleek, and feral.

But he didn't stop there.

His form expanded, distorted, evolved. He rose onto hind legs that were no longer feline. Horns curved back from his skull like obsidian crowns. His claws elongated, gleaming like molten glass, edges glowing faintly silver. The air around him buzzed. What stood before them wasn't just Luka.

It was something older. Something sacred. Something forgotten by name, but remembered by the bones of the earth.

Eris shrieked and lunged. Luka met her mid-air.

The impact detonated through the chamber. Stone split beneath them. Fangs clashed. Claws sparked like lightning strikes. The walls quaked with each blow. Fire licked across the ceiling. Smoke unfurled from the corners. Magic blistered the air.

They were primal. Unleashed. Devastation given form.

Eris's magic was chaos incarnate. Her limbs shifted with every strike, one moment wings, the next gnarled claws, the next tendrils of living fog that coiled around Luka's throat.

But Luka fought like a creature born from the wild places the world had forgotten. He struck low, teeth flashing, ripping toward her underbelly. Deep gashes bloomed along his flank, but he didn't falter.

He couldn't.

Because if he stopped, they'd all die.

Eris roared and conjured a whip of bone from her spine. It cracked across Luka's ribs, sending him skidding into a fractured pillar. Stone exploded. Dust filled the air.

He rose, shoulders heaving, ember eyes burning through the haze. And he growled.

It wasn't a sound of pain, but one of defiance. As if to say: *You want to tear this world apart? You'll have to go through me.*

Eris bared her teeth. Her form flickered, unstable, magic bleeding from her like smoke from an open wound.

Luka didn't wait. He lunged again, faster than breath.

His claw struck her throat. Deep. Final. Eris roared. Not with fury. With pain.

Her monstrous form convulsed. Wings crumbled into ash mid-air. Her limbs buckled, stuttering as the shadows peeled away. Her body collapsed inward, the magic holding her together splintering under Luka's blow.

She staggered back, half-shifted, skin twitching with unreleased energy. Her inhuman eyes locked on Luka with hatred so potent the air itself soured.

"You think this is over?" she rasped. Her voice sounded like cracked glass and old magic. Blood dripped from her chin. "I'll return with time itself as my weapon. You'll beg to undo what's already been done." Then the ground howled. A pulse of wind exploded from her chest. Magic tore free, blistering hot, white-gold and crimson, too bright to look at. The floor groaned beneath them.

And then she vanished, threaded away in a rupture of sound and light. Gone. The moment collapsed in on itself. And then silence.

Luka stood over her where she'd disappeared. He was panting, bleeding, shaking. But he was alive. Barely.

"Celeste!" Ophelia cried, spinning toward her mother's slumped form.

Celeste lay crumpled where Eris had struck her, blood pooling beneath her, twisted at unnatural angles. Her cane lay in pieces several feet away.

"No," Ophelia whispered. "No, no, no." She dropped to her knees, crawling the last few feet, her breath ragged. Her hands shook as she reached for her mother, still warm but already distant. She was gone in the way magic disappears when its source is extinguished.

Alex collapsed beside her, gasping. Her fingers glowed faintly with healing magic, desperate and unformed, but the spell fizzled the moment it touched Celeste's skin. "I can't—" she choked. "There's nothing left to hold on to."

Ophelia brushed matted hair back from Celeste's brow with trembling fingers. Her throat was a vise. No spell came to her lips. No incantation. Just grief, raw and cracking.

"You didn't have to do this," she whispered, not expecting an answer. "You didn't have to give yourself for us. Not again."

The body before her gave no reply. But Ophelia imagined the echo of her mother's strength: fierce, stubborn, resolute to the end. It lived in the silence. It lived in the sacrifice.

She bent her head low, her forehead nearly touching

Celeste's. "I forgive you," she said into the stillness, the words broken and whole all at once. "For everything."

No breath stirred. No final word came.

The chamber dimmed around them. The glowing carvings on the walls faded, the last of Marisante's magic sinking into shadow. The silence that followed was total.

Celeste was gone. The air thickened, grief pressing in like fog.

Brisa knelt beside Alex, who was barely conscious, her face pale and streaked with tears. Mo stood watch near Luka, who was half-shifted and barely upright. Gabriel was beside Ophelia now, silent, blood streaked across his jaw, his hand steady when nothing else was.

He didn't speak. He just reached for her. She stared at his hand for a long moment. Then she took it. Her shoulders shook, not from sorrow this time, but from something colder. Harder. Resolve. There would be time to mourn later. Now, there was a world to save.

CHAPTER

TWENTY-TWO

The world blinked away in a shimmer of light and sound, leaving only the cold.

Ophelia landed hard on the mountainside, knees buckling against the loose gravel beneath her boots. She caught herself with one hand, her fingers scraping rock. The air here bit deeper than she remembered, sharper and more unforgiving, as if the mountain resented her return. Wind cut across the ridge in short, vicious bursts that tugged at her coat and tangled her hair across her face. She didn't bother fixing it.

Every muscle in her body ached, not just from the threading, although that had grown more brutal. Since Marisante, the magic tore at her like glass dragged across skin. But she welcomed the pain. It made sense. Unlike the hollow ache in her chest, where Celeste used to be.

She stood slowly, a cloud of fog forming in front of her. This was the ridge she'd once flown from. When her magic had surged beyond her control, when the threads had pulled her straight into the sky. Back then, she'd felt like the storm itself: wild, untethered, and burning with purpose. She missed that feeling. That belief that power and rightness could exist in the same space. Somehow, those were brighter days, before blood and betrayal and the burden of leading.

That was before everything cracked open.

Now the world felt like an echo of itself, and she was the only one who could hear it breaking.

It took longer than she expected to find the cave. Thick ivy veiled the entrance in tangled curtains, as if trying to shield what remained inside from the world. She pushed through it with trembling hands, ducked beneath the low stone arch, and stepped into the shadows.

The air inside was damp and cool, weighted with memory. Stalactites hung like fangs from the ceiling. The limestone walls glowed faintly, as if lit from within by a patient, golden light. At the back of the chamber, the spring bubbled softly against the stone.

She didn't rush or speak. Instead, she crossed the cavern in silence, her boots reverberating faintly off the walls. When she reached the pool, she crouched and withdrew the moonstone from her pocket. It pulsed against her palm. Familiar. Waiting.

Ophelia stared down into the water. Her reflection looked older. Sharper around the edges. The kind of face that had already buried too much.

She exhaled slowly, the moment rooting itself in her bones.

Then she whispered, "I call upon the bloodline that runs through me. I call upon Galla Placidia."

And the cave held its breath.

Silence.

Then the wind stilled. The water stopped moving.

And the cave breathed.

A glimmer danced across the spring's surface, casting ripples of gold along the limestone walls. The light stretched, coalesced, and from it stepped a woman swathed in flowing white, less ghost than memory, yet more solid than ever before. Her robes sparkled like moonlight on water, and her feet didn't quite touch the ground. Those yellow-green eyes twinkled with something between exasperation and mischief.

"You again?" Galla Placidia said with a sigh, brushing imaginary dust from her sleeve. "Must you always disturb my peace?"

Ophelia let out a sound that was half a laugh, half a sob.

"And you look like you haven't slept in a century," Galla observed, drifting closer. Her tone softened. "What's happened?" she asked.

Ophelia's throat tightened. "Everything," she said, the word cracking open something that hadn't stopped bleeding.

Galla tilted her head. "Then we'd better start at the beginning, nipotina." Galla circled the cave slowly, her gaze tracing the glowing lines of ancient mineral and time-worn stone. "This place is stubborn," she said. "Still clinging to its secrets, even after all these years." Her voice dropped as she turned back to Ophelia. "Much like you."

Ophelia didn't argue. She was too tired for it.

Galla stopped a few paces away, folding her hands in front of her. "You come to me heavy with guilt. Is that what you wanted, child? Absolution?"

"No," Ophelia said quietly. "Just...answers."

"Good. Because absolution is for the dead. You, fortunately, are very much alive," she said.

Ophelia dropped her gaze, tracing a crack in the limestone floor with the toe of her boot. "I let her die. Celeste. She saved us, and I couldn't do anything to stop it. And now Alex is barely holding on. Gabriel's hurt. Luka's..." She trailed off, shaking her head. "I can't tell if I'm losing him or if I never really had him," she said.

"Ah," Galla said softly, walking toward her. "So we've arrived at the heart of it."

Ophelia looked up.

"You fear you've already failed," Galla said. "Failed your mother. Your family. Your twin flame. Your friends. Yourself."

Ophelia swallowed hard but nodded. Galla knelt beside her, her form strangely solid as she reached out and brushed a strand of hair from Ophelia's face. The gesture was gentle, almost painfully so.

"Power does not wait for certainty," she said. "Neither does destiny."

The words sank deep, unsettling something inside her. "What if I'm not enough?" Ophelia whispered. "What if I was never meant to win this?"

"Then you wouldn't still be standing," Galla said.

They stayed silent for a beat. Then Galla stood, her voice changing, layered now with something older. Something sacred.

"You came for guidance. So listen, and listen well. The Kala Ghanta is not gone. It is broken, but not dead."

Ophelia's head snapped up, her worst fears confirmed.

"It remembers," Galla said. "But it will not sing for just anyone."

"What does that mean?" Ophelia asked, heart pounding.

"It means you are not the only one who hears its call. But you might be the only one who can answer it." Galla began to pace again, her form flickering slightly as she moved. "The Bell was created by sacrifice. By love and betrayal. By blood willingly given and taken. To wake it, something more than power is needed."

Ophelia stood slowly, fists clenched at her sides. "Tell me what to do," she said.

"You already know." Galla's eyes glittered. "But you won't be able to do it alone. Not this time."

"The fae?" Ophelia guessed. "You think they can awaken it?"

Galla only nodded.

Ophelia's brow furrowed. "They've already refused us. They don't interfere with supernatural politics," she said.

"They don't interfere," Galla said, "until they do. Until something threatens even their illusions of neutrality. And believe me, child, Eris threatens everything," she said.

Ophelia exhaled, caught on the edge of dread.

"Go to them," Galla said. "Ask again. But not as a beggar. As a force."

Their eyes met. The weight of history passed between them. "You are your mother's fire. Your father's blood. My bones. And your own soul. You are not the pawn you once feared you were. You are the player now," she said.

Ophelia stared at her. "And if they still say no?"

"Then you'll do what the Wildes witches have always done," Galla said with a faint smirk. "You'll make your own rules."

Galla Placidia's expression shifted—not softer, but older. She seemed to radiate something ancient, like the cave itself recognized her as its reflection.

"You want to know how to stop her," she said. "But that's not the right question."

Ophelia stiffened. "Then what is?" she asked.

Galla tilted her head, eyes glowing faintly. "What are you willing to give?" she asked.

The silence that followed felt cavernous. Ophelia's heart pounded. She thought of Luka's blood bond. Gabriel's fury and forgiveness. Alex's tears. Her mother's last breath. And the yawning absence left behind by a man she could barely remember but whose shadow still shaped her life.

"Everything," she said, voice low but certain.

Galla nodded, satisfied. "Then listen well. The Bell of Time was forged in an age before language, when sacrifice wrote history and blood held the future together. Not all that is broken is dead."

She turned, gesturing to the luminous patterns on the walls. As she moved, they glinted and pulsed faintly, like veins under skin. "It was never just a tool. It was a lock. A promise. A reckoning."

Ophelia followed her gaze. "You said it won't sing for just anyone," she said.

"Correct." Galla's voice sharpened. "It calls to many. But it answers only to those who understand what it demands: not power. Not skill. But truth. Purpose. Lineage."

She stepped closer. "You carry more than one legacy in your veins, child. My blood built empires. Your mother's burned them down. And your father..."

Ophelia looked up, startled. "You knew him?"

"He was a storm given form," Galla said with a sad smile. "And you are all of us, Ophelia. Which means you are not bound by our rules. But you are shaped by our mistakes."

The truth rang through her, too sharp to ignore.

"If the Bell wakes," Ophelia asked, "what happens?"

Galla looked grim. "Then time itself bends. And you will have to choose whether to let it break."

A shudder ran through the cave. The spring darkened slightly, the light inside dimming.

"But I can't do it alone," Ophelia said. "You said that yourself."

"Correct again." Galla nodded. "And you won't. But the

ones you need won't follow orders. They'll follow truth. They'll follow fire."

"This is the last time I will stand before you like this," Galla said quietly. "My threads are nearly spent, and the veil grows thin."

Ophelia's chest tightened, but she said nothing. Grief had taught her to expect goodbyes, but never to be ready for them. She squared her shoulders.

Galla's voice grew distant as her form began to fade. "Go to the fae. Tell them the world ends in silence unless they act. Tell them the Bell is stirring. And tell them this: *You are the future they feared.*"

Galla stepped closer, her voice lower now, almost reverent. "You carry us forward. Not as memory, but as fire. And fire does not look back."

Ophelia blinked hard, but the tears came anyway. "I wasn't ready to lose her," she whispered.

"No one ever is," Galla said. "But grief is not a tether. It is a torch."

Their eyes locked one final time.

"When the world forgets its gods, its witches remember."

Then Galla faded, and the cave exhaled, as if the earth itself mourned the loss of its oldest daughter.

CHAPTER

TWENTY-THREE

Ophelia returned to Miramare just after twilight, the last streaks of amber sky vanishing beyond the sea. She barely noticed. The threading had left her unsteady—inside more than out—and the moment her boots touched solid ground, it was as if the weight she'd held off on the mountain came crashing down.

The castle stood in silence, the kind that settled after battle and blood and too many names carved into memory. Wind curled through the halls like a ghost remembering its way home.

She didn't expect to find anyone waiting. But Elijah stood near the main archway, a mug in his hand, his usual warmth dimmed by quiet observation. He didn't speak right away, just looked at her in that way only Elijah could. It was as if he saw every crack and didn't flinch.

She opened her mouth. Closed it again. The grief was too sharp for words.

"You're back," he said finally, stepping forward.

Ophelia nodded, her shoulders stiffening. "I didn't know where else to go," she said.

"I'm glad it was here," he said.

They walked together down the hall, boots scuffing against the floor. No need for words yet. He led her into the small library wing. A fire crackled in the hearth, casting the walls in soft gold. The scent of leather and smoke wrapped around her like a faded memory.

Elijah moved with easy familiarity, like the place belonged to him, not through possession, but through presence. He knew exactly where the second lamp needed adjusting, exactly which cushion had slumped too far into the corner of the couch. He belonged here in a way she never quite had anywhere. Watching him settle felt like exhaling.

She sank into the armchair across from him, exhaustion written into every line of her body.

"I saw Galla," she said.

Elijah lifted a brow slightly but didn't interrupt. She'd told him about her grandmother before, when she'd confessed to him everything that had happened over the last year.

"She told me the Bell of Time can still be awakened. But not by me. Not alone." Ophelia stared into the flames. "The fae hold the key."

Elijah took a slow sip of tea. "So you have a plan, I take it. But that's not what's really eating at you, is it?" he asked.

Her mouth twitched. "No. It's not," she said.

He set the mug aside and leaned forward, elbows on his knees. "You're grieving two mothers," he said gently. "The one who tried and failed. And the one who never got the chance."

The words landed with soft devastation. She blinked hard, but she didn't speak.

"I hated her," Ophelia said at last, the admission falling like ash. "Celeste. For leaving me after I learned she was alive. For protecting Eris instead of me. For being...herself. And then she gave everything. She saved all of us."

Elijah nodded slowly. "That's not a contradiction, Ophelia. That's grief. It's messy. It doesn't require you to choose one version of her to mourn. You can hold the betrayal and the love in the same space. That's where healing starts," he said.

She swallowed, eyes stinging. "And Eris...I know she wasn't always like this. I see glimpses. I hear it in the way Celeste spoke about her."

"But that's not the sister you had," Elijah said. "And it's not the one standing in front of you now."

Ophelia pulled her knees to her chest, curling into the chair. "She's obviously sick, Elijah. Twisted by magic and grief and gods know what else. But if there's a way to reach her..."

"You want to save her," he said softly, naming it without judgment. "That makes sense. You've spent a long time trying to rewrite endings you didn't get to choose."

Her head snapped up. "Then what is this for? If not to save her?" she asked.

Elijah met her gaze, steady and unflinching. "Maybe this war isn't about saving her. Maybe it's about saving yourself. And the people who are still within reach," he said.

The silence swelled between them, dense with everything they'd already lived through.

"You've spent your life trying to understand the people who broke you," he said. "Trying to forgive them. Trying to make sense of the damage. Celeste. Eris. Luka. Even Gabriel, when it hurt too much to hope."

She looked down at her hands. "You think I should let her die?" she asked.

"I think," he said gently, "you need to stop bleeding for people who wouldn't do the same for you."

The fire popped softly in the hearth. She didn't answer.

"You don't have to know how yet," he continued. "But maybe it starts with choosing yourself. Not out of guilt. Not out of obligation. But because you're still here. And you matter. And the world still needs what only you can do."

He reached across the space, brushing her fingers with his own. Steady. Grounding. "You're not alone, Ophelia. And you're not her. You never were," he said.

She closed her hand around his, silent tears slipping free.

For a long moment, they just sat there in the flicker of firelight, with the truth of things too big to name stretching between them.

It didn't last.

The library doors burst open with a crash that echoed through the high ceilings and rattled the ancient hinges. A gust of wind followed, scattering parchment and blowing out one of the candles on the mantel.

Mo strode into the library. "We have a problem," he said without preamble.

Ophelia rose from the armchair, tension spiking instantly in her chest. "What happened?" she asked.

Mo slapped a scroll down on the table. "Eris and the Bell of Time," he said.

Elijah's posture stiffened. "Where?"

"Nivara Island," Mo answered grimly, his voice laced with both disbelief and dread.

Ophelia blinked, her mind scrabbling for a foothold. "No. That's not possible."

"It is," Mo said, already pointing. The scroll shimmered with living magic and lines that crawled and pulsed, drawn not with ink but with arcane force. It was more than a map. It was a living record of magical energies across the oceans. And near the southern edge, a red dot flared to life, ringed in silver and black glyphs that shifted with protective layers too complex to name.

"It's warded," he said. "But the signature is unmistakable. It matches the Bell precisely: frequency, flux pattern, everything. Eris likely moved it there, and she's shielding it with a level of protection that predates most known spellcraft. This isn't just concealment. It's claiming."

Ophelia went still. "Nivara is sacred. It's supposed to be untouched. Mira…" she said, trailing off.

Elijah's head snapped toward her. "What about her?"

"She went back before we went to find you…," she said, voice barely above a whisper.

Mo's jaw clenched. "Then she's not just hiding the Bell. She's desecrated one of the most protected sites in supernatural history. That's not strategy, Ophelia. That's a declaration of war."

The word hit like a curse. For a long beat, no one spoke.

Ophelia's knees went weak. She caught the back of a chair to steady herself. Her thoughts spiraled: Mira, the fae, the Bell, Celeste's sacrifice. All of it circling a single terrifying truth: Eris was steps ahead. Again. "She's already laid the groundwork," she said hoarsely. "And we're playing catch-up."

Mo stepped closer, his expression unreadable. "Then what do we do?"

Ophelia stared at the map. The red light flickered again, casting long, distorted shadows on the scroll. Her pulse beat in her ears, matching it. Mira was there. Celeste had died for this. Galla's words rang in her skull: *What are you willing to give?*

THE LIBRARY BECAME their war room. Books lay in chaotic stacks across every surface, old scrolls curling at the edges like they'd been holding their breath for a thousand years. Maps glowed on the walls with ink that shimmered when touched by magic. Candle wax pooled in forgotten corners. Morning light slanted through the tall windows, fractured into golden shards that cut through the lingering haze of smoke and sleeplessness.

Ophelia stood at the head of the long oak table, her palms braced against the scarred wood. She didn't look at the others yet. She didn't need to. She could feel their weight around her.

Gabriel stood to her left, jaw tight. Luka leaned against the wall to her right, arms crossed, his stillness more ominous than movement. Mo hovered near a shelf, arms folded, eyes narrowed behind his glasses. Elijah sat in a high-backed chair, one leg crossed over the other, tapping a pen against his knee with restless precision. Brisa stood behind Alex's chair like a sentinel, her hand curled tight around the backrest. Alex herself looked drained—too pale and too still—but she was awake now, eyes sharpened.

"We're going to ask the fae again," Ophelia said, her voice even.

A pause stretched.

Gabriel frowned.

Luka muttered something low and indecipherable.

Mo raised an eyebrow but didn't look surprised.

It was Brisa who reacted first. "*Ask?*" she repeated, incredulous. "Didn't they already tell us to go screw ourselves in ten dialects of condescension and three flavors of disdain?"

"They already refused," Mo said gently, but with the weariness of someone who had personally cataloged every insult.

"They did," Ophelia agreed. "And I let them. I asked. I begged. That was my mistake." She looked up now, meeting their eyes one by one. "This time, I'll make them listen."

"And if they don't?" Luka asked.

"Then I burn their illusions to ash," she said. "And I remind them what neutrality costs."

The quiet after that was tight, sharp. Alex stirred, her voice rasping but steady. "You'll need me, then. If you're dealing with the fae—"

"No." Brisa stepped forward, cutting her off. Her tone was firm and unyielding.

Alex turned to her, something stubborn sparking in her too-tired eyes.

"I mean it," Brisa said. "You almost died, Alex. You think I'm leaving your side again? After Marisante? After...everything?" There was no steel behind the words. Just fear, brittle and thin and honest.

Alex hesitated. Then reached out, gently lacing their fingers together. "Okay," she whispered.

Brisa nodded once and then gestured to Mo. "We can run interference with Sofija and Ingrid," she added. "Buy you time. Whatever you need."

"What about threading to the fae realm?" Alex asked softly. "I thought it was impossible."

Mo glanced at Ophelia, then crossed the room and retrieved a thick, leather-bound journal, its spine cracked and lined with strange sigils. "I found something," he said. "In a tablet transcription, half-destroyed and written in Old Akkadian. It referenced an ancient liminal path. A kind of ethereal overlay that intersects our plane with theirs, but only in certain conditions."

He spread the journal flat on the table and pointed to a rough sketch. "It's not a door," he continued. "It's a thread. But it has to be drawn from bloodline, place, and time. The last recorded entry came from a Wildes witch—your ancestor, I think—who crossed over using the conjunction of equinox magic and a lunar-binding spell."

Ophelia furrowed her brow. "That's...complicated."

"It's impossible," Gabriel muttered.

"No," Mo corrected. "It's dangerous. But not impossible. Not for you," he said, looking directly at Ophelia before continuing. "You carry two lines: witch and vampire blood, both ancient and stronger than a full-blood from either line. The fae won't let you walk in through the front door. But this path, the one your ancestor used, doesn't ask permission."

"I can thread to them," Ophelia said softly.

"You can," Mo confirmed.

She turned back to the map. The glow of the Bell pulsed like a heartbeat. "We go to the fae. We remind them what's at stake. And if they don't answer..." Her tone dropped, dangerous and deliberate. "Then I make sure they remember who I am."

The moment stretched, taut and wordless. Tension pooled in the silence. And then, one by one, they nodded. It was time to cross the line no one else dared.

TWENTY-FOUR

The moon hung low and swollen above the Miramare cliffs, casting the library in silver as Ophelia knelt on the worn rug at the heart of the warded circle. Her hands trembled, but the motion was steady. Deliberate. She placed the final strand of bloodroot at the circle's edge, fingers smudged with ash and sigil ink.

Gabriel and Luka stood nearby, silent, watchful. Gabriel looked coiled, tense in a way that spoke of protection more than nerves. Luka...Luka wasn't breathing. Or if he was, it was shallow enough to make her wonder.

"This is different," Ophelia said, her voice low.

"Because it's not a place," Mo murmured from behind her. "It's a plane."

She nodded once and closed her eyes. Her blood began to hum, answering the call before her mind could. The circle flared to life, glowing a molten gold threaded with the deep violet of lunar magic. She reached inward, drawing from her bloodline. Her veins burned.

The air changed.

She spoke the incantation—a blend of Latin and something older, something guttural and bone-deep—and the ground dropped.

Gabriel shouted her name.

The world split.

She wasn't falling. She wasn't flying. She was unraveling.

Time looped inside her. Past and future scraped against each other as the thread tore through dimensions. Her vision fractured into kaleidoscopic shards. Her magic fought her, then surrendered. Gabriel's voice echoed from behind her eyes: "Ophelia!"

She turned. Luka was suspended in the dark beside her, limbs warped in flickers. His eyes had gone golden, slitted. His jaw was half-shifted, teeth too sharp. He growled low, not at her, but at the thing trying to follow them.

There was something in the between. Ophelia felt it reach. A presence that smelled like rot and roses.

Thread, she screamed inside herself. *Thread, goddamn you, THREAD.*

The circle flared. And the world snapped.

She hit the ground hard.

Not stone. Not soil. Something soft but knowing. Alive.

The forest exhaled around her. She rolled to her side, gasping. Her arms were scraped, blood glowing faintly under her skin like fireflies trapped in glass. Her magic recoiled and then stretched, aching.

Gabriel was on his hands and knees, coughing violently. Blood trickled from one nostril. His other hand braced against the earth. "I'm fine," he said hoarsely. "Just give me a second."

Luka didn't speak. He was on his feet, wild-eyed. He turned in a slow circle, chest heaving, hands curled into claws. His pupils were slits. His voice, when it came, was raw. "This place smells like endings," he said.

Ophelia sat up. The air buzzed in her lungs, too thick, too bright.

She looked around.

Colors bled at the edges of vision. Trees towered overhead, silver-veined bark flickering with life-force. Leaves whispered secrets in frequencies she couldn't quite hear. Petals drifted through the air, glowing faintly.

Ophelia touched one tree.

It *sang*. It wasn't sound, but a sensation. A surge of memory: Celeste's hand on her cheek, Galla's voice calling her "nipotina," Elijah's steady presence at her back.

The tree took nothing. But it *knew*.

Gabriel reached for her, grounding them both. "Are we here?"

Ophelia nodded once, her exhale slow and sure. "We are."

Luka tilted his head. "Then something knows it."

And the forest began to move.

One moment, they stood in a clearing, luminance spinning between branches overhead like suspended constellations. The next, the trees bent inward, vines unraveling with fluid grace, revealing a path that hadn't existed a moment before.

Gabriel stepped instinctively in front of Ophelia. Luka flanked her other side, one hand twitching toward the hilt of a dagger at his hip. They didn't speak. Breath was too fragile a thing to waste here.

From the shadows, they emerged. The guards were not what she remembered, not the fae who had once remained aloof while the world crumbled. These were different. Armored in bone-thread and starlight, tall as trees and just as old. Their eyes shimmered with no whites, no pupils, only magic in motion. They held no weapons, and yet she felt every one of them was armed.

They surrounded them in silence, their movements perfectly synchronized, like the trees themselves had sent them.

Ophelia raised her chin. "We come to speak with Aelirian."

The guards didn't answer. But one turned. And the path opened again.

They followed.

The deeper they walked, the less real the world felt. Trees with veins of molten gold glowing around them. Leaves floated in place as if held by remembrance, not gravity. The air quivered with colors that felt like emotions: longing, wonder, dread.

And then, the sanctum. Not a throne room, not a hall. It bloomed around them like a living heart—ribcage arches of petrified bone and glistening root systems, no walls but woven light. The floor was translucent crystal shot through with veins that pulsed like an ancient heartbeat. Overhead, vast canopies shimmered with strands of something that looked like memory spun into silk.

And in the center: Aelirian.

They turned slowly, expression unsurprised. Their silver hair rippled with some unseen breeze, face ageless but not young.

"Audacious," they said, voice low and clear. "Threading into the sacred groves."

Ophelia stepped forward, ignoring the tightness in her chest. "You refused me once. But the world's changed."

Aelirian tilted their head. "So has the price."

Gabriel tensed beside her.

Ophelia held her ground. "We came to bargain," she said.

Aelirian's head tilted. "Bargain implies leverage," they said.

Gabriel didn't speak, but his shoulders stiffened. Luka remained unmoving, a controlled stillness.

"But the war is closer now. The Bell has been moved. The balance is shifting," Ophelia said.

Aelirian took a slow step forward. The ground beneath them bloomed with pale radiance. "And you believe we owe you a shift in stance?" they asked.

"No," she said honestly, quietly. "But if you believe in balance—if you believe in the survival of this world—then you'll hear me out."

There was a long pause. Then Aelirian smiled, wide and unnerving. "Very well, Wildes blood. We shall let you speak your piece."

As Aelirian led them through the shifting woods, the air throbbed with barely contained energy. Then the forest parted, like a curtain of existence being peeled back, revealing a vast space beyond.

The fae court rose before them. Towering columns of calcified brilliance stretched upward, refracting colors that didn't exist in the mortal spectrum. The floor beneath their feet was a smooth surface of petrified crystal and bone, ancient and translucent, laced with veins that pulsed faintly like the roots of a long-slumbering tree. Above them, suspended in air, hung sheets of luminous silk woven with celestial memory. The space had no walls, only archways of woven antlers and fossilized vines that arced into the sky like the ribs of a great beast long buried.

It was ancient. Elemental. And not meant for human eyes.

Luka stepped in behind her, silent and tense. Gabriel kept close to her right side, gaze sharp, taking everything in like he expected it to vanish. Or strike.

The fae moved like wraiths through the court. Some glowed faintly. Others flickered in and out of visibility, leaving only the impression of wings or flame or wind in their wake. No footsteps. No voices. Just presence.

They were led to the center of the space, where Aelirian turned, his robes trailing behind him like liquid dusk. Several other fae appeared at his sides. Elders, Ophelia guessed, though their faces were ageless. They regarded her not with cruelty, but with an eerie detachment that made her stomach turn.

"Do you know what we are, witch?" one of the elders asked, their voice fluid and neither male nor female.

Ophelia straightened. "I know what you're called. Fae," she said.

Laughter rippled through the chamber like the striking of glass. Not unkind, just amused.

Aelirian tilted his head. "We are the stewards of life and death. We aren't gods. We are tenders of what you would call time. Rebirth. Decay. That which is meant to pass and that which endures," he said.

"We were born from endings," another elder added, her voice low and melodic. "And from beginnings that refused to stay buried."

Ophelia swallowed. "Then you know why I'm here."

"We do," Aelirian said, eyes unreadable. "The Bell of Time. The Kala Ghanta. You seek to wake it."

Gabriel stepped forward. "She doesn't want power. She wants to stop Eris. The balance—"

Aelirian raised one elegant hand. "We know what she wants. And we know what she is," he said.

The silence that followed cracked something inside her. "What am I?" Ophelia asked quietly.

"You are a thread unraveled," one elder whispered.

"You are a convergence," said another. "Witch and vampire. Mortal and myth."

Aelirian's voice anchored the room again. "You are blood of the Bell and the echo of a wound that was never closed. The Bell remembers you, though it does not yet sing. But if we help you awaken it—if we take you to what remains—you must understand what that means."

Ophelia's heart pounded. "What does it mean?" she asked.

Aelirian's gaze sharpened. "Time, as you know it, is not a river. It is a pattern. And every pattern requires balance. Light and shadow, birth and rot. Some of us—those bound most deeply to the decay of time—will not survive its resurrection."

Behind her, Luka shifted. Gabriel's jaw flexed.

"You're saying if you help me, some of your people will die?" Ophelia asked, voice low.

"Not die," Aelirian corrected. "Cease. Unmake. Our songs will end, and no one will remember the melody."

The words hit like a stone. Ophelia glanced around the court at the fae drifting through it, the ancient beauty of the place. "I'm not asking you to sacrifice yourselves. I'm asking you to help stop a war. If Eris succeeds, time won't just bend. It will break."

"You think in binaries," one elder said. "Win or lose. Save or sacrifice. We do not."

Gabriel stepped forward. "Then help us understand," he said.

"To right what's been broken," Aelirian said softly, "some threads must be severed. Even sacred ones."

Ophelia's fingers sparked with restless energy. "And if you do nothing? How many others will suffer?"

Aelirian approached her slowly. He stopped barely inches away, and when he looked into her eyes, it wasn't like being seen. It was like being *read*.

"We will deliberate," he said. "Until the next moonrise."

"And if you say no?" Luka asked quietly, his voice low and dangerous.

Aelirian turned to him with the faintest smile. "Then your war will be yours alone." The fae around them disappeared one by one, slipping between ether and nothingness.

A final breeze swept through the court, rustling the starlit canopies above.

And they were alone.

TWENTY-FIVE

The fae court vanished without ceremony. One moment, they stood beneath ribbed arches of bone and starlight. The next, the world disappeared with a soundless snap, and the crystalline floor gave way to moss. Soft, bioluminescent flora faintly pulsed underfoot like something alive and dreaming. No fanfare. No farewell.

Only silence.

Ophelia staggered slightly, catching her balance. The air pressed against her skin like damp velvet, neither hot nor cold, just *other*. It held no scent. No breeze. As if the very concept of weather had been abandoned here.

Trees loomed on all sides, but they weren't trees in the earthly sense. Their trunks curved like cathedral spires, veined with silver light that flickered with no visible source. Some beat in slow rhythm, others stood utterly still. The branches arched high overhead, leaves shifting in color as if filtering emotion, not sunlight. Above them, there was no sky —only a void lit by hanging constellations that blinked like memory.

Gabriel broke the silence first. "Is it always like this?" he murmured, voice hushed.

"I don't think so," Ophelia replied, her voice barely above a whisper. "It's worse."

He shot her a questioning look, but she didn't elaborate. Because it *was* worse. The air tasted like endings. Time here didn't flow; it hovered. Every step felt like walking through a dream someone else had abandoned. The very space around them resisted chronology. Leaves drifted upward. Their shadows lagged behind them, slow and deliberate, like the past refusing to be left behind.

They walked in silence, boots silent against moss that never compressed. Ophelia led, though she had no sense of direction, only a pull. Something old. Something sacred.

The forest thickened as they pressed on. The trees grew stranger, bark etched in runes that shimmered when she looked directly at them but vanished when she blinked. Vines writhed lazily in the distance, curling around empty air. Shadows darted between roots with no visible source. The deeper they walked, the quieter it became, until even the sound of their breath felt like a trespass.

Gabriel's hand occasionally brushed hers. Not possessive, reassuring. But it made her aware of the contrast. Her pulse fluttered at his nearness, but the bond that used to sing under her skin—the one tethering her to Luka—was silent. Not severed. Just...waiting.

Luka walked a few steps behind them. He hadn't spoken once. His expression was neutral, but his shoulders were drawn tight, and his eyes flicked constantly from movement to movement. If the court had disturbed him, this place unsettled him in a way she couldn't read.

It appeared without warning.

A gleaming structure rose ahead, nestled between trees

that seemed to bend protectively around it. It wasn't built; it had grown from this place. Its surface shimmered with hues of pearl, violet, and dusk. Transparent in places. Opaque in others. It looked like a shell that had come alive.

"It's waiting for us," Ophelia said.

No one disagreed.

Luka stepped forward first. His fingers hovered just above the iridescent surface of the wall, and the wall responded like water meeting wind. The membrane shimmered, then folded inward, revealing a corridor bathed in a soft, sentient luminance.

Ophelia stiffened. "It's sentient," she murmured.

"And it's listening," Gabriel said.

They entered without speaking. Inside, the passage curved like a spine, rippling as if inhaling around them. The walls weren't solid so much as stabilized, a dance of translucent mineral and organic weave. The very air changed with every breath, thick with magic so old it had forgotten how to be named.

They passed doorways that weren't doors, just openings that emerged and receded like the sanctum was adjusting itself to their presence. Each room felt grown rather than built: arched ceilings and alcoves with no right angles, no straight lines. Just rhythm. Just a murmur of being.

Ophelia stopped at the edge of one chamber. It glowed silver-blue, soft and inviting, a space made of curves and quiet. There was no bed, only a cradle of vines strung with something like silk and moonlight. A resting place. Gabriel stepped inside, not stopping to see if she followed.

Across the hall, Luka stood in the threshold of another room. The hue inside his was dimmer, cooler and violet-touched. His silhouette was sharp against the glow. His eyes met hers across the corridor. For a long moment, neither of them moved. Luka's jaw flexed, and he stepped forward like he might speak. But then he stopped. His shoulders sagged, just slightly. A man bracing for a blow that never came. He dipped his head once. Then he turned and vanished into the half-light of his chamber. The structure curved shut behind him.

Ophelia paused before stepping inside after Gabriel. He turned, eyes catching the chamber's glow like burnished amber, and for a moment, neither of them spoke. The absence of a door felt symbolic. Nothing between them now. No walls. No excuses. Just the question hanging between heartbeats.

Gabriel took a step forward. "You came."

"I chose you," she said simply. Her voice didn't tremble.

Emotion welled in his eyes, but he didn't speak. He just looked at her—really looked—with that unflinching focus that always unraveled her. But she didn't look away. Not this time.

"The blood bond is nearly silent here," she said. "I thought it was Luka. I thought fate chose him. But it wasn't fate. It was magic. And now that it's quiet...I know. It will always be you."

Gabriel moved toward her like gravity answered to the pull of her soul. His hand cupped her jaw, thumb brushing across her cheek. "Then say it."

She leaned into his touch. "You are my twin flame. My mate. Not because the blood told me. Because I feel it. Because I choose it. And I'll always choose you," she said.

He kissed her then, not urgently or possessively, but with awe. Like he'd been frozen for years and only now remembered how to move. Their bodies found each other naturally, lips trailing from jaw to collarbone as hands unfastened what little clothing remained. It wasn't frantic. It was a sacred, slow offering.

Magic hummed low in her bones, responding to every brush of skin. Her veins lit softly beneath the surface, golden and alive, as if her very blood recognized the moment.

Gabriel laid her down onto the crystal bed, which softened beneath her like moss under moonlight. Strands of radiant filament shifted around her body, cradling her. He followed, kneeling between her thighs, his hand steady on her hip.

"We don't have to rush," he said, voice thick with emotion.

"I want to feel you inside me," she whispered.

He kissed her chest, slow and reverent, his mouth lingering at the curve of her breast before trailing lower. When he entered her, she moaned, a sound of relief and clarity. No more ache. No more confusion. Just the truth of him, inside her.

They moved together slowly, reverently. The rhythm was not frantic or desperate; it was grounding. He kissed her shoulder. Her cheek. Her mouth. And her body answered him with rising fire.

Then, the bond stirred. It began as a hum—familiar, buried. A phantom thread twisting deep in her chest.

Her magic flared, gold and wild. A warning.

"Gabriel," she gasped, hands gripping his back. "Something's—"

The break came like a shattering star. Her spine arched. Her veins lit from within, throbbing with blinding heat. The golden threads—Luka's—flared once, then unwound all at once with violent grace. Her body convulsed, pleasure colliding with power, and her cry fractured in her throat.

Gabriel held her tight, hands steady on her hips, his body shielding hers. "I've got you," he said, over and over, voice fierce and gentle.

A final tremor rolled through her. Then stillness.

She lay beneath him, chest heaving. Her eyes found his. "It's done," she whispered.

Gabriel cupped her cheek, his thumb brushing away a tear neither of them noticed fall. "You're free," he said.

"Not free," she said. "Found."

He kissed her, deep and certain, and moved again inside her: slow, anchoring, and sacred.

Magic moved between them now, but it wasn't the kind that demanded or bound. It was woven of intention and skin and choice. His name left her lips again and again, until it was all she knew. When they climaxed, it wasn't an explosion. It was fusion. Magic shimmered through the opaline chamber. The ceiling hummed. The magic didn't rupture—it harmonized.

When they lay tangled together afterward, their bodies slick with sweat and glimmering dusk, there was no bond, no compulsion, no ancient thread. Just them: chosen and together.

THE AIR in the fae realm was still, but never silent. It beat gently and rhythmically, as if the land itself whispered beneath the crystalline structures and ancient trees. Every root and stone seemed to hum with awareness.

Ophelia stepped barefoot onto the glassy ground outside the dwelling. Behind her, Gabriel slept, his body curled in loose protection around where she'd lain. She hadn't wanted to wake him. Not yet.

She needed a moment alone.

The stars above didn't shift with the hours. They just hung there, suspended in a too-perfect sky. She hated how still they were. No constellations to follow. No North Star to chart a course. Just a dreamscape pretending to be real.

In her hand, she clutched the moonstone Mira had gifted her long ago, its surface cool against her palm. She didn't summon Galla this time. She didn't need to. The warmth it offered was grounding. It was a tether to what she already knew.

Not all that is broken is dead.

The thought echoed, low and certain. That was Galla's answer. And now she finally understood it. The blood bond hadn't died in some grand, violent explosion. It had been undone quietly, like a knot slowly unthreading. She and Luka had stepped out of the world where it was forged, and in doing so, left behind the power, the promise, the pain. It hadn't broken. It had been relinquished.

She hadn't come here to escape. She had come to choose. And now, under a sky that refused to move, she knew what she had chosen.

A soft footfall sounded behind her. She didn't turn, because she didn't need to. The air shifted with him, laced with that strange alchemy of stillness and storm.

Luka stopped a few paces away. His dark hair was tousled, his expression unreadable. There was a weight to him she hadn't noticed before, like something vital had been stripped away.

"You feel it, too," he said, voice low.

She nodded, her fingers tightening around the moonstone. "It's gone."

"No pain. No burning thread," he added, eyes never leaving hers.

"No pull," she agreed. Her voice didn't shake.

For a long moment, they just stood there, the forest around them rustling faintly with leaves that moved without wind. The silence between them wasn't cold. Just final.

When she turned to face him, his gaze was already waiting. Not pleading. Not bitter. Just...tired. As if something inside him had finally stopped fighting.

"I never meant to bind you like that," he said quietly. "I thought I was protecting you. From the world. From Eris. From...yourself."

"I know," she said. It wasn't forgiveness, just truth.

His jaw clenched. "But it wasn't protection. It was control. I didn't trust you enough to let you choose."

There it was. The truth lay bare between them, unvarnished and raw.

"You didn't," she said. Her voice was soft, but it landed hard. "And you hurt me because of it."

He flinched, just slightly. But he didn't look away.

"I wanted to believe it was fate," he said. "That the bond made it right. But you were never mine to bind."

Something in her chest cracked open. Not in pain, just in release.

"We were never meant to be a forever," she said. "Just a moment. One that mattered. But it's over now."

Luka's shoulders rose, then fell in a quiet hush. "Will you miss it?" he asked. The bond. The connection. Him.

She considered. "I'll miss the version of us that might've existed, if it had been ours to choose."

He nodded, gaze heavy but calm. "Then maybe this ending is the only mercy I have left to offer," he said.

They stood in silence once more. This time, it didn't ache. It simply was.

Then Luka stepped back. Just a single step, but it shifted the air.

"Be safe, Ophelia," he said. His voice didn't break. It didn't need to.

Then he turned and disappeared into the shadowed trees, the quiet swallowing him whole. No dramatic exit. No final flare of magic. Just a soft, clean ending.

And this time, she let him go. Fully. Finally. Because she didn't belong to the past anymore. She belonged to herself. And she had chosen her future.

TWENTY-SIX

The sun—or whatever passed for it in the fae realm—had dipped behind clouds that did not move. The once-radiant landscape had dulled, its glow muted as if the land itself held its breath. When Ophelia, Gabriel, and Luka approached the court again, the changes were immediate.

The cathedral-like structure they had entered the day before no longer shimmered with impossible light. The walls, once shifting with color and motion, had solidified into pale stone veined with something that pulsed faintly, like a dying heartbeat. Even the ground beneath their feet had lost its iridescent sheen. Moss crunched instead of breathing.

"It feels...colder," Gabriel murmured, his eyes flicking across the motionless vines.

"They've made their decision," Luka said. Then, softer: "Or they think they have."

Ophelia didn't answer. Her fingers tightened around the moonstone in her pocket. Her magic simmered just beneath her skin, ready. This was the end of the line. If the court said no, there was no one else to ask. No one left who could tip the scale.

As they stepped into the sanctum, the tension crystallized. The air itself seemed denser, thicker, as though layered with unspoken expectation. The inner court was already full. Fae gathered in tiered semicircles, rows of beings so still they might have been carved from starlight and marble. Some shimmered with spectral wings. Others bore thorn-like ridges down their spines. None blinked.

At the center stood Aelirian. No robes. No crown. Only a simple tunic the color of bone, its sleeves bound at the wrists. They looked younger like this, less mythic and more mortal—a faint reminder of a life that might have once known simplicity. But their eyes burned with knowing.

"Step forward," they said, voice amplified unnaturally in the chamber. "This is your audience."

Ophelia moved first, boots thumping across the stone. Gabriel and Luka flanked her, shadows cast in loyalty and tension. She bowed her head but did not kneel.

One of the fae stepped forward. Her eyes were obsidian, hollow as if they swallowed all light. "We have spoken," she said, tone like frost cracking glass. "The risk is too great. To rouse the Bell is to disturb time's balance. And time belongs to none."

Murmurs rippled across the gallery. It wasn't clear if they were in agreement or dissent, but the air trembled faintly with each new voice.

"She is not of the old blood," another fae added, their tone layered in two octaves at once. Their hair shimmered like moonlit smoke. "Her magic is fractured. Vampire. Witch. Mortal. A convergence of instability. She cannot bear the weight."

Ophelia flinched. Gabriel stepped closer.

But Aelirian's words sliced through the chamber. "She does not seek to rule it. She seeks to stop what would unmake us all."

"And what of the price?" the obsidian-eyed woman demanded. "If we help her, there will be no rebalancing. The rot will spread. The elders will unweave."

Luka shifted beside her. "So you'll let the world burn, so long as your own bones are safe in the ash?" he asked, sharp and angry.

A hiss tore through the crowd. One fae stepped forward, eyes glowing, fists clenched.

Aelirian raised a hand. The court stilled.

"We do not survive by clinging to decay," they said. "We are rebirth. We are transformation. And yet we hesitate when one of our own did not." Turning to the court, their gaze swept the rows like a blade.

"She was not born in our cycle," they continued. "Her blood was diluted, disrupted, nearly forgotten. And still, Alexandra came to us, seeking understanding. She honored our rites. She asked the questions we had stopped asking. She bled to prove herself, and we let her."

Ophelia swallowed hard. Alex. They were talking about Alex. Her sister in all but blood. The girl who had walked into the heart of fae magic and asked for belonging, not power. A flicker stirred at the back of the room. A younger fae touched a pendant at her throat. Another looked away, shame in the tilt of his chin.

Aelirian's voice resonated. "She is young by our standards. But do not mistake youth for weakness. She remained when others fled. She reached for us when we turned away. And now she is the one most broken by this war."

Ophelia's breath caught. Her hand gripped the moonstone tighter.

"She is not lost to us yet," they said. "But if we do nothing —if we refuse to act—then we are the ones cutting that thread."

A silence deeper than any she had heard settled over the court. Not stillness. Waiting.

"Call it," said a fae from the gallery. "A vote."

Aelirian nodded.

One by one, the fae extended their hands. Palms up for yes. Palms down for no. The magic tallied with each motion, sparks rising into the air like fireflies. A net began to form above the dais, brilliant and shifting.

The majority were down.

Ophelia's stomach dropped. Her vision tunneled. No. No, they couldn't be saying no. This wasn't just about her. It was about Eris. About Alex. About every thread unraveling if the Bell woke for the wrong Wildes witch.

Then Aelirian stepped forward, and the air shifted. The glow dimmed. The magic paused mid-flicker. They didn't raise a hand or lower it. Instead, they turned a palm inward, pressed it against their chest. Gasps echoed through the sanctum.

"You break the vote?" asked the obsidian-eyed woman. Her voice rang like judgment.

"No," Aelirian said. "I balance it. In times of fracture, we do not vote. We offer." They stepped off the dais, feet touching the ground in an offering.

Even the most stoic among the fae flinched.

"If helping her means death, then let me die first. But I will not watch another cycle be consumed by fear and cowardice."

Ophelia didn't breathe.

"You would sacrifice your place for her?" a moon-haired fae whispered.

"I would sacrifice far more," Aelirian said. "Because I

remember what it is to hope." The words sank like roots into the chamber.

And slowly—hesitantly—one hand turned upward. Then another. The net of light re-formed. Brighter. Stronger. It wasn't consensus. It was unity born from sacrifice.

"It is done," Aelirian said.

They turned to Ophelia. "We will help you. Under one condition."

She stepped forward, steady. "Name it."

"A favor," they said. "One that will be called in time. You will not know when or how. But when it comes, you will answer."

Ophelia hesitated for half a breath. Then she nodded. "Yes. Of course."

Aelirian extended a hand. When Ophelia placed her palm in theirs, the air shimmered. Threads of silver and gold coiled around them, glowing with ancient magic. Binding magic.

The court bowed their heads.

And somewhere—distant but clear—a bell rang once.

And then the silence swallowed it whole.

CHAPTER

TWENTY-SEVEN

The library-turned-war room at Miramare felt heavier than usual, as though the castle had begun to mourn. Magic hung in the air like smoke, thick and metallic, charged with old spells and unspoken dread. Even the torches lining the stone walls flickered more cautiously, their flames too still, as if they, too, were holding their breath.

Ophelia stood at the head of the long table, oak warped with age, divots carved from generations of planning and desperation. Her hands were braced against its surface, knuckles pale. She didn't speak yet. Words felt brittle. Too breakable.

The fae emissaries lingered near the arched windows, statuesque and unnerving, framed in morning light that filtered through clouds. They didn't speak. Didn't shift. Just watched. Silent as frost and just as unyielding. One of them had no discernible mouth, only a shifting ripple of iridescence where their face should be. Another had skin like quartz that pulsed faintly, casting moving shadows along the wall.

Aelirian had not yet spoken, but their presence was

enough. They stood slightly apart from the others, neither part of the court nor apart from it, radiating calm edged in inevitability. The hush around them wasn't dread. It was prophecy. The breath before fate turned the page.

Gabriel and Luka stood on either side of Ophelia, both silent, both tense. For once, neither postured nor argued. Gabriel's fingers twitched near his blade hilt every few minutes. Luka stood unnaturally statuesque, arms crossed. His gaze was fixed on the window, like he could see what waited beyond the horizon.

Brisa leaned against a support column across the room, arms crossed, leg bouncing like a metronome, nervous energy bleeding through her calm. Her eyes tracked the fae delegation like they might try to eat someone. "You sure they're not just bedazzled corpses?" she muttered under her breath.

Elijah, standing beside the fireplace, snorted behind his hand, caught between amusement and horror.

"They can hear you," Ophelia said, not looking up.

"They should hear me," Brisa said louder, narrowing her glare at a tall fae with bioluminescent filigree crawling across their neck like ivy. "Some of them have antlers, Ophy. Actual antlers. I watched one lick a book. For wisdom. That's not even the weirdest part."

The fae in question tilted their head, a ripple of color moving through their crystalline stare. Not offended. Not amused. Simply aware.

Brisa didn't back down. She leaned toward Elijah and added in a louder whisper, "If any of them turn into a mushroom, I am setting this room on fire."

"You better not," Elijah whispered back. "This place is full of dry parchment and emotionally unstable witches."

Another fae blinked—horizontally—and Brisa muttered, "Nope," looking away with a visible shudder.

Aelirian moved, barely, and the shift rippled through the room like a subtle gravitational shift. Ophelia felt it in her teeth. Luka's shoulders drew tighter. Gabriel shifted his weight like he was bracing for impact.

But Aelirian didn't speak. Their gaze landed on Ophelia, unreadable as starlight. Waiting.

Ophelia finally looked up from the table, her attention sweeping across the gathered faces: her allies, her found family, the immortals who might yet decide the fate of time itself.

The room didn't tremble. But the air did.

The heavy tension was broken not by magic, nor proclamation, but by the sound of soft footsteps in the corridor. Familiar. Halting. But steady.

Alex.

She appeared in the doorway like a ghost resurrected, pale and wrapped in a blanket that hung from her shoulders like a mantle stitched from quiet defiance. Her silver hair was pulled back, exposing the bruising beneath her eyes. A thread of dried blood marred her collarbone like a memory someone had tried to scrub away but failed.

"You're going without me?" she asked, voice low but clear.

Everyone turned.

Ophelia's chest clenched. "You need time to recover," she said gently.

"I know," Alex replied with a tired, almost amused smile. "Doesn't mean I have to like it." She stepped further into the room, the fae watching her without comment. Some with curiosity. Some with guilt. One with something that almost looked like respect.

"I don't want a goodbye," Alex continued, reaching for Ophelia's hands. "But I'm not letting you walk into this without saying it." The contact jolted through Ophelia like a thread snapping back into place. Alex's fingers were cold, but her grip was firm. Familiar. Anchoring.

"You always say goodbye like it's temporary," Ophelia said, voice cracking slightly. "Like the world will wait for us to come back."

Alex's smile didn't fade. "Maybe it won't. But that doesn't mean we don't try."

Brisa glanced away, blinking rapidly. Elijah busied himself adjusting his cuffs, his jaw tight.

Alex drew Ophelia into a hug, no fanfare or theatrics. Just the fierce, quiet desperation of two people who had lost too much and still chose to hold on. When she pulled back, she didn't release Ophelia's hands right away. "You'll come back," she said. "You will."

"I'll try," Ophelia whispered.

"No," Alex said, her voice hardening. "You will."

And with that, she turned and walked to the side of the room, her blanket trailing behind her like a cloak. Brisa moved to her side silently. No words passed between them, but Brisa's hand found Alex's and held it tightly.

Elijah was next.

He stepped forward slowly, appearing older than usual, more human than he let most people see. He stood beside the window, casting a halo of pale gold. His voice was quiet but unwavering. "I'm coming with you."

Mo's voice cut through the room. "No," he said.

Elijah frowned, turning. "You don't get to decide—"

"No," Mo said again, firmer now. "You're not a supernatural. You're a mortal. And you're not bound by this world the way we are."

"I'm not helpless either," Elijah snapped. "You think I'll sit here while she—"

"You're the one who'll have to carry us," Mo said. He

stepped forward, laying a hand on Elijah's shoulder. "If we fail, someone has to remain. Someone who can bury the bones."

The silence that followed was leaden. Elijah's mouth tightened. "Just don't give me a massacre," he said.

"No promises," Brisa muttered, swiping at her face. "But if I die, write something badass on my tombstone. Like 'She died with a curse on her lips and a blade in her hand.' Not something soft. Don't you dare write something soft."

Gabriel gave a sharp exhale, barely disguising his laugh as a cough. Luka just looked vaguely alarmed. "Do you think you're going to die?" he asked seriously.

Brisa shrugged. "We're going to a time-warped island filled with cursed blood magic, ancient death gods, and a woman who thinks apocalypse is a personal aesthetic. I'd say fifty-fifty."

"Higher," Gabriel muttered.

"Helpful," Ophelia said, unable to help the half smile that tugged at her lips.

That smile didn't last.

Because Aelirian stepped forward then, their silhouette cutting across the light like a blade. "It is time," they said, voice neither loud nor soft, but absolute.

Ophelia stared down the table one last time—at Mo's quiet watchfulness, Brisa's barely masked sarcasm, Alex's fierce faith, Gabriel's steadiness, Luka's guarded calm.

No one moved. No one questioned.

She straightened her shoulders, stepped out from the head of the table, and took her place between Luka and Gabriel.

"Let's finish this."

CHAPTER

TWENTY-EIGHT

The air changed the moment they threaded in.

Nivara Island emerged like a wound carved from the ocean, jagged and ancient beneath a sky bruised to violet. The sun didn't shine here, not exactly. Instead, a gray-lavender hue shone overhead, as if the heavens had stalled mid-thought. Clouds hung motionless, too dense to be natural.

Ophelia landed in a crouch. Her boots splashed into a thin film of seawater that clung to the slick obsidian rock like blood too stubborn to be absorbed. The ground stank of iron and salt, the scent of something ancient unearthed. Sea spray coated her skin, mingling with the metallic taste of threaded magic still clinging to her tongue. The impact rattled her bones. Around her, the others arrived in staggered flashes: Gabriel, Luka, Brisa, Mo, and the fae delegation led by Aelirian. No one spoke.

The island was wrong.

Everything felt corrupted. Perverted. Stone paths now shimmered with residual blood magic, their edges cracked and curled like parchment left too close to flame. Sacred trees stood blackened and hollow, limbs brittle and scorched, leaves shriveled to dust. Sigils etched into the cliffs glowed faintly red, but not from their own magic. Something else fed them now. Something feral. The symbols bled light in slow drips, like they were weeping.

Ophelia turned in a slow circle. The land itself felt hostile. The wind whistled with a jagged cadence, too sharp and precise. Instinctively, she reached out with her magic and then instantly recoiled. The ground was alive, yes, but in the way a dying thing twitches before it goes still.

"Gods," Brisa muttered, pressing her fingers to a warped tree trunk. Its bark sloughed away at her touch, revealing rot shot through with glowing veins of red. "This place is supposed to be a sanctuary."

"It was," Mo said softly, crouching to examine a cracked ward-stone buried beneath overgrowth. "But Eris has been here. You can taste it in the air."

Gabriel stepped up beside Ophelia, his gaze lifted toward the horizon. The sea had pulled back unnaturally far, revealing barnacled ruins and jagged rocks jutting from the sand. Fish flopped weakly in the distance, stranded in tidepools that should not have existed. "It's like the island is paralyzed," he said.

"No," Aelirian corrected, their voice cool and clear. "It's choking." The fae shimmered with unease. Their luminous forms, once radiant and seamless, flickered with tension, like sunlight filtered through a dying prism. One of them—taller than the rest, skin veined with silver and shadow—lifted a hand, casting a ward that pulsed outward in a concentric ring. The edges of the circle distorted like a mirage, stabilizing their perimeter.

"Her magic is unraveling the very fabric of this place," the fae said. "If we don't reach the Bell soon, time itself may bleed."

Brisa whistled low, pulling her jacket tighter around her frame. "Is this the part where things go completely sideways?"

Aelirian turned to her, eyes opaque and ancient. "That depends. Are you prepared to walk through time's remains?" they asked.

Brisa snorted. "Prepared? No. Likely to do it anyway and curse you the whole time? Absolutely."

A faint chuckle stirred from Mo. Even Luka's mouth twitched, though his hands remained clenched at his sides.

Ophelia didn't smile. Her magic twisted in her chest—not with fear, but anticipation. The air surged with warning, and the ground beneath her feet throbbed in time with something deeper than magic. This island knew her, and it was waiting.

Luka stepped beside her, his movements slower than usual, as if the weight of the place pressed down on his bones. His eyes scanned the horizon, sharp and searching, picking apart the contours of a landscape that felt more mirage than solid ground. Fog moved in tendrils across scorched stone and shriveled grass, curling into shapes that mimicked motion and memory.

"She's not hiding," he said at last, his voice low and grim. It wasn't a guess. It was a certainty.

"No," Ophelia replied, barely more than a whisper. "She wants us to find her."

The wind picked up then, a slow, dragging pull like the island itself was inhaling.

Gabriel's hand brushed hers, warm and grounding. "Then we shouldn't keep her waiting," he said.

But before they could take a step, the shadows between the broken trees shifted, and a figure emerged.

Mira.

She walked as if time meant nothing to her, and perhaps it didn't. Her presence was quieter than before—less light, more shadow—but it carried the weight of prophecy. Her bare feet didn't disturb the ground. Ophelia froze when she saw her eyes. There was no warmth, just the vast stillness of eyes that had watched galaxies spin and fall.

Ophelia broke free of her stillness and rushed to her, arms reaching without thought. They collided in a fierce embrace, arms locking tight, the contact a shield against the chaos rising all around them.

"I thought you were—" Ophelia began, her voice cracking.

"I know," Mira said softly, her hand brushing Ophelia's hair. "But the fates hadn't finished with me yet."

Ophelia pulled back, her hands gripping Mira's shoulders as if to confirm she was real. "You know why we're here. You saw it."

Mira nodded, and her gaze drifted toward the heart of the island, where the very ground seemed to ripple. "I saw it in a vision," she said. "Long ago. Before you were born. Before the Bell went silent. Eris couldn't unlock it, not without you. So she buried it, deep in the heart of this place, hoping to twist time around herself until the rest of the world forgot. But you still have a choice. You can still end this."

Aelirian stepped forward, cloak billowing behind them like a whisper of starlight. "We will lead you to the sanctum. But make no mistake, the moment the Bell awakens, Eris will feel it. She will come. We cannot shield you from her fury, only from her reach."

Mo turned to glance behind them, eyes narrowed. "The outer wards are already breaking," he said. "Two collapsed as we landed. Another's flickering."

A sharp crack split the sky overhead. For a moment, the air shimmered, a kaleidoscope of broken time—images flickering in and out of the mist. A younger version of Ophelia sprinting across the cliffs. A child holding a fractured amulet. A woman —Eris—standing at the center of the ruined Bell chamber, laughing, her eyes full of stars and blood.

Then the visions faded.

"She's bending time around herself," Aelirian said. "And it's beginning to break."

Brisa shivered. "Okay, yeah. Definitely the sideways part."

Mira's gaze lingered on the horizon, but her voice was resolute. "There's still time. But not much. Follow me." And without another word, she turned and stepped into the cracked heart of the island.

The path narrowed as they moved deeper into the earth— no longer a path, really, but a wound tunneled through stone and time. The entrance sealed behind them with a soft hiss, like the island itself was withdrawing into silence. Shadows thickened. Sound fell away. Only the rhythmic crunch of footfalls and the occasional drip of water echoed back to them.

The air was heavy, not just with dust but with something older. Something waiting. Veins of pulsing energy lined the walls—thin threads of dormant magic spiderwebbing through ancient rock. They glowed faintly gold, then blue, then vanished into darkness, like fog fading on a mirror. It didn't illuminate so much as haunt.

"We're close," Mira whispered, her voice nearly lost in the hush. "You'll feel it before you see it."

They descended through switchbacks cut by forces neither natural nor wholly magical. It felt more like the earth had been carved away by thought, or time itself, creating a spiral of descent that bent logic just enough to unsettle.

Faint whispers skittered across the back of Ophelia's mind —words she couldn't make out, but emotions she could feel. Regret. Longing. Warnings.

At one point, the tunnel forked. Aelirian didn't hesitate. "Left. The right passage loops you back into your own past. Some who enter never return."

Brisa grunted. "Well, that's horrifying," she intoned.

"They say time flows like water," Aelirian said, glancing back over their shoulder. "But here, it remembers how to drown."

The final stair led to a landing of pale stone streaked with veins of black glass. Beneath it: the sanctum. They stepped into the chamber like intruders into a cathedral no one had prayed in for a thousand years.

It was unnaturally vast. A domed cavern that stretched into shadow above them. Roots dangled from the ceiling like petrified vines, their tips a soft phosphorescence. They didn't sway, though the air seemed to move. Instead, they pulsed in a slow rhythm.

And at the chamber's heart, half-consumed by vines and time, stood the Bell of Time. It didn't shimmer. It didn't sing. It loomed. The metal was darkened, dulled, and at its base, time itself seemed to warp—light bent in unnatural ways, shadows moved with no source.

"It's not glowing," Ophelia said, voice hollow in the echo.

"Not yet," Aelirian said. "It has to remember why it should wake."

Aelirian stepped forward. Two elder fae trailed behind them, their expressions solemn, their movements almost glacial. One's hair shimmered like frost melting. The other's eyes were twin suns behind a storm. Power radiated from them in concentric waves.

Without a word, they began the rite. The air tightened as they lifted their hands, their palms stained with sigils inked in silvery lines. The chamber trembled. A low, harmonic hum vibrated through the walls. The chant they spoke wasn't recognizable—not language so much as invocation. A blend of vowel and vibration, of memory and meaning.

Magic thickened. The roots along the ceiling recoiled, curling away like they'd been burned. Dust rained softly from above.

Then Aelirian reached inside their robe and withdrew a curved blade. The moon-shaped dagger gleamed with ancient magic. They sliced across their palm without flinching. The elders followed suit. The blood that spilled was not red; it was silver, luminous and slow, like mercury dreaming.

They stepped into a triangle around the Bell, their blood marking the stone in three perfect points. Their voices rose.

"Blood that remembers," Aelirian intoned. "Power that bends but does not break."

"We restore what was never meant to be lost," they said in unison.

A vibration rippled through the chamber. The Bell began to glow. Not all at once. First, a faint beat at its core. Then another. Slow. Rhythmic. Like something sleeping remembering the shape of air.

Ophelia stepped forward, not entirely by choice. The pull wasn't physical; it was ancestral. Cellular. Her magic responded before her body did, spiraling under her skin in patterns that hurt and healed at once.

She didn't notice when Gabriel moved behind her. Didn't hear Brisa whisper something like a prayer. Didn't see Luka shift his weight like he was preparing for a fight that hadn't begun yet.

Because the Bell saw her. And it was waking.

Aelirian turned to her. Their voice was steady, reverent.

"It will only respond to one who is not bound by time," they said, "but strong enough to hold it. You are both."

Ophelia's mouth was dry. "What do I do?" she asked.

Aelirian extended their arm toward the Bell. "Touch it," they said. "And choose the thread."

The energy intensified. Her magic surged in her blood, radiant and coiling. Her fingers trembled.

And then she stepped forward.

The Bell welcomed her.

Ophelia reached out, fingers outstretched, her magic humming in her bones. The Bell reverberated once beneath her hand, warm and familiar. And then it *opened*.

Not like a door. Like a *wound*.

Threads of gold and silver and blood-red, spiraling in dizzying arcs around her. Each one shimmered with a different echo: a laugh, a scream, a heartbeat. She saw her mother's eyes. Elijah's hand reaching for hers. Gabriel's mouth forming her name. Luka's fury. Eris's tears.

A thousand lives. A thousand possible Ophelias. All flickering at the edge of becoming.

Then—

"NO!" Eris's voice ripped through the chamber, a banshee's howl of rage and grief. Her form burst from the far wall, smoke and shadow and bone, lunging toward the Bell.

Aelirian moved, runes flaring like constellations reborn. Fae light collided with corrupted shadow.

But Ophelia didn't flinch. Because this wasn't Eris's thread to choose. It was *hers*.

She closed her hand around the curve of the Bell and whispered, "I choose."

The Bell rang.

One pure, sonorous note. It vibrated through bone and blood and memory, through stone and star, echoing across every version of time that had ever been.

The air shattered.

The chamber fractured.

Reality *unraveled*.

Gabriel shouted her name, but she was already gone, swept into an eruption of possibility and converging realities.

Time fractured like glass. Futures bled into pasts. And at the center of it all, Ophelia fell—not down, but *through*.

She didn't scream.

She let go.

And the world burned behind her.

TWENTY-NINE

The air was different here: thicker, older, humming with the weight of centuries. Ophelia stumbled as the thread released her, boots skidding on ancient moss-slick stone. She caught herself with one hand against the base of a ruined pillar, her chest heaving, vision dimming with the residue of too many timelines. Her magic sparked, burning toward something inevitable. She was here. Wherever here was.

Above her, trees arched like sentinels. They were massive things, silver-barked and alive with dormant runes. Their roots braided through the ruins, anchoring what was left of the structure that time had tried and failed to erase. The columns were carved with layered languages: witch glyphs swirling into fae sigils and vampire blood script, all coexisting in impossible harmony. This place wasn't sacred because of what it held. It was sacred because it had not forgotten.

The glow filtering through the canopy wasn't sunlight. It was remembrance made radiant. It made her skin shimmer softly, a glow curling around the edges. Every breath she took tasted like dust, like old spellwork and forgotten names.

She walked slowly, each footfall whispering across a path that felt alive. Vines recoiled as she passed, then twisted back into place, as if reluctant to release their grip on the past. Every ruin here seemed to vibrate with echoes of the past that didn't quite belong to the present.

And then she saw it: the obsidian pedestal, cracked but upright, at the heart of a ring of runes.

Ophelia blinked. Recognition slammed into her.

She knew this place. Not from memory, but from a vision. From prophecy. From stories whispered in dreamlike fragments.

This was where the Bell had been born.

Her pulse skittered. She moved toward the pedestal, and the runes at its base glowed—first red, then gold, then something deeper. As if responding to her presence. As if welcoming her home.

And then: a familiar voice behind her, low and certain.

"You came," he said.

She turned, heart in her throat.

He stepped from the shadows, his form outlined in soft illumination. His silver-streaked hair fell to his shoulders, and his eyes—her eyes—watched her like someone who'd already lived this moment a hundred times.

"Leander?" she asked.

He inclined his head. "I dreamed of this moment. Centuries ago."

Her throat closed. "I thought I'd never get to ask you anything. And now I don't even know where to start."

"You've already started," he said, turning toward the ruins. "Come."

They walked in silence through the temple that time had nearly swallowed. Birds called from high branches. Wind stirred, and every step echoed like a memory replaying itself.

"This is the site of the Kala Ghanta's creation," Leander said as they reached a wide, circular platform carved into the earth. "The witches believed they could use molten gold, obsidian, and blood to bend time. To save lives. Stop wars. Rewrite mistakes."

Ophelia stepped closer to the center, where an obsidian pedestal rose, blackened and cold.

"I saw them," she whispered. "In a vision. They weren't just determined. They were terrified," she said.

"They should have been," Leander murmured. "They succeeded in stopping a war—but created something worse. The Bell became sentient. Insatiable. It tethered itself to whoever wielded it. Loyalty. Legacy. Sacrifice. It demanded it all," he said.

"And when they tried to unmake it?" Ophelia asked, already guessing at the answer.

"It refused," Leander said. "It bound itself to its creators through blood magic. The tethering spell made it impossible to destroy without sacrifice. If broken, it would unravel the very timelines it touched."

Ophelia's stomach twisted. "It's still tethered to me."

"Because it remembers your blood," he said, meeting her gaze. "But I sealed the last spark of its original magic here. Bound it to a future I knew might come. A moment I dreamed of. You were the one who could end it."

Ophelia knelt beside the pedestal. The runes beneath her feet glowed red, then gold. Her body thrummed with ancestral recognition. A ripple of time stirred around her like the breath of an ancient god.

She looked up at him, her voice trembling. "Will you tell

me about her? My mother? The way you saw her, before everything fell apart?"

Leander's mouth softened. He sank to one knee beside her, eyes distant. "Celeste was starlight and fire. She believed in every lost cause, every wounded thing. She was fierce and brilliant and too brave for her own good."

Ophelia blinked back tears. "Did she love you?" she asked.

He gave a small, sad smile. "Yes. And no. We were never meant to last. But we burned bright while we did. She loved differently than others: complicated, fractured, but real."

Ophelia bowed her head. The grief was different here. Sharper. Cleaner. As if time stripped it of excuses.

Leander unsheathed a silver dagger from his belt. Its hilt was carved in a spiral. "To awaken it, you must offer your blood. And your intent. But be warned. If you destroy the Bell without sealing the tether, its energy will tear through everything. Every moment it ever touched."

She hesitated. "Will I be able to get back?" she asked.

Leander didn't answer.

"You knew this would happen," she said quietly, not an accusation.

"I've lived a long time," he said. "I watched your mother. Your uncle. Your sister. And you. I shaped what I could from the shadows. But this was always your moment."

Tears burned her eyes. "And now you'll die."

He smiled. "I was never meant to last this long. Time only held me together so I could help you reach this."

She took the dagger from him. Her fingers trembled.

"Blood for truth," she whispered.

"Blood for finality," Leander replied.

She sliced her palm. Her blood dripped into the shallow ring on the pedestal. And the world convulsed.

A deep hum rose from the stone. Wind tore through the trees. The glowing glyphs flared to blinding white.

Leander staggered back, eyes wide. "Remember who you are! Not her shadow, her opposite!"

And as the Bell began to awaken, Ophelia screamed her promise into the wind.

"I'll end this!"

She dissolved and disappeared into light.

It felt like she was falling through herself.

Time shattered and reformed around her in shivering threads. Memories and half-lived moments started to spin past in a blur too rich, too fast to hold. She was everywhere and nowhere at once, threaded into the heartbeat of every version of herself. A thousand lives she might have lived. A hundred deaths that never came. All of them colliding in the now.

She saw Elijah—young and nervous—standing in the doorway of a sunlit bookstore, his tie askew, his cheeks flushed with hope and nerves. And then Sebastian, leaning against the counter with that sly, sideways smile, unfolding into laughter the moment their eyes met. She watched the moment unfold like a page turning: Elijah offering a coffee he didn't drink. The beginning of something gentle and real. They didn't see her, but it didn't matter. They had found each other. And that had always been enough.

Next: Mira. Sunlight flooding a small yoga studio in New York. Ophelia, barely in her teens, angry and confused. Her limbs trembled in downward dog, Mira's calm voice guiding her breath. It wasn't just yoga. It was the first time in years she felt her body wasn't betraying her. Mira had said, *"You are allowed to take up space."* And she had believed it.

Then the park. Central Park, tangled with evening mist. She saw herself running, wind slapping her cheeks, lungs burning. She rounded the path and froze, because he was there. Not Luka the man. Luka the jaguar. Sleek, watching. Dangerous. She remembered the way he hadn't pounced, hadn't run. Just stared, as if seeing something inside her that even she didn't know yet. It had both terrified and thrilled her.

Other moments now. Younger. Smaller.

Her hands trembled in a hospital bed, too many wires and not enough air. Celeste was gone. The nurses whispered. The magic flared uncontrolled. And still, no mother. Just silence.

Another flash: sitting on the roof with Alex, watching the stars blink in patterns she tried to decode like prophecies. Her loneliness had been so vast it filled the sky. She had screamed her mother's name like a curse.

Then: Gabriel. Their first meeting. He stepped through the shadows like a predator—beautiful, lethal, other. She'd hated him on sight. Too smooth. Too cold. But then he looked at her, not through her, not around her. At her. Like he was reading her story on the inside of her skin. She should have run. Instead, she'd stayed.

And then Eris. Ophelia saw glimpses of her sister in a hundred forgotten and missing frames: childhood laughter tangled with screams. Moments that never existed. The two of them chasing lightning bugs. Eris braiding her hair. Then fire. Then teeth. Then nothing. She felt the ache of never truly knowing her and of losing someone before she had the chance to love them fully.

And now Celeste. Her mother's final breath heavy in her lungs, the image still raw. She had given everything to save Ophelia. She had chosen her, at last.

All of it unfurled around her. The joy. The fury. The wrong turns and the right ones that had cost more than she'd wanted to pay. The people she had loved. The ones she had lost. The monsters she had faced, and the parts of herself she'd thought were monstrous, too.

And still, she didn't flinch.

She could feel the threads swimming around her. Threads she could pull. Paths she could change. There was power in this place. Power to rewrite everything. To save her mother. To undo the bond before it ever formed. To have never met Luka. Or never lose the innocent version of Eris. To leave Gabriel behind. To never be found at all.

But she didn't reach for any of them. Instead, she stood still. And she whispered into the crucible of time, "I wouldn't change a thing." Not because it had been easy. But because it had made her who she was.

And she was enough.

The light flashed.

And the thread began to pull her back home.

Then: impact.

Ophelia slammed into the altar chamber with bone-jarring force. Her body struck the floor, a sharp crack echoing through the airless space. The impact stunned her. Her hands scraped against the ancient stone, and smoke curled from her fingertips as if her very magic had tried to cushion the fall. Her palms stung, raw and blistering. Blood bloomed beneath her skin, glowing with residual power.

She coughed once. Twice. Then drew a shallow breath, lungs aching from the transition. The air was thick with charred ozone and something older, scorched magic clinging to every surface like ash after a wildfire. She blinked up at the ceiling, heart thundering. The glyphs carved there had gone dark.

The Bell of Time was gone. The pedestal that once anchored it stood fractured and blackened, split through its center like a broken crown. The runes that had pulsed with memory were silent now.

It was over.

They had destroyed it. The Bell had been forged to answer choice, to bend the fabric of time around desire, desperation, and power. But Ophelia had given it nothing. No plea. No correction. No rewrite. In the face of infinite power, she had chosen stillness. And that, paradoxically, was the act that broke it. A force meant to serve will could not survive being denied one. The Bell had waited for her to shape the world. Instead, she had accepted it.

She had looked into the heart of her past, her pain, her power. And she said *no*. No to rewriting. No to erasing. She had stood still. Chosen herself. And in that quiet, radical act of surrender, the tether snapped. The spell unraveled. And time was finally free.

"Leander?" she called, her voice raw, panic mounting in her throat. It echoed through the hollow chamber, unanswered.

Then, movement. From the edge of the shadows, a figure stumbled into view. He looked like a myth unraveling. Blood streaked Leander's tunic, seeping from a jagged wound at his side. One hand clutched the gash, the other trailing limply behind him. The magic around him fluttered, threads of light breaking apart midair, as if the world itself could no longer hold him together.

Ophelia scrambled to her feet and rushed to him, catching his weight as he collapsed into her arms. His skin was cold and too pale, his body trembling from effort.

"It's already inside me," he whispered. "The rupture."

"No," she said, clutching him tighter. "There's still time—we can find a way—"

"There is no more time," Leander said, a faint smile pulling at his lips. "Time is the thing we just killed."

His breath rattled in his chest as he sagged against her. "I always knew I wouldn't return from this," he said.

He lifted one trembling hand and pressed something into hers: a small, rune-carved stone that pulsed with a soft red light. Its warmth sank into her skin like the touch of a blessing. "A moira left this for me. She said I'd know when to give it to my daughter," he said.

She stared down at it. Her fingers closed around the stone like a lifeline. "You knew I'd come? That I'd be your daughter?"

"Of all the futures I dreamed..." His voice caught, and for the first time, she saw the depth of his love. The longing. The loneliness. "Yours was the one I hoped for," he said.

Tears streamed freely down her face, hot and bitter.

"I don't want to lose you," she said.

"You never had me," Leander whispered. "But you carry me now. That's enough."

The magic around them began to unravel. Cracks split the air itself. The chamber flickered—sometimes whole, sometimes fading—like a reel of film skipping frames.

"You have to go," he said, his voice now barely audible. "Now. Or you'll be caught in the rift. You'll fade like I am," he said.

Ophelia clutched the stone to her chest. It beat like a second heart in her hands. "I'm scared."

He reached up and cupped her cheek with surprising steadiness. "So was I," he said. "But fear is not weakness. It's the doorway to purpose."

The wind began to rise. It was pure energy. Raw, coiling, hungry.

Leander pushed himself upright with the last of his strength. His eyes glowed once more, not with pain, but with pride. "Remember this: You are not an echo. You are the Bell's final chime."

Then he raised his hands, and magic erupted from the stone that began burning in her hands. Gold and flame spiraled into a vortex of unraveling light. The threads she had broken began to seal, drawn shut by the strength of his final spell.

"You are what I always hoped for," he whispered.

And Ophelia vanished.

THIRTY

The light tore her apart before it stitched her back together.

Threading had never been gentle. But this was annihilation. Ophelia fell through time like glass through flame. Her body unraveled at the seams, bones vaporizing, blood boiling into threads. She wasn't falling through space; she was falling through moments. Spinning fragments of the life she might have lived if she'd made a different choice. Or if she'd failed.

A version of herself broken and alone, cradling Gabriel's corpse in the ruins. Another chained in shadow, eyes hollow, her magic a leash gripped in Eris's hand. A third who never came back at all.

The thread pulsed once—violently—and tore all the other selves away. And then came the impact.

She slammed into the earth hard enough to make the world shudder. Her knees hit the scorched ground, ribs knocking together, breath punched from her lungs in a ragged, shocked gasp. Her skin seared against the heat. Pain bloomed down her spine like fire beneath her flesh. She choked on smoke and ash, flames of fury incarnate.

The world reeked of burning time. She blinked once. Twice. Her vision swam in waves of violet and gold.

Nivara was still burning. Magic hung heavy in the air, coiling like smoke from a dying star. Fire twisted overhead in unnatural spirals, suspended mid-collapse. Some of it reversed, as if the flames had forgotten time was meant to run.

The sky didn't crack with storm clouds, but with seams of molten light. It was as though the world's skin had split open and was struggling to hold itself together. Everything around her screamed—metal, magic, voices—an ocean of noise crashing over her head. Somewhere, someone was sobbing. Somewhere else, something was laughing. It was hard to tell the difference anymore.

Ophelia pressed her palms to the scorched ground. Her fingers were shaking. Her body wasn't broken, but she was no longer whole either. She had been taken apart. And now she was here. The battle hadn't ended. It had only waited for her.

A jagged sob tore through the haze. "Ophelia?" Brisa asked. The voice was hoarse, raw with disbelief. And then a blur of crimson hair and clanking metal collided with her. Brisa dropped to her knees and threw her arms around Ophelia with a force that knocked the air out of her lungs. She shook with the effort of holding herself together and failing. Her hands curled into Ophelia's back like she might fall apart if she let go. "You came back," Brisa whispered, voice cracking. "You fucking came back."

And then, just as quickly, she leaned back, tears streaking her smoke-smudged face. "I swear to all the weird little gods, if you ever thread yourself through time again without warning, I will kill you. And then I'll bring you back and kill you again. Understand?"

Ophelia gave a short, choked laugh. "Okay," she said.

Brisa sniffed and wiped her eyes with the back of her blood-slick glove. "Damn right."

A shadow loomed behind Ophelia. Gabriel. He didn't speak. Just dropped to his knees beside her, gaze raking over every inch of her as if trying to memorize her all over again. His hands hovered near her face, trembling, as if afraid she might dissolve under his touch.

Ophelia reached for him first. That broke the spell. He cupped her face in both hands, his thumbs brushing away soot and tears with reverent care. His eyes burned with something desperate and undone.

"You came back to me," Gabriel said, voice breaking like a wave against her name.

She leaned into him. "I came back to you," she said.

He kissed her, a bruising press of lips that said everything he couldn't. His lips trembled against hers. When they pulled apart, his forehead still rested against hers, his breath warm and uneven.

Behind them, Brisa exhaled sharply. "Okay, I'm happy for you two. But if you start screwing in the ash field, I'm walking straight into enemy fire."

Gabriel snorted. Ophelia laughed, even through the tears.

"No time to celebrate," Brisa said, pulling back. Her voice steadied. Her blade flashed in her hand again.

Ophelia rose on shaky legs, swaying slightly. Gabriel steadied her, then stepped aside so Ophelia could see the battle before her. It wasn't over. But they had a chance. The scene before her seethed with fire and fractured earth. The noise was relentless: the crack of spells colliding, the shrieks of dying supernaturals, the earth groaning beneath the weight of unraveling time.

Using blood magic, Eris had raised an army. Sigils carved into her arms bled freely, each drop a sacrifice to the spell. The bones of Marisante stirred beneath the earth, clawing their way through cracked stone and charred soil. Skeletal figures—wrapped in the shredded remains of ceremonial robes, their spines twisted unnaturally, eye sockets glowing with sick green fire. Even ghosts emerged. Hovering. Watching. Their faces stretched in silent screams, hands flickering in and out of solidity. Not illusions. Not remnants. These were the bound dead, shackled to Eris's will.

The blood magic didn't just animate them...it rewrote their purpose. Gnarled skeletons formed tight phalanxes, shields raised in unison, swords lifted high. The ghostly warriors didn't drift aimlessly; they hunted with purpose, descending on the living like a coordinated wave. They fought without mercy and without pause.

They fought for Eris, forced by her.

But the alliance of supernaturals fought for peace and to hold the line.

The fae were the first to meet the horde, their silver magic cutting arcs through the air like falling stars. Wings of energy stretched from Aelirian's back—neither illusion nor fully real —moving with terrible, ethereal grace. Other fae shimmered in and out of sight, their movements more art than violence. Weapons made of crystallized light flashed through the corrupted ranks, slicing with the sound of shattering glass. Their eyes burned with old truths. Their hands moved like those who had seen the end of empires.

And still, they fell.

A fae archer released one final glowing arrow. And then her body flickered, unraveling into motes of light. A spell-scarred witch collapsed to her knees, mouth still open in the middle of a chant, before a spectral blade found her throat. One by one, the frontline faltered, pressed back by the sheer volume of the dead.

The alliance did not break.

Mo raised walls of rock infused with earth. His magic clung to the ruins like ivy, shielding the wounded, holding the ground.

Brisa cut through the fray with wild precision. "You want creepy?" she yelled, dodging a ghostly spear. "I'll give you creepy!" She rolled beneath a swinging axe, jammed her dagger into a revenant's skull, and grinned like a madwoman.

Luka stalked the battlefield and tore through the dead like a force of nature. One moment, he was a jaguar, muscles coiled beneath ink-dark fur, fangs tearing through a spectral revenant with a guttural noise. The next, he shifted mid-run into a massive black bear, slamming into a cluster of risen soldiers with the full force of his weight. Bone cracked. Then he twisted again—hawk, wolf, something scaled and ancient—never staying in one form long enough for the enemy to adapt. His transformations weren't graceful. They were savage. Tactical. Primal responses to whatever abomination came at him next.

Ingrid held a crumbling barricade with three other witches, their arms locked, chanting a weaving spell between them. Blood dripped from her temple. Her eyes never wavered. "We don't give ground," she muttered like a vow. "We don't give ground."

And still the dead surged forward.

Each death ached in Ophelia's chest like a weight that would never lift.

And at the center of it all was Eris. She stood on a raised dais of cracked bone and molten stone, surrounded by a spiral of ruin that throbbed with malevolent intent. Her body was barely holding shape now. Veins of corrupted magic crawled across her skin, glowing red-gold like fissures in cooling lava.

Her hair—once a wild crown of black—had transformed into living flame, flaring and twisting as if trying to escape her scalp. Her shadow moved independently, twitching and elongating in grotesque shapes that hinted at beasts she had summoned and could no longer shift to.

She was beautiful in the way lightning was beautiful. Terrifying in the way prophecy was terrifying. An oracle unmoored from her thread. A mirror fractured too many times to reflect the truth.

Eris raised her chin, and when she spoke, her voice split the air. Too many voices layered beneath her own. "You came back," she said, every syllable slicing the air. "Did you really think you could change what's already written?"

Ophelia stepped forward, the fire of her power simmering low and lethal in her palms. Her magic whispered across her skin, restless and sharp. Behind her, Gabriel moved with her, never touching but ever-present, silently syncing with her own heartbeat. "I didn't come to change it," Ophelia said, her voice steady, but her bones humming with dread. "I came to end it."

A part of her wanted to look away. To shield herself from what Eris had become. But she didn't.

Because she also saw what Eris *could* have been. There, in the bones of her posture, in the remnants of grace still visible beneath the war-torn robes and cracked skin. A seer. A girl who could have held Ophelia's hand in the dark and whispered dreams instead of doom. A sister.

But now she was this.

Eris's body shifted again, contorting as a bestial form tried to force its way free, a lupine maw snapping open from her abdomen before folding back into her ribs with a wet, sickening sound. Her skin stretched, split, healed, and glowed all at once. The blood magic sustaining her army was leeching her dry. She was unraveling even as she stood.

Brisa darted past Ophelia in a streak of crimson and rage, slicing through a corrupted vampire with a scream of grief. Mo knelt beside a fallen witch, his hands stained with earth and magic, whispering spells to fortify the crumbling perimeter.

From the cliffs above, the fae archers released volley after volley. Their arrows burned with celestial fire, but most shattered against the shields Eris had woven from shadow and bone. Still, they fired.

And still, they fell.

Eris lifted her arms. And the battlefield convulsed.

Rifts tore through the ground, yawning open like hungry mouths. From the depths crawled horrors—bone-winged beasts stitched from corpse and curse, shrieking shadows that slithered without shape or mercy. The sky itself groaned as time buckled above them, violet and black clouds rupturing to reveal streaks of blinding gold and unknowable dark.

"Still pretending to be free, sister?" Eris called, her mouth curled into a jagged smile. "Still trying to defy what we are?"

Ophelia didn't answer. Not yet. She was watching. Feeling. Mourning. Because for all her fury and fire, she was afraid. Not just of Eris. But of what had been lost to make her.

"I'm not your sister anymore," Ophelia said. Her voice was quiet. Final. And then she ran headlong into the danger.

Fire rippled beneath her heels, magic roaring up her spine like a battle cry. The air between them thickened, warped. Each step forward bled into fractures of time, a thousand moments threatening to collapse beneath her. She saw Eris at the center of it all: a queen of ruin, her body barely holding shape. Her skin cracked and burned, runes slashed across her arms like old wounds reopened. Her shadow twisted in the air behind her, forming and unforming into beasts with jagged limbs and eyeless faces.

They collided.

Ophelia's fire met Eris's blood magic in a searing shock-wave that shredded the space between them.

Eris drove a spear of crimson light toward her heart. Ophelia parried, flame wreathing her arms. The impact rocked the earth. Her magic snarled against Eris's, a living force that clawed, resisted, refused to be consumed. Her body trembled with the effort of holding the line.

"You never understood what we could be!" Eris shrieked. "You were supposed to rise with me! We are gods!" she said.

"No," Ophelia gritted out. "You wanted power. I chose purpose."

Eris laughed, vindictive and furious. She flung both arms outward. Chains of blood magic erupted from the ground, lashing toward Ophelia like vipers. She countered with a wall of golden flame. The magic met with a screech that rattled the air itself, a screech that echoed with ghost voices.

Time stuttered.

Dark magic hit her square in the chest, cracking her shield. Her breath vanished. A flash of Sebastian. Leander. Celeste. The visions tore through her. Her magic faltered.

Eris saw it and seized the opportunity. "You were never strong enough to finish this," she said, voice thick with shadow.

Ophelia tried to rise. Too slow.

Eris's final strike crashed into her chest. The world shattered around her.

She hit the stone like a falling star. Her shoulder cracked against the rubble, her head whipping to the side. A scream tore from her lips before darkness swallowed it. Her last sight: Eris towering above her, radiant with ruin.

And then, nothing.

THIRTY-ONE

Ophelia couldn't breathe. She couldn't move. Pain licked every nerve. The world had narrowed to the taste of metal on her tongue, the thunder of her heartbeat against broken ribs. Her limbs refused to obey. Her vision was smoke and shadow.

And then, Gabriel was there. He caught her before she hit the rubble again, arms wrapping around her with a ferocity that bordered on desperation. One arm locked around her waist. The other flung outward to deflect a barrage of cursed shards meant to tear them both apart. His jaw was tight, crimson dripping from a gash above his brow, but his grip held firm.

"I've got you," he said.

For a beat, she sagged into him—because it was easy. Because it felt good. Because he was safe.

But even as she leaned into him, she felt the jolt—sharp and hot—where something had hit him. His shirt was torn along his ribs, darkening fast. Blood seeped between his fingers where he pressed a hand against his side. "You're bleeding," she said.

"Not important," he said, jaw clenched. "You are." He pulled her back to him, as if he could protect her from the chaos around them.

But safety wasn't what the world needed from her now.

She pressed a trembling hand against his chest and met his gaze, iron rising in her voice. "Let me go," she said.

His breath hitched, but he didn't argue. Didn't try to stop her. He stepped back with reverence, not retreat. Doubt clawed at the edges of her mind. She was tired. Her bones were smoke. Her magic felt shredded, scorched thin at the seams. But then something deep inside her cracked wide and luminous.

A flare of heat bloomed in her chest, not frantic, but steady. Gold light surged through her veins, wrapping around every fracture like thread spun from starlight and fury. The pain didn't vanish. It was there. But it no longer ruled her.

Ophelia rose. Not stumbling. Not weak. She rose like fire remembered its shape.

And then she moved.

The next strike Ophelia launched tore across the battlefield like a comet, searing a path of molten fire. It hit Eris square in the chest. Her robes shredded. Her hair flared around her like a burning halo. She staggered, but it wasn't enough. Not yet.

Behind them, the battlefield was bleeding magic. Aelirian's cry rose through the chaos, sharp and bright. One of the elder fae collapsed beside them, unraveling into strands of light as corrupted witches surged forward. Mo stood atop a shattered altar, arms outstretched. A cyclone of earth and ancestral spell-work whipped around him, carved from both grief and resolve. He fought not just with power, but memory, summoning protections older than the Alliance itself.

Brisa carved a path through the cursed dead, blood and sweat streaking her temple. One arm hung useless, but her eyes gleamed with rage so wild it bordered on sacred.

Ophelia wavered. Her vision narrowed. Power sputtered at her fingertips.

Gabriel was suddenly there, pressing his hand to her chest, grounding her again. "You're not alone," he said, low and raw. Her heart found its rhythm. Her fire returned.

She turned back to Eris.

Her sister was already rising again. Cracks veined her skin like obsidian glass, pulsing with blood magic. Her body shifted into restless shapes...wolves and serpents, until reforming.

"Let's finish this," Ophelia said.

Eris screamed—an unholy, fracturing sound—and hurled a spear of black flame. Ophelia caught it between her hands. Her palms singed, but she didn't flinch. She twisted it, transformed it—black to gold, then to silver, then into something that pulsed with silence. With choice. With endings. She hurled it back. She staggered backward, and then the landscape buckled.

The air itself split open. Magic distorted. The duel slipped sideways, becoming something stranger. Threadwork unfurled in every direction, invisible seams pulling at the fabric of time. The world blurred.

Ophelia raised her arms. Light poured from her fingertips, not just flame now, but woven golden magic threaded with memory, grief, and choice. Every moment that had shaped her. Every loss that had refined her.

Eris screamed as she struck, her power faltering. She staggered. And then she began to come undone. Her body cracked. Fissures bloomed along her arms and chest, glowing with ruptured magic. Her mouth opened in a soundless scream as tendrils of red-gold power writhed from her skin like smoke made solid. The blood magic sustaining her—and everything she'd raised—was splintering.

"You were supposed to become me," she gasped, stumbling to her feet. Her voice was no longer booming with false prophecy. It was raw and unguarded. "You were supposed to lead beside me."

Ophelia stepped forward, her magic curling around her like a living thing. "I wasn't meant to become you," she said softly. "I was made to free you."

The magic inside Eris howled. It tore loose with violent desperation, screaming out of her ribs, her throat, her spine. Her veins glowed like molten cracks in rock. The power had hollowed her out. And now it wanted release.

Then the army broke. Across the battlefield, the ghosts convulsed, jerking mid-step, then crumbling like ash in the wind. The spectral remnants flickered once, mouths open in eternal agony, then vanished. No explosion. No scream. Just release.

The bone-forged monsters let out keening wails as their bodies twisted and collapsed, their forms unraveling into marrow and rot. The dead dropped where they stood. Those still bound by cursed sigils convulsed once and were gone.

A silence swept across the ruins, aching and unnatural. Eris's body bowed. Her knees struck the ground. The glowing cracks across her skin began to widen, splintering her apart from the inside.

"I didn't want to destroy. I just..." Eris's eyes found Ophelia's, wide and wet and young again. "I wanted to be loved," she said.

Ophelia's throat tightened. She stepped closer and knelt. "I know," she said. "But you built a kingdom from the bones of people who loved you anyway."

Eris sobbed. Magic shook loose from her ribs like wind

tearing petals from a flower. Then, without violence, without rage, Ophelia reached forward and laid a hand over her sister's heart. She didn't speak a spell. She didn't need to. She simply *let go*. The blood magic binding Eris's soul cracked open.

And Eris came undone. *Unbound.* Her light poured into the air, golden and wild and aching. A memory of a girl who might have been. And then she was gone.

For a heartbeat, the battlefield stilled. No screams. No thunder. Just stillness.

And then, Gabriel's breath hitched. He staggered back, eyes going wide—like his body had just remembered it was dying.

"Gabriel?" Ophelia asked.

He dropped like a felled star, his knees buckling before she could reach him. Blood poured from his side, soaking the charred earth in a widening stain.

"Gabriel!" Ophelia sprinted toward him, slipping on the rubble, magic flaring at her fingertips. She dropped to her knees so hard that something in her leg gave way. But she didn't care. Her hands were already on him, glowing with unsteady light as she willed the wound closed.

"Stay with me," she pleaded, pressing her palms over the wound. Her magic crackled, wild and chaotic. "Don't you dare leave me now."

His eyes opened. Barely. Just enough. "You did it," he rasped. "You ended her."

She shook her head, tears burning tracks down her face. "Not if I lose you. Don't say goodbye. I won't survive it."

Her power sputtered in her hands. It wasn't enough. Her vision blurred. His pulse was fading. Too slow. Too shallow. Had he been struck in the heart?

Gabriel's bloodstained hand rose, slow and shaking, and rested over her chest, right above her heart. "I follow you," he whispered. "Only you."

Her tears fell freely now, dripping into his open wound, mixing with all the things they had never said.

And suddenly, she knew what she had to do. But it would cost her.

Her breath hitched as she looked down at him. "Gabriel," she said, voice raw. "If I give you my blood now…it will bind us. It will heal you. But you once healed me with your blood. You know what that means."

He didn't speak. He didn't have to. His eyes, dark and infinite, held hers. He remembered. The bond Luka had once forged in desperation. How it had nearly ruined her. How she had torn it apart to reclaim her agency.

And now, she was the one holding that power. Now she had something Luka hadn't given her: choice. A blood bond wasn't just survival. It was surrender. It was knowing every thought, every feeling, every heartbeat. And it was forever.

She could walk away. Let someone else try to save him. But deep down, she knew it had to be her.

"Gabriel," she whispered, voice shaking, "I need you to be sure. Because if I do this, we can't take it back. Not this time. Not ever."

His gaze didn't waver. "Then bind to me," he said. "By choice and by love. As twin flames and life mates."

She didn't hesitate. She bit her wrist. The skin broke with a sharp snap. Blood welled, rich and golden-red.

Their eyes locked.

"I choose you, Gabriel," Ophelia said, the vow leaving her lips in a whisper.

"And I choose you, Cinis," Gabriel said. His voice was a breath, but it held a lifetime.

He took her offering. And the world shifted. Magic surged between them: sacred, soft, and steady. Her blood threaded into his. His into hers. The bond flared to life, not with pain, but with clarity. It was warmth. Light. A connection forged not out of fear or grief or war. But love. Ophelia felt the tether snap into place with a finality that was both terrifying and utterly right.

This was not destiny. This was theirs. Gabriel's breathing steadied. His pulse grew stronger beneath her hand. He blinked once. Twice.

Then he smiled. "That's better," he said.

Ophelia collapsed forward, burying her face in his chest. She sobbed, not just from relief, but from everything she had almost lost. From everything she had finally allowed herself to claim.

Brisa stumbled toward them, bloodied and wild-eyed. "Okay," she croaked, wiping at her face with her good hand, "that was romantic as hell. But if you two start making out while I'm over here leaking organs, I swear to all the gods—"

Ophelia laughed, a deep, hearty laugh. They were still here. And Gabriel was hers.

The battlefield didn't echo the sound. It absorbed it. Swallowed it whole. Around them, the world had gone quiet in that uncanny, reverent way that follows only devastation. Like the earth itself was holding its breath.

Ash drifted from the sky like snow. Flames crackled quietly in the distance, low and tired, nothing left to devour. The air was thick with smoke, blood, and the remnants of magic burned to its last breath.

She stood slowly, helping Gabriel to his feet. He leaned on her for a moment, just long enough to find his footing, to remember gravity and pain. Then he straightened. His hand stayed in hers.

Around them, the cost revealed itself. Fae warriors stood still among the fallen, their silver blood mixing with red, their armor dented and luminous. Some knelt beside the dead.

Some simply vanished, shimmering into light and returning to that dreamworld. They were going home. Returning to the stasis from which they'd come.

Aelirian knelt beside a fae child warrior, eyes closed, one hand pressed to the young one's heart. A silent invocation passed their lips, spoken in the oldest tongue, carried away by the wind.

Ingrid moved quietly through the ruin. Her face was streaked with soot, her hair wild. She paused over each fallen witch, whispering something soft and sacred in a tongue Ophelia didn't know. Her fingers touched each brow in turn, as if to ferry their spirits home.

Brisa leaned on a broken pillar nearby, face pale, one eye swelling shut. But she was grinning faintly, bloodied sword resting across her knees. "I hope someone kept score," she muttered. "Because I want credit for every one of those undead bastards."

Ophelia gave her a tired smile. "We'll carve it in stone," she said.

And then she turned.

Luka stood at a distance, half in shadow, half in light. His shirt was torn, one arm streaked with blood, and he looked… like something ancient. Something unmoored. Their eyes met, and for a heartbeat, the bond that once existed between them trembled. It was like a thread in the wind, still catching sunlight but no longer tethered.

He nodded once. A gesture not of anger, not of farewell, but of recognition. Of release. And then he turned and walked away. She didn't try to stop him.

Gabriel's fingers threaded through hers again, warm and certain. She squeezed them back.

"What now?" he asked, voice low, reverent.

Ophelia looked out over the ruined horizon. Fire still smoldered in the distance. Rubble stretched in every direction. But the air no longer vibrated with battle. It held something else now. Possibility. She turned to him, the bond between them humming like a promise in her chest.

"Now," she said, finding his eyes, "we begin again."

CHAPTER

THIRTY-TWO

The stars shimmered above Miramare Castle, too bright for a sky that remembered war. The wind had gone soft, no longer screaming with magic or soaked in ash. The world had quieted. But not forgotten.

Ophelia stood barefoot in the courtyard where so many things had ended and begun. The rocks beneath her feet were cool and worn, etched with invisible scars of the battles waged here. Magic hummed faintly through them, not volatile anymore, but mournful. Reverent. Like they, too, were remembering.

She pressed her palm to one of the marble columns, the gesture unconscious. Here was where she'd fought Luka during training, their bodies colliding in a haze of sweat and half-swallowed feelings. Here was where Gabriel had once kissed her after a narrow escape, his blood warm on her skin, his love a fire she hadn't yet dared to name. Over there, a bench where Brisa had once doubled over and muttered, "If one more fae stares at me like I'm a haunted love letter, I'm setting something on fire."

Ophelia's throat tightened. These stones had seen her become something more than the girl who once ran through the woods with a power she couldn't name or control. More than a girl who'd lost her mother. And then found her and so much more.

They'd seen her become herself. And now she was leaving. Not for a mission. Not for a battle. This time, there would be no return. She let the truth settle like dust in her lungs. "I'm not coming back," she whispered aloud. Her voice didn't shake. She had come not to fight or fix or save. But to say goodbye.

Celeste had once whispered to her, "Some places don't live in time. They live in truth." She followed that whisper now, closing her eyes and stepping into the thread.

It wasn't something Sofija or Galla had taught her, or anything etched in Mo's oldest grimoire. This magic didn't require runes or incantations. It answered only to blood...and to the quiet promise between one breath and the next.

The thread unfurled in her palm like silk soaked in moonlight, delicate and humming with ancient life. It pulsed once. Twice. Then again, syncing with her heartbeat until she could no longer tell where her body ended and the magic began.

The world stilled. Then tilted.

A low vibration hummed up through her bare feet. The air rippled around her. Light fractured into golden filaments, dancing like ghosts across her vision. They whispered as they spun familiar voices without mouths, ancestral echoes threaded into the very marrow of her bones.

Come home.

The courtyard blurred, colors bleeding into one another like wet paint on paper. Ophelia's breath hitched. The thread wrapped around her wrist now, glowing brighter with every passing second, tugging her gently forward with invitation.

Time faltered. Space folded.

And then, like stepping between heartbeats, she slipped into the liminal.

The sky was not a sky. The ground was not ground. Just twilight and mist and memory, blooming open like a story she had already lived. Archways rose from ivy-covered earth, leading nowhere and everywhere. Around her, a garden bloomed luscious and untamed. Above, two moons glistened in a velvet sky, twins mirrored beneath her feet as if she stood at the seam between worlds.

At the center of it all: Celeste.

She stood barefoot among lilies, clad in a flowing white dress. Her silver-streaked hair fell loose, curls bouncing around her shoulders. Her eyes were aglow, not with magic, but something gentler. The weariness that had clung to her during life was gone. She looked like the mother Ophelia remembered from childhood dreams.

"Hello, my love," Celeste said, her voice quiet but steady.

Ophelia's throat tightened. "Is this real?"

Celeste smiled. "Real enough."

Ophelia took a step forward. And then stopped.

Just beyond Celeste, standing in the dappled light beneath a break in the trees, was another figure: tall, dressed in silver and navy, silver hair curling over his collar. Leander.

His features were softened, younger. The weight of centuries had slipped from his shoulders. His gaze met hers, warm and full of something unexpected.

Pride.

And then, another figure stepped into view. Eris. Not the monster. Not the tyrant. But her sister, whole. Her eyes and aura were calm. The twisted rage was gone, replaced by something Ophelia had never seen in her before: stillness.

"They're here," Celeste said gently. "Because you brought us peace."

"I don't understand," Ophelia whispered.

Celeste gestured to them all. "This place doesn't obey the rules of life or death. It reflects what might've been, if healing had come sooner. If forgiveness had been allowed to grow."

Ophelia turned to her mother, eyes full of questions. "Why didn't you ever tell me? About Eris. About him," she added, nodding toward Leander. "Why did you let me grow up believing I was alone?"

Celeste's smile dimmed into something sadder. She took Ophelia's hand, fingers cool and steady. "Because I thought silence was protection," she said. "Because I was afraid that knowing too much would shatter you before you had a chance to become who you were meant to be," Celeste said, her voice breaking. "I'm sorry I left. I'm sorry I lied. I loved you so much I forgot how to be brave."

Ophelia leaned into her, forehead resting briefly against her mother's. "You did what you thought would protect me."

"I did. And I was wrong." Her voice was quiet, threaded with ache. "I was trying to keep you whole. But in doing so, I left you to wonder why you were fractured," Celeste said.

Ophelia shook her head gently. "I've made my own mistakes. I've kept my own secrets. I know now how hard it is to choose anything when everything feels like loss."

An audible breath caught in Celeste's throat.

"You loved me," Ophelia said. "Even when I couldn't feel it. That's what matters now."

They embraced each other in the center of the luminous garden, the weight between them released. When they finally parted, the pain in Celeste's gaze had softened into something quieter. Pride. Tranquility.

Then Ophelia turned to Leander.

He stepped forward, reverent. "You carry the very best of both of us," he said. "And none of our failings."

Ophelia smiled faintly. "I carry those, too. But I've learned not to let them lead," she said.

Leander's eyes shone. "Then let me leave you with this." He raised his hand and brushed two fingers to her brow. "May your power serve you, but never define you. May your heart remember joy. And may you always choose your own becoming."

And then Eris stepped forward. She didn't ask for forgiveness. Didn't apologize or justify. She simply stood beside Ophelia, gaze turned up toward the twin moons overhead. For a long moment, they said nothing. Just stood in the stillness between what had been and what could have been.

Finally, her sister faced her and smiled. It wasn't the sharp, wicked thing Ophelia remembered from the battlefield, but something much sadder. "You saved more than just the world," Eris said quietly. "You saved me from becoming a tragedy told in only one voice."

A sound stirred behind Ophelia. She turned, and there he was. Ophelia's throat closed. "Sebastian..."

He stood beneath an archway bathed in the moonlight, its silver glow softening the lines of his face. He looked younger. Unburdened. "Hey, kiddo," he said, his voice low and warm. "It was the honor of my life to raise you. To see you become who you are."

Tears welled in her eyes, but she smiled. "You were a wonderful father. And I forgive you. I know Elijah does, too."

Sebastian's eyes shone, and his voice caught. "Thank you," he said. And when he opened his arms, she didn't hesitate. She stepped into them and lingered, not for the past, but to the peace between them now.

When Ophelia released him, the ache in her chest hadn't vanished, but it had settled.

Leander stepped beside Celeste and took her hand.

Together, they looked radiant, like something once shattered had finally been stitched whole.

"Our bloodline was a wound," Celeste said. "But you didn't just stop the bleeding, Ophelia. You rewrote the story."

She lifted her free hand into the air. A single golden thread spun down from nothing, gleaming with quiet power. It shimmered between her fingers, warm and alive, as she offered it to Ophelia. "This was meant to bind," she said, voice solemn. "Now, it can anchor."

Ophelia accepted it into her palm. The thread pulsed gently through her fingers—not with force, but with something steadier. Belonging.

Celeste's smile deepened, touched by something lighter than relief. "It's time for us to go."

Leander nodded once, his gaze steady. "You are everything I once dreamed my legacy might become."

Eris stood beside them, her expression calm, free of regret or pleading. Just whole. "I'll see you," she said, "in the spaces between."

And then the light began to rise, not violently or in rupture, but with gentleness. Final. Sacred. The garden glimmered. The archways began to dissolve, like breath on a mirror.

And just before the courtyard reclaimed her, Ophelia saw two more figures framed in a final archway. Galla Placidia stood radiant and regal, her long hair wild and her gown flowing like water. Her eyes gleamed with familiar mischief, undimmed by time or memory. At her side stood Alaric, cloaked in deep blue robes. Not ghostly. Not burdened. Whole.

They stood hand in hand, a pair restored.

Galla met Ophelia's gaze across the mist and winked, one last spark of irreverent joy. A smirk curved her lips, as if to say, *"You did it, Nipotina."*

And then they vanished.

So did the light.

Ophelia landed in the courtyard with a force that stole her breath.

As she returned, her knees buckled on impact, palms scraping hard against the cool stone. For a heartbeat, she thought the world might shatter again, but it held. She held. Barefoot and trembling, she drew a ragged breath, lungs aching as the magic inside her recalibrated. It surged, stuttered, then quieted, settling into something new. Not sharp. Not shattering. Whole.

The sky above Miramare was just beginning to brighten, the first blush of dawn brushing the horizon. Stars still shone faintly in the thinning dark, and overhead, the moon hung full and pale, watching. Waiting.

She tipped her head back, throat tight. "Goodbye," she whispered, voice barely more than breath.

To her mother. To Leander. To Eris. To Sebastian. To Galla and Alaric. To the broken bloodlines and the stories rewritten.

Her fingers opened. In her palm, the golden thread pulsed with a steady glow. She brought it to her lips, kissed it once, and then pressed it gently against her heart. The magic stirred, warm and willing. The thread melted into her skin, disappearing beneath the surface. It wasn't gone. She would carry it forever.

She stood slowly, her shadow stretching toward the rising sun. This was not a return to the life she had left. It was the beginning of the one she had chosen. And peace—true peace —was no longer a dream. It was hers.

EPILOGUE
TEN YEARS LATER

The waves lapped gently at the shore, a rhythmic hush that had long ago replaced the sound of screaming spells and splitting sky. Nivara was a memory. Miramare, a scar. This was home now.

The island—unnamed by cartographers, known only to those who'd once bled for the world—stretched in a crescent of white sand and endless sun. Jungle bloomed behind their villa, wild and fragrant, with flowers that hadn't yet agreed on a color and vines that crept into the windows like they belonged there. Birds cried from the treetops. The sea shimmered in blues so deep they looked painted, layered with stories the tide never stopped telling.

Ophelia stood barefoot in the sand, her hair damp from the swim, a sarong clinging to her sun-warmed skin. She held a half-melted popsicle in one hand and a paranormal romance book in the other. Both still guilty pleasures. Two pairs of small footprints raced ahead of her down the beach, one set zigzagging wildly, the other more deliberate but just as fast.

"Girls!" she called, barely bothering to sound stern.

The two curly-haired shadows shrieked with laughter and bolted toward the tide. One of them—the bold one—held a glittering conch shell high like a trophy. The other—quieter, sneakier—grinned over her shoulder, already plotting her next escape.

Ophelia didn't chase them. Not yet.

She just stood there for a moment, letting the sun kiss her shoulders. Her toes were buried in the sand, and her heart was steady in a way it hadn't been in years. This was the kind of peace no spell could conjure. It had been forged the hard way: in blood, in sacrifice, in the binding of ancient debts.

Behind her, footsteps. Familiar enough that her breath caught with recognition before he even spoke.

"Let me guess," Gabriel said, slipping an arm around her waist. "Someone swiped a relic and made a run for it."

"It was your idea to tell them about magical artifacts," Ophelia said, leaning into him.

"It was also your idea to teach them how to cast circle wards," he muttered. "Our youngest is using them to trap sea crabs."

She tilted her head up and smiled into his chest. "You love it."

"I love you," he murmured.

His hair was longer now, kissed by the sun. His stubble had gone from strategic to scruffy. But his eyes—steady, solid brown—were the same. They always would be.

Just offshore, his sailboat bobbed lazily in its mooring, sleek and sea-worn, painted the color of storms. They took it out often, sometimes with the girls, sometimes alone. But they always had the wind in their hair and a silence that didn't need filling. It was their other kind of magic. The kind made of wind, salt, and choosing not to run anymore.

From the shaded porch behind them, Brisa's voice rang

out. "They're going to bring home another cursed rock if you don't intervene!"

Ophelia raised her hand in lazy defiance. "It's a beach day, not a crisis."

"You say that," Brisa muttered, "until something hatches."

Alex, draped across a pile of sun-faded cushions, burst into laughter. "Says the woman who tried to ward a watermelon last week because it 'felt off.'"

Brisa flipped her off without turning around. Alex only giggled harder.

Laughter drifted from inside the house—Mo and Elijah arguing about who made the better mango cocktail. The windows glowed amber in the late light.

The vampires and fae had kept their promises. There were no guards. No wards humming at the property line. Just a house full of people who had chosen peace over power. And they'd earned it.

No one spoke of the war anymore. Not unless it was quiet. Not unless it mattered.

And even then, they always ended the story with something else.

Gabriel pressed a kiss to her temple. "They're growing up," he murmured.

"They are," Ophelia said, watching the girls chase waves that would never catch them.

A breeze swept in from the sea, carrying the scent of salt and hibiscus. The world was quiet, save for the ocean's lullaby and the laughter of children.

Gabriel slipped his fingers between hers.

And for a moment, Ophelia just looked at him and really saw him. The man she had chosen. The one who never stopped choosing her.

Not because of fate. Not because of magic. Because they

had walked through fire together. And come out holding hands.

She leaned into him, her voice low and sure. "We made it," she said.

He kissed her softly. "We did."

A beat passed.

Then she smiled again—slow, certain, endlessly in love. "It was always you, Gabriel."

ALSO BY CARRIE VIXENHART

THE WILDES WITCH TRILOGY

Eye of Fire, Book 1

Out of Ashes, Book 2

Flames of Fury, Book 3

AUTHOR'S NOTE

Thank you for diving into Ophelia's world of magic, mystery, and untamed passion. If you enjoyed this journey, I'd love to stay connected.

JOIN MY NEWSLETTER

Want exclusive sneak peeks, updates on future books, blog posts, and behind-the-scenes content? Please visit my website and sign up for my newsletter! www.vixenhart.com

SOCIAL MEDIA

Let's keep the conversation going! Follow me on social media for updates and a glimpse into my writing life. @carrievixenhart

ACKNOWLEDGMENTS

This book wouldn't exist without my amazing support system. First and always, to my daughters, thank you for being the loving and magical humans who keep me tethered to joy (and reality). I move through the world buoyed by your love and strength. I'm sorry I've spent so many nights with Ophelia; please don't hold it against her.

To my family: You are the soundtrack, the subplot, and the full dramatic arc of my life. Our story is as unbelievable as it is unforgettable. Someone should write a book about us. Wait a second...

To my friends: Thank you for the never-ending encouragement, the emotional triage, and for pretending my 4 a.m. voice notes were normal behavior. Your faith in me made the madness worth it.

To Steaver Beaver: Thank you for truly seeing me—and letting me see you right back. You're in these pages more than you know.

A special shoutout to my Wildes Witch early readers: Alison, Allison, Amy, Brigette, Elayna, Kelly, Keri, Lara, Lindsey, Lynn, Mary, Melissa, Rebekah, Tara, Toni, Virginia, and Wendy. Thank you for your honest feedback, sharp critiques, and occasional ego checks. You made this trilogy better, stronger, and infinitely less embarrassing. I couldn't have done it without your brutal brilliance (and your kindness in telling me when something made no sense).

In loving memory of Lynn Lightfoot. Your stories were unforgettable. Your creative genius deserved a wider stage, and the world is dimmer without you in it. We miss you deeply, especially the endless quest to come up with synonyms for limp.

To my phenomenal editors—Alex Harpp, Leanne Rabesa, and Jamie Ryter—thank you for helping me shape this chaos into something I'm truly proud of. Your insight, patience, and sharp eyes made all the difference. And to Sarah Hansen of Okay Creations, your cover art is everything I dreamed of and then some.

To Alex, Amy, and my entire yoga community: Thank you for keeping me grounded, flexible, and (mostly) sane, both on and off the mat.

To my Shelf Love crew: Your enthusiasm, unfiltered reactions, and deep appreciation for questionable decisions and gloriously unhinged plot twists have carried me through. I'm so glad I found this community.

Stories don't start on the page; they begin in the moments we live, the people we love, and the echoes we carry. From first spark to final page, thank you for being part of the magic.

ABOUT THE AUTHOR

A free spirit at heart, Carrie Vixenhart's passion for life has carried her across the globe. She delights in sharing new wonders with her daughters, both through travel and the magic of books. Carrie is perpetually drawn to the ocean, where she feels most at peace. A dedicated yogi and aspiring sailor, she dreams of one day exploring the world by water. Fueled by a bottomless coffee cup, she weaves high-suspense urban fantasy packed with steamy romance and supernatural drama.

instagram.com/carrievixenhart

tiktok.com/@carrievixenhart

amazon.com/author/carrievixenhart